WINDOW OF TOLERANCE

.

WINDOW OF TOLERANCE

A NOVEL

SUSANNA CUPIDO

TIDEWATER
PRESS

Published by Tidewater Press
New Westminster, BC, Canada
tidewaterpress.ca

978-1-990160-36-3 (print)
978-1-990160-37-0 (e-book)

Front cover illustration: Tracy Hetherington, tracyh.ca

LIBRARY AND ARCHIVES CANADA CATALOGUING IN PUBLICATION
Title: Window of tolerance : a novel / Susanna Cupido.
Names: Cupido, Susanna, author.
Identifiers: Canadiana (print) 20240388976 | Canadiana (ebook) 20240389026 | ISBN 9781990160363
(softcover) | ISBN 9781990160370 (EPUB)
Subjects: LCGFT: Novels.
Classification: LCC PS8605.U74 W56 2024 | DDC C813/.6—dc23

Canadä

Tidewater Press gratefully acknowledges the support of the Government of Canada.

For my mum, my dad, and my sister.

CHAPTER ONE

The first thing that Marta noticed about Thomas Zimmerman that day was that his feet were bare.

She only noticed this at all because she happened to be looking at the floor. The linoleum tiles were white, slick with wax, a polar landscape divided into neat and symmetrical squares. The walls of the room were white, too, but it was nearly impossible to tell anymore. Every spare inch had been papered over with posters, bright and shiny colours, snappy slogans—and faces. Lots and lots of faces. Not the same faces as the ones who sat in the hard-backed metal chairs—not tired, not grey—but perfectly round ones, with blobby, cartoonish features. Smiling face, frowning face, crying face, thinking face. If a person ever got stuck, they could pick out the one they felt closest to and say: *Today, I feel happy. Today, I feel sad. Today, I feel. Today.* In the counselling centre on Barrington Street, statements that started with "I feel" were always safe. They were something to fall back on.

Shaw, whose turn it was to speak, was falling back on one now. "I feel like happiness is probably very different for everybody," he said. "It's a very—it's a very subjective thing. I don't really know what I'd call it. But I feel like a lot of things do make me happy, like . . ."

In his hands was the soft red ball that had made its way around the circle of outpatients, one to the other, awarding everybody their turn to talk. Shaw's knuckles were white, his fingers sunk down all the way to the second joint in the leathery stuff of the ball. Marta

1

figured it was only this that was stopping him from reaching up to scratch his nose or pick at his lip or rub his moustache. He did that last one a lot, she'd noticed, and in a compulsive kind of way, as if the act of rubbing would bring him good luck. As far as she could tell, it never had.

"Like, going for long walks somewhere quiet, going to the park, to the public gardens, or down to the pier, and just . . ."

Shaw looked at the ceiling while he talked, and most of the others looked at Quyen, the therapist whose job it was to lead the weekly sessions, but Marta kept her gaze fixed on the patch of linoleum directly in the centre of the circle of chairs. And that was why, when Thomas Zimmerman came in, she noticed his feet first.

They were bare, which was the most particular thing, but it took her a moment to realize this—they were so coated with mud that it was almost impossible to make out an inch of the skin underneath. What little could be seen was a coppery brown and veined, all whorls of scab-flesh, peeling flakes of dead tissue. Marta looked at his feet and at the marks they left behind, a trail of dirt across the white squares. She watched them cross the circle, then turn, shuffle, as Thomas Zimmerman lowered himself into the only empty chair. He sat, and his bare feet rocked back and forth for a moment, heel-to-toe, heel-to-toe, and then lined themselves up neatly along the seam between the floor tiles.

To Marta's left, Shaw was still talking, bravely fumbling his way to the end of the sentence. "—so, it's, ah, it's been really helpful, just being able to have some clarity on things," he said and reached up to rub his moustache. "And . . . and, yes. To contemplate things, to get perspective. So."

He eased his white-knuckled grip on the ball and then offered it to Marta, who took it from him automatically. She cradled it against her chest.

"Thank you, Eugene," said Quyen and then, "Marta?"

She had the ball, but nobody was looking at her. They weren't even pretending, now—they were just watching Thomas Zimmerman. He sat there rigidly, his dark hair in a cloud, fine like floss, and his eyes very bright, and didn't say anything. He was wearing a stained brown duffel coat with a sheepskin lining that looked so old it was faintly fungal, and there was dirt ingrained deeply into the knees of his worn denims. His feet stuck out from under it all, bare and muck-caked and strange. In the chair to his left, Nat Ryerson wrinkled her nose and leaned away from him; to his right, Allan Baird, the youngest regular of the therapy group, was grinning widely, his round face split open.

"Marta?"

In the four months that Marta had attended sessions at the centre, she'd only seen Thomas Zimmerman at a handful of meetings and had never heard him speak. Whenever the ball came around to him, he'd passed it silently along; the second that each session ended, he'd been gone. Maybe that was why she was only noticing now that he had the slightest gap between his front teeth. It gave a division to his smile, parting it neatly in two. As she looked at him, his gaze, which had been shifting restlessly around the circle, face to face, settled on her. Their eyes met.

"Marta," said Quyen, "is there anything you'd like to share? Any thoughts about happiness?"

People were whispering to each other, now, low and conspiratorial. Somebody laughed. It was the faintest of sounds, stifled quickly by a hand over the mouth, but Marta recognized it all the same. And Thomas Zimmerman sat looking at her, cracked lips slightly parted and his tongue flickering between them, wetting them again. There was a glassiness in his eyes, she noticed—a sheen across them, the same as the polish on the linoleum. She thought she recognized that, too.

Marta looked down at the ball in her hands. "Yes," she said. "I think we should take a break, please. I think we should maybe step out for a while."

"This is the men's washroom," Thomas Zimmerman said, motioning vaguely to the pair of steel urinals against the far wall. He had a mild, easy kind of voice, just a fraction higher than Marta had been expecting.

She leaned over the sink, tearing a length of paper towel from the dispenser and then wetting it under the taps. Her own reflection winked at her through the smeared glass of the mirror, the proportions slightly distorted—her long nose warped a fraction longer, her bleached hair becoming a static haze around her head. "So?"

"This," he repeated, enunciating the words painfully, like he thought she hadn't heard, "is the men's washroom. You can't come in here."

"I won't tell if you don't," said Marta and grinned gummily at her face in the mirror. It was something that Quyen had recommended in last week's session—smile for fifteen seconds at a time, whether you wanted to or not, and you could trick your brain into releasing the right kind of chemicals again. Fifteen seconds off, fifteen seconds on, you conned your way into being cured. She doused the paper with soap and then scrunched it into a wad, dissolving soggily between her fingers. "We'll get cleaned up, okay? C'mon, you stand over here—I'll help."

He stared at her, looking slightly stricken. "You don't have to . . ."

"It's all right, you know. It's no big deal."

Slowly, haltingly, he leaned up against the sink, and Marta crouched on the tiles in front of him. Carefully, she began to clean the dark, clogged dirt from his feet. Long strokes, following the line of each ridged vein, and she could feel him starting to tremble. She was conscious of him watching her now, too, and she tried to remember when she'd last touched anybody so gently. She couldn't, but that didn't mean much—she barely remembered anything, minute to minute. That was the thing about depression. It had taken the past first, and then it had taken the future, and then she had been left out at sea, stranded in the vanishing present.

"I've been there," she told him. "I took some pills one time—ketamine, you know—I got so fucked up I couldn't even breathe. I had to go out to the parking lot for, like, an hour and just walk around in circles. Really bad kind of trip, yeah?"

Expectantly, she looked up at him, but he didn't say anything. He just kept watching her. High as a kite, she thought, and chased clumps of frothing suds down his ankles, wiping the last traces of mud away.

The ground around the parking lot of the Fairview Lawn Cemetery had been muddy, too, and the soil had been wet and warm and *humming* when she'd bent down to touch it. There had been down-headed dandelions growing there, and the dead husks of milkweed plants, and she could vaguely recall finding this strange. The grass in the graveyard itself had been trimmed so neatly, after all. But she'd walked around the edge of the parking lot, around and around, feeling the humpbacked asphalt rising to meet her with each step, and after an hour that could have been nearly a day, Dina had come out to find her and had said—

"All done," said Marta, and dropped the accumulated wads of paper in the trash can. She went to wash her hands, but the soap dispenser was empty. Still leaning against the sink, Thomas Zimmerman was working his tongue between his teeth, a look of real concentration straining the fine lines of his face.

She gave up on being indirect. "So—what did you take?"

He blinked so slowly that she could see the entire sequence of it, footage played in slow motion: down-down-up. Long eyelashes fanning on his cheeks. "The bus," he said. "From the North End, down to the top of Barrington Street. I walked from there."

Her turn to blink now. "No, I mean, are you on something?" And, when he only looked at her warily, his tongue protruding slightly where his teeth parted, she went on, "I wouldn't tell anybody, if you are. I mean, I wouldn't snitch you out or anything like that. I get high most days I come here. You wouldn't get in any kind of trouble. It's cool, you know. It's really okay."

"What's okay?"

"I just mean," said Marta, "if you're having some kind of bad trip, you might feel better talking yourself through it. Telling me. That's what this therapy thing is all about, yeah?"

"I was going to do the dishes," he said.

"Yeah?"

"I was going to do the dishes," said Thomas Zimmerman, "but Joe MacLeod was in the sink."

And he pressed his lips together, like that explained everything and there was nothing more to say.

The meeting had broken up, and it was every outpatient for themselves, whipping up a feeding frenzy around the table of handouts—the buffet of snacks and the stacks of printed worksheets, the photocopies of Quyen's diagrams and charts, the free colouring pages you could fill in with markers and crayons later on. Half the reason that anybody went to therapy at all. Shaw was standing hunched over the table, scooping up leftover snacks into his jacket pockets—silvery, crinkled packets of fruit gums, crackers, granola, sunflower seeds—when Marta elbowed in beside him.

"Hey, man."

"Hey," said Shaw. "Where did you go? You missed the whole end of the meeting. We're supposed to make lists of all our support figures."

She only clicked her tongue, impatient, and reached past him to snag a juice box and a couple of bags of pretzels. Slim pickings, but she liked the printouts best, anyway, and most people didn't touch those. She liked the maps of the tenderest parts of the brain, mantras to stick on the bathroom mirror and chant every morning, odds and ends of psycho-philosophic prayer. "Do you know somebody called Joe MacLeod?" she asked him, taking a worksheet from the top of the pile.

Shaw was a regular and, as a regular, knew pretty much everybody on the Barrington Centre circuit. He'd done his twenty weekly sessions—the ones everybody got, if they had an insurance provider to cover it—a long time ago and had kept coming back for more each year, twenty and twenty and twenty *again*, over and over. It was the only place in the province that would take him. His name was on the waitlist for a therapist, a psychiatrist, a pastoral counsellor—nobody ever called him back. In the purely technical sense, he was still seeing his family doctor down in Yarmouth where he'd grown up, but ever since the pandemic his in-person appointments had been replaced with a series of increasingly sporadic phone calls and a string of prescriptions sent to him by fax. Sertraline thinned his thoughts, fluoxetine clotted them; he took lithium for suicidal ideation, propranolol for the tremors that lithium gave him, and valium for his anxiety about the propranolol. And every time the carousel of the counselling centre tried to wheel Shaw back out into the world, he hit another crisis and got sent right back.

"Joe went to therapy sessions here a couple years ago," he said. "Way before your time."

"Yeah? I wouldn't have met him ever?"

"I don't think so. He's . . . he's passed, now."

"Oh," said Marta. "So, I guess he's probably not living in Zimmerman's sink."

Shaw stared at her. He had a good kind of face for staring—his eyes protruded from their hollowed sockets, uncanny, and she could see the latticework of red veins there and the perpetual wetness that always seemed to be welling up. "What?"

"Just something Zimmerman was saying. Joe MacLeod, in his sink. I told him I'd help him out with it."

"You told . . ."

"Zimmerman, yeah," said Marta, and glanced over her shoulder. She could see, through the open door of the session room, a bare sliver of Thomas Zimmerman. He was waiting out in the hallway, his arms folded tightly over his chest as if he were trying to hold his own ribcage together and his head tipped back toward the ceiling. "I think he's tripping out," she said. "Like, he's on something serious. Some space-cadet shit. Like that stuff they do in South America and your whole brain breaks up, hits the outside edge of the universe. Rockstar shit. Real shit."

"You should tell Quyen then."

"And, what, narc on him? Call him out in front of everybody? Fuck off, you saw how they were all staring at him before."

"But counsellors are trained to handle that stuff. You could just tell Quyen and—"

She folded the worksheet, tucking it into her pocket. "Are you kidding? He could hook us up with a dealer, maybe."

"Well—"

"Look, I'll see you later, okay? You go easy, man."

"Stay free," said Shaw, and then rubbed at his moustache again. Marta bumped his elbow gently with hers and left him there, a lobster-faced man with crackers in his pockets and the skin under his septum raw and red in the counselling centre lights.

There were dishes piled up all across the counter in Thomas Zimmerman's kitchen, and crumpled ramen wrappers spilled out from under the lid of the garbage can in the corner. The calendar hanging from a nail on the wall was last year's and a month behind, still showing the snowman of December. Studying it, Marta shivered and hugged her sides. It was a rotting kind of day, everything with a sheen of ice over it, and she'd had to pick her way between puddles all the way up the street, wet seeping through her boots.

Thomas Zimmerman hadn't seemed to notice the cold at all—his feet on the threadbare carpet were the colour of a bruise and swollen taut with chilblains. He had brushed past her and was standing at the window where, among the accumulated gunk of dust and the shrivelled remains of houseflies, a single porcelain ornament perched incongruously bright on the sill. It was a shepherdess with a black-fleeced lamb nestled in her arms. With the very tips of his fingers, Thomas Zimmerman fidgeted with the statuette, turning it delicately one way and then the other, so that the shepherdess looked first out the window, then at Marta, and then at the mounds of dirty dishes. The lamb's eyes were closed—it wouldn't look at anything.

Neither would Thomas Zimmerman.

He was embarrassed, Marta realized, and she forced herself to grin again. "All right, man. So, this is the sink, yeah? This is where you saw him?"

He nodded, tucking his chin close to his chest; he touched the shepherdess's head like a benediction.

Marta leaned over the sink and looked down the drain. She was pretty sure that Joe MacLeod wasn't down there, but it didn't hurt to check. Squinting, she saw nothing but a rime of food scraps and stray hairs congealed around the rim of the drain, and a couple dead fruit flies caught up in it. And there was a rank smell around the sink, too, sweet and rotten and strangely familiar. It took her a few moments to place it—it was something like the reek she caught off her father sometimes, bending down to kiss his cheek goodnight or sitting across from him over supper. A fog of halitosis, decaying gums, the stinking stuff of years.

When Marta straightened up again, she saw that Zimmerman

was still by the window, still not looking quite at her. "Did—eh, does Joe MacLeod have bad teeth? Like, has he got cavities and stuff?"

Another nod.

"Oh," she said and considered this for a moment. Then, before she could think twice, she stuck her fingers down into the drain, feeling around in the slick dark of the pipe. Something clung to her skin, thick muck like melting fat between her fingertips. With a wince, she wiped her hand on her jeans, then asked, "Do you think we could have some tea?"

"If you want."

She watched as he took the kettle from the stove and left the kitchen, giving the sink a wide berth as he went, and—a few moments later—heard water splashing somewhere off down the hall. Today, she thought, we're addressing the problem, not the symptoms. She liked the way that sounded in her head—it had a ring of authority to it. It sounded like something that Quyen would say in a therapy session. *We're addressing the problem, not the symptoms.* In her mind's eye, she saw it written in block letters on poster board, pinned up in the meeting room of the counselling centre. That's what she would say to Shaw and the others later, giving them the run-down on the whole thing.

Alone, she checked the kitchen cupboards—they were mostly empty: a few packets of lentils, rice, beans. Little insects that flew up in a cloud, fluttering their graphite wings in her face. There was a single pill bottle too, nestled among tinned peaches in the cupboard by the stove; this, she noticed, was full, and the printed sticker on the side said it had been prescribed to Thomas Zimmerman by a Dr. Simon Greene a little under a week ago. The tablets were an ugly rust-red and the label said "Risperidone." She hesitated over these for a moment; Allan Baird had told her once that antipsychotics were the one type of medication there was no point stealing.

"They're awful," he'd said. "You don't get high; you just get sick. We did a whole unit on them, studying prescription drugs. They give you seizures."

At the time, Marta hadn't been particularly impressed. She rarely was when Allan was talking—he rubbed her raw sometimes, only twenty years old and nearly six years younger, but always carrying himself with a kind of druggier-than-thou superiority. She wondered sometimes whether he'd started his pharmacy degree to get access to heavy-duty opioids or purely for the trump card it gave him, winning every argument on the subject.

She'd said, "Everything can give you seizures."

"Seriously," he'd told her, his grinning round face anything but serious. "You don't want to fuck with antipsychotics. Your breasts would start hurting and all this runny stuff would come out of your nipples. Full-body nightmare. You'd hate it."

Marta, snagged by the memory, felt a phantom twinge in her chest. You couldn't trip on antipsychotics, anyway—she was pretty sure about that—and people didn't keep their best drugs in cupboards, either. If Zimmerman was on anything worth stealing, it would be LSD or DMT or one of the other certified brain-fuckers, sealed in tinfoil and kept hidden away cold in the far back of the refrigerator. That would be it. She left the pill bottle alone and poked around in the bottom cabinets instead, where she found a baking soda box and a bottle of vinegar. The bottle was nearly empty, and grit crunched under the rim of the lid as she twisted it off. She poured the soda down the sink first, then the vinegar, and watched as they foamed and spat, spurting up like she'd lanced an artery.

Thomas Zimmerman returned with the kettle, and they stood in silence and waited for the water to boil. When he'd filled the teapot, Marta took the kettle from him and poured the rest of the boiling water slowly down the drain, rinsing out the remnants of the baking soda and vinegar. She could hear it all gurgling together in the pipes, the congested-throat noises of a clogged drain clearing. "You keep doing that every couple weeks, I think you won't have a problem with Joe MacLeod anymore," she said. "You just have to keep the drain clear, so shit doesn't get caught up all the time. Bad smell. Seen it happen tons of times at work."

It was impossible to gauge the expression on his fine-boned face; an isolated muscle twitched, just one, but the rest was perfectly still. "Work," she repeated, not sure if a little spasm around his jaw spelled confusion or something else entirely. "I'm a night janitor— over at the university, you know? Clean a lot of sinks, smell a lot of rancid shit."

He looked at the pot. "Do you like milk in your tea?"

"Naw, just plain is fine," said Marta, who didn't really want tea at all. Now that the sink was cleared, the ghost of Joe MacLeod exorcised, she felt a little awkward, uncomfortably dissected under the lens of his stare. Leaning up against the refrigerator door, she imagined that, hidden away behind it, a little foil wrapper of dimethyltryptamine was waiting for her. The fridge was humming, it was humming, tantalizing—but she could hardly go looking around for drugs with him watching her. She was starting to get cold and cramped around her stomach, too; reflexively, she dipped her hand into her jacket pocket, fishing around for her lighter. "Do you mind if I smoke in here?"

"No."

"Thanks, you're a real one."

Her fingers brushed furled paper. She wormed the joint out and then wedged it between her teeth as, with a snap and click of metal, she coaxed a flame from the lighter. "So, you don't have a—" she inhaled sharply, watched the light strike up as the paper caught "—a smoke detector and shit, yeah? We're cool? 'cause the one we got back home is awful. You light up, two seconds later it's going off."

Somehow, Thomas Zimmerman had found two clean mugs

among the general detritus of the kitchen. He arranged them on the counter, lining them up with the same precision with which he'd angled his feet on the linoleum floor of the counselling centre. Carefully, he poured for them both, and then stood with his cup cradled between his hands, staring down into its milky constellation.

"My little sister, you know," Marta went on. "Dina. She's basically a smoke detector all on her own. Crazy sixth sense for this kind of stuff. She can smell weed ten kilometres away against the wind like she's a bloodhound. I can't get away with shit anymore—drives me nuts."

She snickered, leaking strands of haze between her teeth, and it dawned on her then that she might be talking too much. Even out here, something of the influence of the therapy group still lingered; it got into your head, sometimes, and you started oversharing compulsively, putting it all out there when politeness dictated you keep it in. She raised her mug and, while she was working out how to juggle the joint from mouth to hand long enough to take a sip of tea, quick enough so that she wouldn't be wasting too much smoke, Thomas Zimmerman said, "What do you think happiness means?"

"What?"

"In therapy, you had the ball, but you never said. What's happiness?"

The air in the kitchen was getting thick with smoke now, a veil coming down between them. Marta squinted, sniffed hard—she could feel the wildfire haze in her lungs, harsh at the back of her throat. A thick plume of ash was hanging from the end of the joint, and she tapped it off against the rim of her mug before it could scatter on the floor. "I don't know," she said and laughed. In the smoke, she thought she saw the parking lot of the Fairview Lawn Cemetery and the edge of someone's face, long gone and too familiar, but she knew it was nothing. "I guess I probably had some of it, at some point. Whatever it is, I did have it."

"Yes," he said and put his tea down on the counter. "Thank you for helping me, Marta. It was kind of you."

She hadn't known that he knew her name. She hadn't known that he knew her at all, really, except as another face in the circle of chairs, another voice between the four white walls of the session room. After a while, he took the mug from her hands, making the tea swirl and the ashy remnants of the joint bob up and down in the waves, a buoy out in the harbour. "Be careful how you go," he said. "The man who lives in the next apartment puts bones in the walls sometimes. You shouldn't let him hear you."

Marta nodded, pleasantly high and numb to the words themselves but listening, still, to the soft swell of his voice. "Sure," she said and realized too late that she was already in the corridor and that the door was between them—that it was closed and she was alone in the hall where he was not. Too late, too, to go hunting in the fridge, to ask him who his dealer was or, once more, what he was taking. She stared at the door for a moment, then rubbed her nose, sniffed, and cleared her throat with a painful rasp.

"Stay easy," she told the panelled wood, and then she sniffed again and, feeling stupid, turned quickly and went down the hallway, playing pattycake off the walls as she rolled from one to the other. Alone, she walked home through the smoke-laced haze of the city and, walking, practised smiling to herself in fifteen-second turns. Fifteen seconds off and fifteen seconds on. Every off, she wondered how long it would be before she was happy, and every on, she thought about Thomas Zimmerman.

CHAPTER TWO

The tin was empty. There was still a little bit of accumulated grit at the bottom and a strong reek of weed, but it was empty. Marta shut it again with a snap and shoved it back in its hiding place under the narrow mattress of the fold-up bed. She checked the other stash spots too, even though she knew there wouldn't be anything there: first, the shoebox pushed to the back of the closet, buried under old coats, and finally the little alcove behind the radiator grill. The radiator was on, cranked up high, and it blew gusts of moist air across her face as she knelt in front of it. When the metal contracted in the January chill, it always made a creaking sound like a woman breathing very softly, very slowly, and some nights Marta threw a blanket over the grill to muffle the noise. Now she ignored it.

There was nothing in the alcove either.

Marta straightened up, a tickle in her lungs from the dust she'd raised, and then ground her clenched fists into the ache behind her eyes. We're addressing the problem, she thought, and not the symptoms. Blinking hard, she looked around again, but there was nowhere else in the room to look; the only space not occupied by her bed was filled with plastic clothes racks, ghosts under their hanging sheets, and the washing machine pushed up against the far wall. The window was open. Through it, the parking lot of their building, ringed with a scattering of shabby sycamores; the South End sprawled beyond, the harbour with its dockyard-maze of shipping containers and scaffolding, and the lone construction crane looming over it all like a grotesque praying mantis. A cold wind was getting in, making the sheets billow around her legs, the door rattle in its frame.

The door was closed—she always kept it closed now and would have locked it if there had been a lock—but a long glass panel ran down the middle, set into the wood. The glass was fogged, nearly opaque, but blurred and fragmented shapes moved behind it.

Stepping out, she found her nephew, Nicholas, sitting at the kitchen table, a bowl of cornflakes at his elbow and his homework spread out in front of him. Her father was there too, tearing the tops off paper sugar packets and emptying them, one after another, into his mug of coffee. The Klausners lived in an open-concept apartment, but its dimensions had been drawn so narrowly that the room felt more claustrophobic than spacious. From his spot at table, Nicholas only had to lean sideways to pass his grandfather another handful of sugar packets; from his recliner in the living room, Jacob Klausner could watch the morning news on the little television set that perched on top of the fridge. The light of the screen threw deep crevasses into his leathered face, his jowls sagging like the flesh of a jack-o'-lantern left rotting on a stoop.

Today's headlining story was that trial dates had finally been set for the demonstrators arrested during the city-wide protests of eighteen months ago. Someone who'd assaulted a cop, someone who'd vandalized the statue of Winston Churchill in front of the old library. "Affordable housing for all," scrawled across the back of the great man's coat. Vagrancy had been a growing concern in Halifax for decades, but the housing crisis had come to a head in the summer of 2021, said the news anchor. Endemic, he said, as the cost of living rose.

"Nicky," Marta said, "was your mom in my room last night?"

"I don't know."

"You didn't see her in there, tidying up and shit?"

"Watch your language," said Jacob Klausner.

Marta turned to him, appealing. "Did you see her? I told her, I didn't want her going in there when I'm at work. I *told* her—"

"She has to," he said. "It's not just your room, anyway, it's the laundry room as well. How else is she going to do the laundry? If you don't want her touching your things, you should try washing your own clothes for once."

Nicholas was looking down at his homework again. "What is Nova Scotia famous for?"

"Seafood and violent knife crime," said Marta. Quickly, she crossed the kitchen counter and began to rake through the top drawer, through layers of accumulated tissues and throat sweets and old Christmas cards. Nothing. Nothing in the other drawer either, and nothing in the corner cabinet, among the old porcelain dishes and the miniature snow-globes that her mother had once collected. Dust and cobwebs and nothing. "She likes doing it, Dad, 'cause it gives her an excuse to poke around. Jesus Christ, if she threw my stuff out—"

"I told you to watch your language," said Jacob, and then, to Nicholas—"It's got to be fish. Fish and lobster."

"I need five. It's due today, first period."

"So, you just put different types of fish. Put, uh—put mackerel and whitefish and cod and salmon and trout. Put that."

There was nothing on the kitchen counter, either. She gave up looking and opened the fridge instead, rooting around the precarious stacks of Tupperware containers until she found the remnants of last night's beef goulash. Dina had left some on the counter for her, covered in Saran Wrap with a note stuck on top, reminding her to please rinse the plate this time—but Marta had been too bone-tired to eat it. She always was, coming off the night shift, the ozone-reek of cleaning fluids sticking to the inside of her lungs like an infection. At the university, the janitorial staff were only given bottles of a biodegradable eco-liquid to clean with; nearly three years in, Marta hadn't bothered to learn its name, but she knew that it smelled like the first breath of a thunderstorm.

"Where *is* Dina, anyway?"

Jacob had angled back his recliner so that he could keep an eye on the television above her head. "She went to take the garbage out."

"Why? I said I'd do it on my way down. I told her."

He only shrugged, reaching for his coffee mug again.

In between mouthfuls of goulash, Marta stole a pen from Nicholas's pencil box and took the opportunity to pick away at her *own* homework: the sheet from last week's therapy session. The page had "My Support Systems!" printed at the top and, below, four concentric circles, spreading out across the page like someone had dropped a pebble into water. In the knot of the smallest circle, "me"; in the next one, "family"; the next, "friends"; and lastly, "community." Marta spread the paper flat on the kitchen counter and stared down at the blank rings, which were waiting, accusatory. The "family" circle was the easiest, with a clear and exact answer. She scrawled: DAD. DINA. NICHOLAS. But there was still so much room in the ring that she felt compelled to put down something more, if only just to fill up the blank spaces. After a moment she added: AUNTS AND UNCLES AND COUSINS (KLAUSNER SIDE). Then the same again, except with MACLACHLAN SIDE tacked onto the end instead. Crossing the H of MacLachlan, a spattering of ink from the pen's nib, dark against the clean page.

She looked at the mark and it became a spread of birds' wings. A flock of crows—*murder* of crows—in funeral attire, flying endless circles around the parking lot of Fairview Lawn Cemetery.

Up on the screen, a representative of the Halifax Regional Police was standing across from the old library, telling the camera that every effort had been made to treat the transient individuals in question with dignity and consideration. Only the most violent agitators had been charged. The first round of trials was now expected to begin in May, but advocates from the Open Hands Charity Foundation had already expressed their intention to demonstrate outside the courtroom. Behind the policeman, Marta saw the lone statue of Winston Churchill hunching his shoulders against the wind. It looked like there were still traces of white graffiti on the back of his coat, but maybe that was only bird shit.

"You'd think they would've seen it coming," said Jacob. "You can't just set up your tents on Spring Garden Road like that, with the tourist shops and the town hall and everything, and expect the police to shake your hand and wish you luck."

"Um," said Marta, noncommittal, sucking on the end of her pen. The empty circles were bothering her, but Quyen never checked that anybody had actually done the worksheets. The worksheets, she always said, were only for *them*.

"And punching police officers, setting things on fire—"

"Um."

For a moment, he eyed her sideways over the rim of his mug, and she could tell he meant to tease her before he even opened his mouth. His humour—where *she* was concerned, at least—had gotten increasingly clumsy over the years, each punchline slotted gingerly into place and left dangling a beat too long, like he was afraid she wouldn't get the joke otherwise. Before, they'd cracked each other up on a fairly regular basis; once, he'd made her blow chunks of broccoli out her nose she'd been laughing so stupid and hard, and her mother had threatened to make them both leave the dinner table. He only ever kidded her with kid gloves, now. Wetting his lips, he said, "*You* weren't there, were you? Weren't a ringleader, eh? We won't be seeing *you* up in court."

Clunk. Marta watched the attempt at a joke plummet to the floorboards, where it joined the collection of empty sugar packets scattered at her father's feet. "Not as far I know, Dad," she said and gave him a listlessly anemic grin.

In truth, she couldn't remember where she'd been or what she'd been doing during the summer demonstrations of 2021, although the date itself was enough to piece together a rough picture. Approximately a year after the pandemic had definitively put an end to her job at the House of Blues and she'd switched to janitorial work, approximately a month before the landlord had bumped the rent up *again* and she'd moved back in with her family—no clear memories, everything a soupy haze of sunlight in the attic room she'd rented for herself in the North End, the opposite side of the city. Laying on a futon in that attic, perfectly inert and packing the bowl of a pipe while the sun blazed through the skylight over her head. That was where she would have been, probably, while a protestor was scrawling words on the back of Winston Churchill. But that was only a guess.

At the table, Nicholas turned a page in his notebook. "Why do tourists visit Nova Scotia?"

"Because it's less boring than New Brunswick," said Marta.

"Something longer than that. I have to fill up three whole lines."

"Write in bigger letters," said Jacob, and then—"Change the channel, Marta. All this protest stuff, these court cases, it's giving me a headache. Put on the hockey highlights, eh?"

Marta found the remote behind the cornflakes box and was still flipping through the channels when the apartment door opened and Dina came in. The Klausner family lived three floors up and the six flights of stairs had left her slightly out of breath, her face flushed and whisps of dark hair escaping from her tight ponytail. She was already wearing the starched uniform of the car dealership where she worked most days, and every movement was accompanied by a crisp rustling of fabric.

"Another cold one," she said and leaned down to pick a stray cornflake off her son's collar. "You make sure you're wearing your scarf and gloves at recess. Marta, why don't you heat that goulash up in the microwave? It only takes a minute."

"I'm all right," said Marta.

"Well, sit down and eat it out of a real bowl, anyway."

"I'm all right," she said and shovelled another spoonful of goulash into her mouth to show how all right she was; mumbled and thick, she went on—"I was gonna do the garbage on the way out, you know. You didn't have to."

"I just thought I'd get it done early. You can go to the superstore instead—we're nearly out of eggs and there's no milk left."

"I can't," said Marta. "I've got therapy this afternoon."

"Oh," said Dina, and it seemed for a moment as if she was going to say something else, too, but instead she only began taking dishes from the draining board and putting them back on the kitchen shelves. Each one, she looked at for a moment, held up to the light, and for every two that went onto the shelves, one more went back into the heap of dirty dishes in the sink.

"It's your last month there," said Jacob. "Isn't it?"

Marta had been watching the stack of dishes in the sink rise higher and higher, each one rejected—she'd been the one to wash them the night before, coming in from work, and she squinted hard, trying to see what particles of contamination her sister was finding. "What?"

His eyes darted left and right; he wanted to be looking at the television again, she could tell, but now that he'd asked the question, he'd committed himself to it. "Your last month at the centre," he said. "I thought they only gave you twenty sessions. And you've been going since the beginning of October, haven't you?"

"September," said Dina.

"Right. So you'll be done by the end of the month, won't you?"

Marta blinked. "Oh—sure. Yeah. My insurance as a university employee covers twenty, anyway. But they let you come back for more, sometimes, if you really need it—if you're a bad case or you're having a crisis or something."

"Good," said her father. "But that's just for the ones who need it, right?"

It wasn't what she'd been expecting and, for a moment, she was caught off-balance—skewed, she stared at him, her spoon suspended halfway to her mouth, dripping chunks of goulash. She was suddenly aware of a certain quiet in the room, an absence of sound she'd barely been noticing before; Nicholas's pen was no longer scritch-scratching across the page and Dina, at the sink, was arranging the clean dishes with exaggerated care.

"Sure," she said. "Yeah."

It wasn't something that she'd thought about—not lately, at least. In the week that had passed since she'd washed the dirt from Thomas Zimmerman's feet, since she'd banished the ghost from his sink, she'd barely thought about anything else at all. What she'd say when she saw him again, whether he'd talk to her. Had he come down off of whatever head-trip had fried him out? And, if he *had* come down, would he want to see her again? He wasn't on Instagram or Facebook—she'd checked—but would he swap phone numbers, agree to stay in touch?

The smile on her father's face went right through her. "So, your last month. That's great. That's really something to be proud of."

"Thanks," said Marta, and then—"I mean, yeah. Yeah, I probably would have stopped going sooner, but I like seeing the guys, Shaw and Allan and Nat and all, and hanging out with them and stuff. I'm almost ready to be done with the whole thing. Good to go." She dropped the empty Tupperware in the sink, then briskly, "Speaking of being good to go, Nicky, we'd better make some tracks if I'm walking you to school. Go brush your teeth, yeah? Wagons west."

And she waited until the boy had vanished into the bathroom before she turned to Dina, dropping her voice to an accusatory whisper, "Have you been taking my stuff?"

"Of course not."

"I bought six joints last week," she said, "and now there's nothing left."

"So? You probably smoked them all and forgot about it."

"I wouldn't. I dropped, like, thirty bucks on them. I wouldn't just *forget.*"

"You forget things all the time."

"I'm not a teenager," said Marta. "And you're not my fucking parole officer. You don't have any right to go through my stuff."

For a second, she sensed that they were teetering on the very edge of it—a real fight, a real shit-kicking, just like the old days—and she braced herself for it. It wasn't the missing joints that she minded, exactly—she hadn't been planning on smoking up before the therapy session, anyway—but the absence of them, the place where they should have been but weren't, and the ground pulled out from under her. This, the shock of it, was what she couldn't stand. She braced herself for the argument, but Dina only tucked her hair behind her ears again and then smiled, crisp and painful, and that was worse than anything. She said, "I need to put Nicky's lunch together. And could you please make sure he's there before the bell this time? He was late to homeroom attendance yesterday and I got a call from the teacher."

It was only after she'd left Nicholas at the school gates—in time for the bell, but only barely—and caught the bus back downtown that Marta had time to fill in the "friends" section of her worksheet. SHAW, she wrote, in slanting block capitals. ALLAN. NAT. They were her friends in the loosest sense of the word, the same way she imagined that people made friends in prison or in the trenches of a battlefield—they could shoot the shit together between sessions every Tuesday, stand shivering outside to smoke or to swap horror stories of the side effects they'd gotten off various substances, but that was the extent of it. And again, she found herself hitting a wall—there were no more names to write. She'd lost touch with her school friends when they'd all gone away to university; her musician friends when she'd lost her job at the House of Blues; her unemployed friends when she'd gotten the janitorial gig. She'd fallen out of touch with all of them and *they'd* fallen away from *her*, peeled away like eggshells by each round of forgetting, and at the core of it—what?

Marta looked down at the worksheet and then out the bus window. They were crawling down the main artery of South Park Street, clogged with morning traffic, and last night's snow was turning brown and sludgy in the gutters. Taking the turn, the bus splashed through a puddle and sent mud splattering up in thin streaks across the window. Marta stared at it. After a moment, she bent over the page again and wrote: THOMAS ZIMMERMAN. Then she crossed that out, scribbling the letters over and over until she'd nearly worn through the page. It didn't feel quite right to have him there, but it didn't feel right to leave him off completely either. He wasn't family or a friend or a community, whatever that was, but he wasn't nothing, either. He couldn't be, when he was still writ large across the inside of her mind.

She thought about it for a while, and then wrote his name outside the string of circles, floating off by itself in the sea of white.

Thomas Zimmerman.

There. That was better.

At the Barrington Centre, the group therapy sessions were meant to start at noon on the dot, but that was only on paper—in reality, most of the outpatients trickled in late, and Quyen rarely started the meetings before 12:15. The scattering of early-comers usually sat waiting in their chairs, looking at their phones or making stilted little attempts at conversation, but Marta generally liked to hang around in the hallway, where she and Shaw could read the assortment of flyers pinned to the communal bulletin board. The current favourite had been put out by the Nova Scotia branch of Alcoholics Anonymous, with a cartoonish picture of a wine bottle and "Problem Drinking?" written underneath. They could generally get a lot of mileage out of that one.

This week, it was Marta who started them off, entirely confident that Shaw would join in.

"*I* got a problem," she said. "I can't drink a fifth of whiskey without falling over."

"Nobody will pick up my bar tab," he said.

"Tequila makes my nose tickle."

"I never know how to pronounce 'daiquiri' right."

"You guys are immature as fuck, you know," said Nat, breezing past them and into the session room on a gust of floral perfume. "And your material's getting stale, too. You did the tequila one before."

Marta grinned, unperturbed. She'd gotten off the bus a few stops early to visit the weed dispensary on Dresden Row, and the joint she'd bought to replace the ones Dina had thrown away was now scratching pleasantly at the inside of her trachea. Thomas Zimmerman hadn't arrived yet—she'd stuck her head around the door twice to check—and she wanted to wait and meet him in the hallway. Say something to him, quiet and conspiratorial, before the session started. Maybe ask if he'd been keeping his sink clear.

"My dad took me to an AA session one time," she told Shaw, just conversational, meaning to pass the time. She wasn't quite sure if she'd mentioned it to him before, but he nodded encouragingly, eagerly, and so she went on, "Not for drinking, just for the weed and pills and all. The symptoms, y'know, and not the problem. I think it was the only kind of therapy he'd ever heard of, so he thought—why not try it, yeah?"

"Right on."

She giggled. "It didn't stick."

"No?"

"Naw, it was too many rules—too many for a teenager, and I was only about nineteen back then. I said, the only 'twelve steps' *I'm* taking are the ones between here and the door, and I'm getting the fuck out of here."

As the anecdote unfolded, she'd grown increasingly sure that she *had* told it before, but Shaw still gave the punchline a dutiful snicker. "I used to do AA back in Yarmouth," he said. "We did meetings in the basement of our church. They were nice people, very nice, but I only went a couple times."

"For drinking?"

"No," said Shaw. "Not for drinking."

They both studied the bulletin board in silence for a while after that, and Marta amused herself with holding her tongue exactly parallel to the roof of her mouth, waiting for it to turn dry and puffy. There was a new flyer on the board this week, this one issued by Open Hands. It was minimalist in design, featuring a single black-and-white image—a photograph of a brown paper bag, slightly rumpled and grubby-looking. The caption below, printed in accusatory block capitals, read: DO YOU KNOW THAT MANY HOMELESS WOMEN HAVE TO USE PAPER BAGS INSTEAD OF TAMPONS? And below that, in smaller and less confrontational print, an exhortation to donate any extra toiletries or sanitary products to the next Open Hands charity drive.

Marta was fascinated by this. "That can't be true, can it? Why would you ever do something like that?"

"Well—I guess they can't afford anything else," said Shaw.

"But why not just use toilet paper? It's softer, yeah? I mean, imagine having a brown paper bag scraping up your vagina. It's gotta be fucking *agony*, man."

He coughed and then, with a reflexive kind of haste, rubbed his moustache. "We should go in pretty soon, eh? It's almost twenty past."

Marta looked up and down the hallway, but the crowd had thinned itself down to nothing, no sign of Thomas Zimmerman. Reluctant, she followed Shaw into the session room and took the chair to his left in the circle. The chair to *her* left, she draped her coat over and shooed away the other stragglers. She'd decided already that she would save it for Thomas Zimmerman, when he came.

But he didn't come.

CHAPTER THREE

The last session in January and the last of Marta's twenty, the word of the week was "resilience," and there was an empty chair where Thomas Zimmerman should have been. It cut the circle of attendees in two and Marta couldn't stop herself from circling back to it, over and over, the same way you could push your tongue into the gap of a missing tooth. She leaned into Shaw, who—in the seat to her right—was already contorting himself into his usual hunch of discomfort, twisting his knotted hands like he was trying to peel himself out of his own skin. "D'you think Zimmerman's okay?"

"I guess," said Shaw, and pried his hands apart in order to fidget with his moustache. "People miss sessions sometimes."

"Yeah, but not coming in almost a month, and that day, you know—being out of it like that . . ."

She'd written her phone number on a slip of paper and held it, now, between finger and thumb, smoothing out the creases. Already, she'd planned out exactly how she'd give it to him—just casually, after the session was over, and with just the right amount of easy-going indifference so he'd know it wasn't a come-on. Low voice, all the most masculine mannerisms. *Just if you want to hang out some time. Just if you ever want to talk about shit.* No big deal, no hassle. It was hard to strike that balance sometimes—to tell a man you just wanted to be friends, no hetero-compulsive schtick necessary—but she thought that Thomas Zimmerman might understand. He hadn't seemed much affected by conventions.

"He's probably fine. I thought you said he was just tripping out."

"I'm not sure," said Marta. She'd thought it over enough times by now that she'd begun to doubt that he'd been on drugs that day at all. He hadn't talked like most of the druggies she'd hung around with in the past; he hadn't seemed high, exactly, just quiet and reticent and odd. "When I was over at his place, I saw some antipsychotics. They don't prescribe that stuff for nothing—if you're just a bit fucked up in the head or whatever. If he was having, like, some kind of crazy psychotic episode or—"

She broke off as, two seats down, Emma put her finger to her lips, shushing them; at the head of the circle, Quyen had snapped the cap off her marker with a decisive little click. The outpatients all went quiet, watching the therapist as she turned toward the board and wrote on the tacked-up page, in big block letters: RESILIENCE.

"Today," she said, "we're going to talk about resilience. What does it mean to find resilience in ourselves? How do we recognize it in others? What does this—" she tapped the marker against the whiteboard for emphasis, leaving a little blotch of black under the S "—really mean to us? Going forward, how can we incorporate it into our personal wellness journeys? Now, I'm going to pass the ball around, going right to left this time, and we can all take turns to just give our thoughts about resilience, and what it means to us. And if you don't have anything you feel like sharing right now, you can just pass the ball along to the next person, no problem—okay? You can start, Marta."

Caught off balance, Marta kneaded the ball in her hands, fumbling around as she tried to draw her thoughts together and very aware that people were looking at her. She'd been wrapped up in thinking about Thomas Zimmerman, eyeing the door where he would have—but wouldn't, wouldn't—come walking in, and so she hadn't had as much time as she would have liked to concoct a good answer. But she knew pretty well that it didn't really matter what you said, because usually nobody was listening. They all had the same look, now, turned in on themselves and distracted, racking their brains for what they would say when the ball came to them. "Um, I think," she began, and her fingers sank deep into the rubber, flakes of latex skin peeling away; words and words and words, everybody staring but nobody listening, and she'd held the ball how many times since that first day, twenty weeks ago? She couldn't remember. "I think it's good to be resilient. Yeah. I mean, I got diagnosed with clinical depression when I was eighteen. Almost a third of my life, now. And thinking back, I've been through some pretty bad times and the fact that I'm still here, I'm still going . . . it probably means something. So that's good."

She looked to Quyen and, winning a blinding smile and a nod of approval, passed the ball to Leslie Anderson on her left, then sank back into her chair with a feeling of pure relief. Down the road to Thomas Zimmerman again, she could check out, she could stop listening, except—

"I don't mean to disagree with you, Marta," said Leslie, "and I completely respect your opinion, your experience, but I think 'resilience' is a pretty problematic concept in itself. I can only speak for myself, but just getting through these ordeals didn't make me more resilient. It didn't make me stronger or anything like that, and it's just damaging to try and claim otherwise."

Marta sat up again. "I didn't—"

"Please," said Quyen, and put a finger to her lips. "Marta, you'll get the ball when it comes around again. It's Leslie's turn to talk."

"She's talking to me. How come I can't talk back?"

"You'll have your chance later."

The ball went to Emma next. "I totally agree, one hundred percent," she said. "I think it's very reductive to frame mental health issues in terms of resilience. It just sends the wrong message, doesn't it?"

Quyen was nodding encouragingly from her whiteboard, accepting their remarks with the gentle enthusiasm she showed every speaker, but Marta was stung, on edge again and seized with a gut-sunk irritation. Going first, getting the ball rolling, she'd said what she thought had been some safe-sounding bullshit, and now they were all pulling the rug out from under her. Staring at her. She was trembling again and so she folded her arms tightly, pinning her hands against her ribs to make them go still.

The ball went silently along to Allan, who tossed it in the air and then caught it again. "No comment," he said and gave Marta a wink.

She could have killed him.

Appealing, she turned to Shaw, but he was ignoring her. He had taken the ball in his turn and was gripping it like a lifeline, looking from the whiteboard to Leslie and Emma, and back again. "Yes," he said and began to rub skittishly at his moustache. "It's, yeah—I agree."

The ball went back to Quyen again. She smiled around at them all, a lighthouse beam cutting through the sea of stormy faces. "Those are some very interesting perspectives, definitely. Leslie, Emma, I completely understand where you're coming from, it's completely valid, and we'll definitely take that feedback on board when I'm planning our next season. Maybe there was a better word than 'resilience' to use to express this concept. So, we'll send the ball around one more time and everybody will have another chance to pitch in, okay?"

This time, Marta gripped the ball white-knuckled, trapping it—and her failing hands—between her knees to keep the shakes from taking her. She felt obliged to justify herself now, the odd one out in the group and a certified holder of Incorrect Opinions. "I guess I just meant that being resilient isn't something you get, something you become, it's just a quality you already have. I was already resilient, and I feel like that's why I'm still here. That's all. I get what you're all saying, but that's just what it means to me."

She passed the ball along to Leslie, who was looking faintly triumphant. Done, she sank deeper into her chair—she looked for the road in her head, the way out, and didn't find it.

"I think it's important that we challenge that idea," said Leslie. "I think it's important that we move beyond outdated terminology. Trauma is trauma. There's no inherent quality that will help you get through traumatic situations or preserve your mental health. There's just nothing."

The ball continued its slow circuit, everyone stumbling on their own words and agreeing clumsily, Shaw and Allan and all of them, but Marta wasn't listening anymore. Her annoyance had gone beyond simple embarrassment; there was something about the whole thing that rubbed her the wrong way. That even in a room where there was supposed to be no wrong answers, no judgment, they had still made her feel ashamed. The betrayal of it, compounded with Thomas Zimmerman's continued failure to appear, was nearly unbearable. When the session was over, she didn't stop to fill her pockets at the handout table one last time or say goodbye to anybody, but went straight out the door and down the hall, going quickly down the stairs. Her last session, the last of her allotted twenty, and they had made her ashamed.

Shaw caught up with her in the lobby. "Are you okay?"

She rounded on him. "Why were you agreeing with them? Do you really believe that shit? You think it's *problematic* to call yourself resilient?"

He was rubbing his moustache again. "I mean, everybody's opinion is valid. You gotta be polite—"

"Polite? Fuck that, man—what does it even mean?"

"I'm just saying, I get it was bad in there, it was a bad vibe, but I don't know why you're so upset."

"They made me look like an idiot," said Marta, and then, feeling suddenly and terrifyingly close to tears, blinked very hard. "I'd always back you up on everything, Shaw. I would. Even if you didn't mean it, you could have agreed with me."

"I'm sorry," said Shaw. He was holding a wad of paper in his hand, and he reached out, now, offering them to her with a hopeful look in his watery eyes, and that stung Marta raw all over again; she knew Catholic contrition when she saw it. He still didn't understand why she was angry, what he'd done to hurt her, but he would carry the stupid, useless guilt of it all the way to the confessional box on Sunday.

"I picked up some extra colouring pages," he said.

"No, thanks."

Still, he held the papers out to her. "Maybe you can give them to Nicholas."

"Listen—" began Marta, hoarse and tearful, then broke off abruptly. Be easy, she thought and breathed. "Whatever," she said. "It's not a big deal."

"Do you want to get supper?"

"No," she said and he looked so pathetically aggrieved that she doubled down on the notion immediately, seizing on the first idea that came to her—"I think I'm going to go check up on Zimmerman," she said. "Just to see if he's okay, you know. Just to be neighbourly."

Alone, she struck out for the artery of Quinpool Road. Alone, she looked up at the sloping, scrubby birch trees that grew out front of Thomas Zimmerman's apartment building. She'd lit a joint on the way over, and the weed gave her a strange heavy feeling at the back of her cranium, as though a weight was pulling her gently down toward the earth. Everything of her anger over resilience was gone, leeched away into the fog, and she'd stopped shaking completely. Now, the back of her neck ached, there was a tingle around the hands, extremities, around the pipes of her ears, and she was perfectly exhausted.

Marta stood on the sidewalk outside the apartment and stared at the birch, and at the rows of windows beyond, trying to remember exactly which one Thomas Zimmerman might—at any moment—look out of. The haloed lights of the cars passing in the road washed over her, throwing her shadow up against the brick wall of the building. She raised her hand, lowered it, and so did her shadow—it waved to the window where Thomas Zimmerman wasn't.

She could smell petrichor, damp earth and leaf mould, and she looked at the birch tree, and thought about

Dina's hand, in the parking lot. Dirt on her fingers.

whether Thomas Zimmerman ever looked out his window and saw it. She could see now that the bark was browner, darker, toward the base of the tree and then faded out as it grew higher; paler and paler, until the topmost branches were like the sepia tone of an old photograph. In these thinned-out branches, she could see little birds, dark and flashing, landing on the outer limbs, bobbing, then still. And it looked to her, in that second, as if the tree might fade on into the infinite, a ladder stretching all the way to the outermost edge of the universe, and that the birds were climbing it now, and so could she.

Somewhere out across the city, a train whistle sounded, and the noise was so loud that Marta started, her stomach twisting. She'd felt it in her bones, like the train was crashing right down the street, right on top of her, and she'd been afraid. "Jesus Christ," she said and rubbed her eyes furiously, jamming her fingers into her sockets so hard that dots swam in the dark behind her eyelids. Blinking, blind, she stepped up to the front door of the building—quickly, before she could change her mind, before the train could touch her, she went in.

Through the first set of doors, she stood in the between-place of the apartment block, looking at the row of buzzers and the list of tightly printed names beside it. There was no "Zimmerman" there at all. She went through the list twice—nothing. For a moment, she wondered if she could possibly have gone to the wrong building, but she hadn't. She remembered the cracked, yellowing tile in the entryway. It was all the same, right down to the dead flies silhouetted on the glass of the fluorescent strip light. Leaning closer, she looked at the list again. The number on Thomas Zimmerman's door had been thirty-six, she was almost sure of that—she remembered looking at it as the door had swung shut in her face. But the name listed on the registry for Apartment 36 was C. Standish.

Marta hesitated for a moment longer, rocking on her heels. There was always the possibility, she figured, that Thomas Zimmerman had moved into the apartment only recently, and that C. Standish had been the tenant before, and the landlord hadn't got around to changing the buzzer listings yet. She pressed the button for the apartment and waited, fidgety and teetering from boot to boot, while the distant drill sounded. Nothing. She pressed it again, then one more time. She tried the door and waited a minute longer—still, no answer. In the static crackle, she thought she could hear water running, down a drain, or into a bathtub. That was the other thing. You heard about it happening pretty often, doing the therapy circuit, and it seemed like they were always found in the bath. Marta had never been able to understand why.

Resilience, she thought, and her tongue felt very thick in her mouth all of a sudden—she was hitting the dry end of the high now and, as the tide receded, the rocky ridge lines of paranoia were rising again. All of them staring at her, crows perched, passing the ball from beak to beak. She looked at the list of names again, selected one at random. H. McNamara in Apartment 12 didn't answer when Marta pressed the button, and neither did A. Beaton in Apartment 24, but she got lucky on F. Comeau in Apartment 27. The buzzer went twice before a voice broke through the static roar, very small and far away. "Yes?"

Marta leaned in. "Hey," she said. "Um, hello—" Already, half-reflexively, she was skipping up an octave or two into the clipped, bright voice that was a few years younger. More like Dina than her. "Sorry to bother you, but I live on the floor above, in—in Apartment 36 and I forgot my keys. I was wondering if you could just buzz me in?"

There was a brief pause, long enough for Marta to get skittish in the lie, and then, "Sure, no problem, honey."

"Thanks."

There was a loud click as the door unlocked, and, quickly, she tugged it open, went through to the lobby, and then into the stairwell. Going up to the third floor, she retraced the route that Thomas Zimmerman had led her along that afternoon. When she looked down, she half-expected to see the muddy marks of his bare feet on the stained carpeting. In the hall, counting off the apartment numbers from thirty, she seesawed wildly from one possibility to another. He was fine, he was upset, he was fine, he was having a psychotic break, he was in the bath with bloodied flowers blooming from his wrists. He was fine. Knocking on the door of Apartment 36, Marta remembered a conversation she'd had with her father months ago, trying for the who-knows-what time to convey to him the particular strangeness of depression, the sheer and awful fear of it.

It's like I'm thinking about bad stuff happening so much that it's happening all the time. Her voice quiet and hoarse in the living room one evening while Dina was putting Nicholas to bed.

He hadn't understood at all.

Nothing bad is happening, Marta. You're fine.

But it's happening in my head. I'm just kind of sitting here and it's already happening. It's like I'm stuck living the worst day of my life, over and over, just by thinking about it.

She hadn't been able to make it clear to him; she'd been able to tell by how his attention drifted, how he'd squeezed her hand and smiled, like she was only the most distant of acquaintances. But she thought about it now—that, somehow, Thomas Zimmerman was alive and dead, that she was telling the paramedics how she'd found him in the bathtub and telling Shaw what an idiot she'd been for worrying when nothing at all was wrong, and all this happening at once, playing out in the theatre behind her eyes. Then the door opened and it was a possibility that she hadn't considered at all: that the person standing there wasn't Thomas Zimmerman, but somebody else.

It was a younger man, narrow and pointed-looking. "Were you the one buzzing?" he asked, and drummed his fingers on the doorframe, an impatient little rat-tat-tat. "If you're soliciting for something, now's really not a good time."

Marta blinked. She looked past his shoulder, to the number on the door: it was 36, she hadn't been wrong about that, at least. "Um," she said. "Yeah. Yeah, sorry, man—I was looking for a guy I know, but I guess I must have got the wrong apartment or something . . ."

She trailed off—she was looking past him, still, and had caught a glimpse of the kitchen behind him; the counter overflowing with dirty dishes, the calendar on the wall with its date-expired picture of December's snowman. It was the same apartment. She could even see the package of baking soda, still where she'd left it by the unclogged sink. The man was saying something terse, uninterested, starting to swing the door shut again—quickly, she stepped forward. "Sorry, this is Thomas Zimmerman's place, yeah? He lives here, doesn't he?"

The man looked at her with a new attention, but no particular warmth. "You a friend of his?"

"Well . . ." She gave a one-shouldered shrug, surrendering to the complexity of this philosophical dilemma. "I don't know. We go to the same therapy group."

He stood back a little, letting her sidle past him and into the kitchen. "At the Barrington Centre?" he asked her, sharp and wary, like he was trying to catch her out in a lie. There was a bruise on his left cheek, she noticed—a dark splotch just below the eye, the deep red of bloodied meat.

"Yeah. Yeah, I just came by to check up on him. He hasn't been coming to meetings lately, so . . ."

She looked around, then back at him—she craned her neck with deliberate nosiness, squinting through the kitchen door and into the dark of the hallway beyond. She wanted him to stop staring at her that way, distrusting, faintly disconcerting. She smiled at him. "I'm Marta."

"Chris," he said.

"It's good to meet you, man. So, you—you're a friend of his?"

"It's my apartment," said Chris Standish.

Marta stared at him. "Oh," she said. "I was here just a couple of weeks ago. I didn't know he had a roommate."

"He doesn't," said Chris turned impatiently and followed her into the kitchen; restless, he opened a drawer, shut it again, shifted a few dishes around the counter in an aimless kind of way. Not restless, Marta thought, looking at the edges of him, drawn taut and sharp like flint. He was angry, rigid with fury, and every angle of his narrow face was tight with it. Residual kind of anger, she thought. The sort that settled under the skin and stayed there a long time. "He doesn't," said Chris, "live here anymore. He's gone."

"What?"

"He doesn't live here."

"What?" Marta said, echoing, blank in the close reek of the kitchen, which was still haunted with the halitosis ghost of Joe MacLeod, the spectre of the dirty sink. She couldn't make sense of it. Blank, she looked around the room, at the door, like Thomas Zimmerman might appear any second. "Since when?"

"Two weeks. Or maybe closer to three, I guess. He hasn't been here since the beginning of January, anyway."

Just after she'd seen him, then. She couldn't understand—first at the counselling centre and now here, he'd vanished completely; in her mind's eye, she had a sudden vision of an invisible hand holding some giant eraser, carefully scrubbing all traces of Thomas Zimmerman from existence. Some incomprehensible magic act from a stage show. Witness the amazing disappearing man. She blinked, feeling the synapses snap and fire sluggishly in her brain—a consequence of the weed. "Maybe I'm not, ah, understanding you properly . . ."

He rounded on her. "He's gone. He left. That's all there is to understand."

She blinked again. "And you're his—?"

"*Was* his. It's crazytown, impossible—you can't live with somebody like that. Seeing stuff, hearing stuff. You can't live. Crazy. I told him he wasn't staying if he quit going to therapy. He's gone."

"Where?" she asked, finally getting her thoughts in line. "Where did he go? Is he okay?"

"Sure, when isn't he?" said Chris, who only seemed to have heard the last question, and Marta was reminded suddenly of the way people always talked in the therapy circle—not listening to each other, or even to themselves, only running through whatever list they'd been compiling in their heads. Words and words, the flow of it, and sometimes it seemed like they wouldn't stop talking until somebody made them. She'd opened that vein herself, too many times to count. "Shit, he's always cozy with his dozen friends who aren't really there. You can't have a relationship with somebody like that—it's crazytown, twenty-four hours a day. Midnight, all night, talking to friends he doesn't have, or cheating with the ones he does—" He broke off abruptly, looking at her with fresh suspicion. "You're not sleeping with him, are you?"

Marta blinked. "Oh—no. Christ, no."

"I mean, it's not my business anymore. We're broken up now, so. So, if you want to buy that ticket, take the ride, you can go for it, you can—"

"Seriously," she said, knowing that it was hopeless. Still, she tried, spreading her hands wide and easy, palms out, like he'd be able to see her lack of interest, her essential indifference to the entire arrangement.

"I'm not saying that I'm a saint," Chris went on, and his mouth was very wet now, flecks of spit flying, contortions of the face that Marta had seen in the mirror all her life, "but I'm not crazy. I have a job, my name's on the lease, I can't live in the not-real world. I have a job. He threw out all our food, he said it was rocks and gravel and shit, we couldn't eat it. I'm not saying I didn't know, you know—I knew he was in therapy, and he was getting help for mental health stuff. I get it, I get anxiety like a bitch, but I know how to take responsibility for myself. I know."

"Listen, I'm just—"

"He doesn't want to get helped. He wants to stay out all night and fuck strangers, and talk to the wallpaper and get lost, and piss himself, and get worse. He wants to get worse. You know what I mean, right? You go to therapy with him, you see what he does—right?"

"Yeah," said Marta. She was hearing him and hearing, too, not the voice of the therapy circle—not her voice—but Dina, now. The Dina of nearly three months back, a silhouette through the fogged glass of the bedroom door, whispering just loudly enough to be overheard. *But she doesn't want to get better, Dad. She just wants an excuse not to grow up already. She could go to those meetings every day for the rest of her life and it wouldn't make a real difference.*

Jacob Klausner's voice had carried even farther—two-thirds deaf in one ear and getting deafer, he'd lost the knack of whispering years ago. These things don't happen overnight, he'd said, and Marta had watched his shadow-shape splinter in the fog, expand, as he'd put his arms around Dina. *You can't force it. She's not crazy, she's not bad—she'll get bored. She's just not one of the bad ones.*

"He wants to get worse," said Chris, "and then he expects me to just live with it? I pick him up from his doctor's appointment and the second we get home he's throwing all our food away. He told me he's never going to therapy again. I told him to move out. It's insane. What the fuck am I going to do with that?" This time, he didn't wait for her to answer, but, abruptly, like a train of thought redirecting itself mid-track, threw the hall door wide open. "If you're friends, you can take his shit with you."

"I'm not—" she began, but he was already gone. Marta listened to him rummaging around somewhere off in the apartment, knocking things over. She looked down at the toes of her muddied running shoes and, beneath them, at the kitchen tiles. There were a few stray traces of lingering dirt there, and something else, too; something that caught the light when she turned her head. Little fractal shards of something pale, water-coloured, caught in the crannies between each tile. When she shifted her foot, she could feel the fragments crunch, faintly sickening—she looked at the windowsill and saw that the porcelain statuette of the shepherdess and her lamb was gone.

A moment later and Chris reappeared, carrying an overflowing cardboard box, which he pushed into Marta's arms. Automatically, she took it, swaying back, and she saw that it seemed to be mostly clothes and a few battered paperback books. A pair of Doc Marten boots were balanced precariously on top; she had to catch these under her chin, awkward, clutching the box against her chest.

"I was just going to leave it all out on the curb, anyway," he said and then, appearing to misread the look on her face, added quickly, "It's all there, all his personal shit. Everything from his drawers, everything he was keeping stuffed away crazy places, hid under the mattress and shit. I cleared it all out. If he wants anything else, he can fucking sue me for it. You can tell him that when you see him."

"All right," said Marta. "I'll tell him, if I see him."

Half out in the hallway, she paused on the threshold, wedging her foot into the path of the fast-closing door, stopping him. "Hey, I'll give you my number, okay? And if he comes back here, or—or you talk to him again or something, can you ask him to call me? Just so I know he's okay and all."

"I'm not talking to him—"

He tried to close the door, but Marta leaned into it harder. "Sure," she said quickly, "but he's probably gonna be back here, sooner or later, hassling you about stuff. People like him can get real paranoid, you know? I can help smooth shit over. Just call me."

Reluctant, Chris nodded, and she rattled off for him the number for the shitty old phone she'd gotten hand-me-down from her dad. "Don't hold your breath," he told her. "But I'll call you."

"Thanks," said Marta, and grinned at him, hollow and beatific and loathing. "You be well. You have yourself a good one."

"Asshole," she said, alone, to the drab carpet and the number on the closed apartment door. The neighbouring door, Number 38, had been open a crack—it shut, suddenly, and the sound made Marta flinch. The man next door kept bones in his walls, Thomas Zimmerman had told her. Be careful how you go, he'd told her, but he was the one who had gone.

"Asshole," she said again, and laughed, reedy and stupid and unsure of herself, between her teeth. "Fuck–ing ass–hole."

CHAPTER FOUR

Quyen's office was the group therapy room in miniature, a hollow shell of space, cluttered up with comfortable armchairs, scatter rugs, pillows, and the walls plastered with more posters, more cheery slogans. Marta took the chair nearest the window, but only a few inches of it—she sat perched on the very edge, hands on her knees and halfway standing, and felt that the overstuffed cushions were trying to suck her downwards. Awkward, she grinned; awkward, she looked down at her fingers, examining the frayed edge of a hangnail. "Thanks for seeing me. I know I'm not really an outpatient any-more, but I just wanted to ask—"

In the chair opposite, Quyen was smiling; even out of the corner of her eye, Marta could see the white of it. "Don't worry about it," she said. "Consider it a freebie, pro bono. How are you feeling?"

"Fine," said Marta, and gnawed on the hangnail. It was snow-ing outside, the mix of ice and sleet that blew in off the harbour, drowning everything in a soupy haze. There was a slight pause, but only a very slight one. Some therapists would let the silences drag on, waiting to see if more could be dredged out of you, but the trick had never worked on her—she had gotten the knack of spacing out, staring blankly into the near distance and fading away from her own eyes, and could almost always wait for the quiet to blow over.

"How's the transition been, getting back into the swing of things? Everything okay at work?"

"Oh, great. Yeah. Still doing the evening shifts, so it's nice and quiet."

"And with your family?"

"Great."

"And you haven't been experiencing any more periods of elevated distress? I know, in the past, you mentioned experiencing some intrusive thoughts—troublesome thoughts—about a few things. That hasn't been an issue at all?"

"No. No issues."

"No thoughts about your mother—"

"No," said Marta. "But I actually only came 'cause I wanted to ask you about Thomas. Thomas Zimmerman, you know, from the group."

She watched the woman carefully, but the smile never slipped. "Oh?"

"D'you know why he stopped coming to sessions? Was there something wrong?"

Not even an inch; instead, it only seemed to calcify, becoming thicker and more opaque, blocking her out completely. "I mean, obviously I can't share the details of Thomas's situation with you—with anyone. Our mission is to create an open, safe environment for our people to connect, to *share*, but we still have to be confidential about each other's struggles."

"Right," said Marta. "But did he just up and quit? Is he not coming back?"

"I don't think Thomas will be coming to any more sessions," said Quyen, "for the foreseeable future. We loved having him here, of course, and—"

"Is it because something happened?"

"You'd have to ask him personally, of course. My impression is that he decided—and this is only my impression, you know—that treatment here isn't *quite* the right fit for him. But I can't speak to that."

"Oh," said Marta, and took a moment to digest this, looking out the window. Sleet blurred the glass, warping the cityscape beyond like someone had pressed their thumbprint to it; she could vaguely make out the spire of St. Matthew's Church, where she'd attended service every Sunday for the first eighteen years of her life, swamped by the steel and concrete rising around it. She wasn't used to listening to what Quyen said with any particular kind of attention—painstakingly, she forced herself to take the words apart, looking for something to hold onto. "D'you mean," she asked, "that he's getting treatment somewhere else, instead?"

Quyen had let the smile drops, but it was only for a moment—she sucked in her cheeks, seemed to be working the muscles there for a moment, then put on a fresh coat of cheer. "That's not something that I can speak to, as I said. Is there a reason you're asking all this, Marta?"

She shrugged. "Just worried about him, I guess."

"I hadn't realized you two were close."

Marta wondered if she should say what had happened when she'd gone back to Thomas Zimmerman's apartment—what the man, Chris, had told her. Again, she shrugged. "We aren't. I mean, I was hoping to get to know him better. Hang out. I guess I kind of wanted to talk to him again before I left."

"Oh," said Quyen, and made an odd little twitch with her hands, lifting them from her lap then dropping them back again. It took a moment for Marta to realize that she'd been reaching for the pad and pen that weren't, this time, sitting out and ready on her desk; it was the therapist's reflex to jot down a note, to record this new quirk of mental disturbance. "You know," Quyen said, "there can sometimes be a temptation to, ah, *displace* our feelings of care, of obligation, of guilt, onto other targets. New targets. When we have unresolved feelings, it can be very easy to—"

Marta bit down hard on her finger, gnawing the cuticle. "Right," she said. "But I was just asking, I was just curious. It's not a big deal or anything. No feelings."

"But how *are* you feeling?"

"Fine, like I said."

"I mean, generally. Going forward. How do you feel, in yourself?"

In yourself. It was, Marta thought, the beginning and end of the problem—that she was in herself, and always had been, and didn't know how to be anywhere else. "I feel a lot better," she told Quyen.

"You don't have to feel better."

"I really do, though. I mean, I don't know if I'm totally in control, I still get sad sometimes, but I feel a lot better than I did before I started coming to sessions."

"Really?"

"Really," said Marta.

Sleet off the harbour, settling a grey blanket of sludge over the city. It would be tricky, heading down the hill toward home, and she knew already the sidewalks would be covered in a slick layer of ice and she'd have to go slowly, shuffling along with her arms held rigidly out at her sides and bobbing like birds' wings, bowled along down the sidewalk by the wind, but fuck it, she couldn't wait to get out there and feel it, all the same. Get out of here.

She said, "I don't really think about her anymore. So. You know."

"I'm sorry to hear that," said Quyen, and sounded agonizingly sincere about it, too. "That was never the goal here."

"It was for me," said Marta.

And the other problem was, she thought, watching the flecks of rain smear the window, that therapists only ever knew her at the worst times of her life. They didn't see how she had been before and so she struggled to explain to them what had happened—that she had been better back then, and that something had happened to her. Something had changed. She'd once had and she'd once lost. Of course, if they *did* know her from before, she wouldn't be able to tell them anything—no more than she could have told her father or Dina. That was the awful paradox of therapy, and of being born with a lead tongue and a mouth that shut like a trap. A hole in the dirt where your mind should be. Marta reached up and rubbed at the closed mechanism of her jaw, counting the seconds before she could be gone.

"I want you to imagine that you do get control of these emotions," Quyen was saying now. "Where do you see yourself heading now? What kinds of things do you think you can do?"

"I can be more social," said Maria, and was rewarded with an encouraging nod. "Spend more time with my family. I can, you know—I can be more present with them."

"What else?"

"Um, I could . . . I could give back to the community."

That won her an approving nod. "We're partnered with Open Hands, you know. That charity that advocates for the unhoused, the homeless. If you want, I could send you an email with their information."

"Great," said Marta, hopeful.

But she wasn't in the clear yet. "What else?" asked Quyen.

"I could spend more time with my friends. Maybe take some college courses. I could, um, I could have more hobbies. Do stuff. Start doing roadie work again, now the pandemic's over and they're doing concerts and in-person shows again. I could—" she hesitated, grinned a little self-consciously, aware of the stiltedness of it—"I don't know, I guess I have an idea in my head about what other people are doing, having happy lives, being normal, so I guess—I guess that's what I want. That's what I want to do."

"What do you think those people do? What do you think is important?"

"Um."

Quyen took a pen from the jar on her desk and handed it, along with a fresh notepad, to Marta. "Go on. You can write it down, if you want—I think it will be helpful for you. What do you see? What do you think is important?"

Marta took the pad and pen, and was surprised when the other woman began to turn away from her, tipping her head like she had asked Marta to strip off all her clothes and was trying to preserve her modesty. Obliging, Marta uncapped the pen between her teeth, and—mindless, balancing the pad awkwardly—scribbled down a few words.

When she looked up again, Quyen was still half-turned away, but she was smiling again, something a little softer, a little easier, than her usual nursery-school beam. When Marta opened her mouth, Quyen interrupted her quickly, "You don't have to tell me what you wrote. Actually, I think it's better if you don't. But I hope you do manage to get there, sometime soon."

"Thanks," she said. "And—thanks."

It was all she could think of to say.

"I hope you find what you're looking for."

"Me too," said Marta. She looked at the pad, where she had written:

CRAZYTOWN PEOPLE IN SANITY CITY. DRIFTWOOD PIECES AND BITS OF BLUE AND BOTTLE GREEN BEACH GLASS AND THE VIEW OVER THE CITY, STEAM AND SMOKE RISING UP, THE GREY SKY. AND TUESDAY, AND THURSDAY, AND FRIDAY, AND IT'S ALRIGHT, I THINK. IT'S ALRIGHT.

She read it with no memory or comprehension, and wondered what it meant. She uncapped the pen again and wrote underneath, in careful looping letters: *Thomas Zimmerman.*

"I still don't think you should look at it," said Shaw. "It's private property."

"So?" said Marta, and blew a long stream of smoke at him, and at the box, which sat forlorn on the bedroom floor between them.

"So *don't*. He shouldn't have given it to you at all—it's an invasion of privacy."

As if to punctuate this point, he turned head sharply away and bent over his worksheet again.

"I didn't *ask* him for it," said Marta. "He pretty much made me take it. He flipped the fuck out, man. A textbook case of Quyen's neuro-aggressive, uber-controlling relationship-figure-shit. You know. Detrimental influences and obstacles to our ongoing mental health journeys. That kind of guy."

She had retreated to her favourite place to smoke, which was sitting upside down and sprawled half-off the bed, with her legs propped up on the radiator, her bare feet jutting out the window. The day's earlier sleet had settled in a thick crust on the window-sill and she could feel ice stinging her ankles. She liked this very much—the radiator's heat scorching the backs of her knees, the cold wind on her toes, and the wedge of grey South End cityscape she could see out the window. It gave her an infinity kind of feeling, like she was out at sea or floating in space. "I'm an uninvolved observer in this whole thing. I'm not invading shit."

"All right," said Shaw, pacific, and gnawed on the end of the pen. "Come on, I haven't even done question one yet. It says I have to name five things I can see."

Marta stubbed out the joint against the radiator grill. It was breathing again, the awful in-out-in-out, but she was reaching the stage of intoxication where she barely noticed it. When she kicked her feet, her heels skimmed the tops of the skyscrapers that clustered around the harbour. "A box. A cardboard box," she said.

"Come on, man . . ."

"Write it down," she said and lowered herself crabwise onto the floor beside him, dizzy as the blood ran strange, skewed in her system. She blinked hard, raking her fingers through her tousled hair; spaced-out astronaut coming out of orbit. "Number one, a cardboard box. Two, a pair of Doc Marten boots—" she shifted the boots out of the way, fished out a paperback with a lurid pulp-ish cover, bright colours and a girl in a silk nightgown—"Three, a copy of *Children of Fortune*. Four—"

"Seriously, stop," said Shaw. "It could be really private stuff in there."

He scrawled "wallpaper" and "bed" on the fourth and fifth lines, and then read question two aloud to her. "It says—'four things I can touch.'"

"One, a T-shirt," said Marta, who had shifted the books aside and was combing through the clothes now; the fabrics were all rough against her fingertips, stiff, like they'd hardly ever been worn. A few things still had the tags attached. "Two, a wool sweater. Three, plaid pajama pants."

She went through each one with the perfect attention that smoking always brought about, the world diminishing down until it was exactly the size of a single cardboard box; two T-shirts, a sweater, a raincoat, boxer shorts, a pair of jeans—she didn't know what she was looking for, exactly. Still, taking each relic into her hands, she felt the picture of Thomas Zimmerman come into sharper focus.

Shaw had retreated into cold silence, casting occasional wounded looks at her over the top of the page. He went on to question three, which was about what you could hear, and stopped asking her for answers. Marta didn't mind. She could hear the distant sound of traffic in the street, the sound of Dina clattering around in the kitchen, the television playing in the next room—all that was muted. More immediate, more real to her now, was the crackling of Thomas Zimmerman's clothes in her hands, the soft rustling of fabric as she folded each item carefully and set it to the side again.

Question four. Weed drowned most things out, but she half

imagined that she could smell something musty, mildewed, and the ever-present reek of spoiled food—the ghost of Joe McLeod again, making himself known.

Question five. She tasted—what? What was there?

At the bottom of the box, her fingers found a clutter of little things, accumulated detritus that had drifted down; a few pens, a cigarette lighter, a half-empty pill bottle of prescribed antipsychotics, a tangled pair of earbuds, and—she blinked, turning it over in her numbed hands—a phone. "What the fuck?"

Shaw looked up. "What?"

"Where the fuck would he ever go," said Marta, "that he wouldn't bring his phone with him? Who moves *anywhere* without taking their phone?"

"Maybe it's an old one."

"Maybe," said Marta, and, hunching over the phone, fiddled with it for a moment. She pressed the power button, and the screen switched on in a blaze of light. The battery was at sixty-three percent and, after a moment, a series of notifications began to pop up, almost too quickly to read; there were seven missed calls, two voicemails, fourteen unread texts. The most recent of these flashed across the screen for a split second, and Marta caught sight of the sender's name—*MOM*, in screaming capitals—and a brief snippet of a message: *talked to the doctor again . . .* Then it was gone. When she tried to flick the phone open, it refused: it was password-protected.

"—Marta," said Shaw, and she looked up; she could tell from the way he was staring at her that he'd been talking for a while, and she hadn't heard. "You should have taken it back to the Centre with you," he said. "Given it all to Quyen."

"Aw, she wouldn't help him. You didn't hear the way she was talking to me today. All the bullshit, the displaced feelings, whatever-the-fuck. Whatever's happening with him right now, it's real. *She* wouldn't understand."

"So what? They'll have his contact information in their system, they can tell him to come pick up his stuff."

"But he doesn't have his phone."

"Then they'll call his family or something, his emergency contact number. Jesus, I don't know—it's just not our business. They probably do this kind of stuff all the time."

Marta was looking down at the phone again, pressing the power button off and then on. The picture that Thomas Zimmerman had set as his lock screen was a slightly blurred photograph; a man who Marta now knew to be Chris, standing down on the pier, with the grey water and the distant smudge of Dartmouth shore behind him. She thought about the shattered shepherdess and her little black lamb, shards of porcelain across the kitchen floor, and the way that Chris had talked. *Crazytown.* The person who Thomas Zimmerman cared about enough to keep a photograph on his phone, and he'd talked that way about him, would have put all his possessions out on the curb. And Zimmerman had left without taking his phone, without taking nearly anything.

And he was gone.

And there was broken porcelain on the floor.

"I guess," she said and carefully began to pile Thomas Zimmerman's jumbled collection of belongings back into the box. She pushed it under the bed, out of sight, stood slowly up. "I'm hungry. You want anything from the kitchen?"

"Not really."

He had bent over the worksheet again, nearly done filling in the page with his careful, slanting scrawl; she looked down at the top of his head, the hair prematurely thinning across the scalp, and felt a twist of something like guilt in her stomach. She knew pretty well that he was right, that she *should* just give the box to Quyen to take care of and forget about the whole thing, but—*There was porcelain on the floor.* Her mind turned to sluggish molasses as the high took effect. *And Thomas Zimmerman walks with bare feet. Jesus Christ, what happened? What happened?*

She let herself out into the kitchen, closing the fogged-glass door to the bedroom smartly behind her, so that as little as possible of the weed reek would escape. As quietly as she could, she moved to the cupboard, fishing out a loaf of bread. Still, Dina looked up sharply from the stove.

"Dinner's going to be ready in an hour," she said.

Marta tore a fistful of fleshy flaxseed bread away, stuffing it into her mouth. "So?"

"That's practically half a baguette."

"I can eat," said Marta indistinctly, "whatever the fuck I want."

From his recliner, her father looked up, shooting her a reproving scowl as he put a finger to his lips; he and Nicholas were watching television together. She shrugged, apologetic, still stung, and slipped back into her bedroom with a feeling of pure relief. She just couldn't breathe with them all looking at her, their distrust running off her like rain.

"She talks to me like I'm a criminal or something," she told Shaw, throwing herself down on the bed with an asthmatic squeal of bedsprings. "Like *she's* the one three years older and I'm her little sister. Like I'm fucking twelve, man."

He sat beside her, looking faintly relieved; she wondered if he was just glad to be talking about anything that *wasn't* Thomas Zimmerman. "Yeah?"

"It's driving me crazy."

"Everybody's family drives them crazy sometimes."

"Not like this."

"Maybe it's because she's a mom now. The parent thing. You know, she just gets used to treating Nick like that, so she kind of treats you the same way . . ."

"No, she started doing it even before he was born," said Marta.

"She's been like that since—" she broke off abruptly, reached into her mouth with two long fingers to tangle a bit of dough out from between her teeth, dripping spit—"I don't know, I don't remember. Since forever. A long time."

She lay back on the bed, wiping her fingers on the old comforter and letting her legs hang down over the edge, and—after a moment—Shaw lay down beside her, shoulder-to-shoulder, and knee-to-knee, audible crack of his spine as he stretched out. He was still holding the worksheet in his hands and Marta took it from him, lifting the crumpled paper up toward the ceiling to read, so that the light could shine through, then letting it drift down over her face. Clean white sheets, coming down over her; she remembered lying in bed with Dina, giggling, while their mother made the bed up around them, throwing the blankets high in the air, a billowing canopy. White sheets over her face. Beside her, Shaw was breathing very shallowly. There was a rigidness in him that even weed couldn't thaw out, and she thought that she could feel him trembling.

"It's just bullshit," she said, and the paper crackled and wafted up with every breath.

"You could always move out," he said. "You wouldn't have to deal with her at all, if you weren't living together."

"I can't afford it," said Marta, but she hadn't really meant Dina, anyway—she'd been thinking about Thomas Zimmerman's box under the bed. "Minimum wage cleaning toilets, and I can't afford to move anywhere, pretty much. I couldn't even afford living *here*, if I wasn't babysitting Nicholas, and when he gets older . . ."

"It's cheaper if you split rent with somebody. You could—"

There was a sharp knock on the door and the bedsprings creaked as Shaw sat up very quickly, smoothing down his shirt and raking his fingers through his thinning hair, all in the approximate four seconds before Dina opened the door. "Are you smoking in here?"

she asked, leaning against the doorframe and sniffing, sharp and accusatory. "It smells awful."

Marta squinted at her from under the paper. "Nope. Less drugs, more hugs—that's how I live my life, you know."

"Grow up."

"I will," said Marta. "I'll grow up, and up, and *up*, like a fucking tree, and I'll keep growing until I get to the stratosphere, and you just can't see me anymore."

Shaw started to giggle. He put his hands over his mouth when Dina turned her stare on him, tucked his chin down, but the laughter escaped in bubbles from between his fingers.

". . . and *up*, and *up*, and *up*—"

"I wanted to let you know that dinner's on the table in ten minutes," said Dina, and looked over Marta as if she wasn't there. "You're welcome to stay and eat with us, Eugene. I bet you must be feeling pretty hungry right about now."

The soft click of the door swinging shut was enough to jolt Shaw into silence—he stopped giggling, but his shoulders still shook. Marta put her hands up, pressing the sheet of paper across her face until it was a mask, pushing her thumbs down over her eyes until she saw stars spin behind her eyelids. *Next time she comes in, I just won't be here. I'll be like Thomas Zimmerman. I'll just be up and gone.*

"Everybody's family drives them crazy," said Shaw again.

Up and gone, thought Marta, and felt the mattress springs creak under her, a twinge just below her ribcage—she watched the stars spin and kaleidoscope away from her while, in her mind's eye, she followed the thread of sensation down, down, and came to the box under the bed. The cellphone in it. Aloud, she said, "D'you know who Zimmerman's mom is?"

CHAPTER FIVE

Thomas Zimmerman's mother lived on Morris Street, where a row of narrow old townhouses slanted down toward the harbour. There were seagulls perching on the shingled rooftops, clustered around the smoking chimneys, and they—the birds, the smoke, the chimneys—were all slanted too, all leaning into the wind. The sidewalk was coated in a thin sheen of ice, and Marta picked her way down the sidewalk slowly, the box of Thomas Zimmerman's possessions balanced awkwardly on her hip. She stopped every block to fish her phone out again, checking and re-checking the directions that Shaw had given her. *It's a house on Morris Street, with the yellow paint and the little fence outside. One of those widow's walks on the roof, I think.* He'd only been there once or twice, accompanying Zimmerman home after sessions. "A while back," he'd said and made a face like the memory went down sour, then added quickly, "He never invited me in or anything."

His tone had struck Marta as funny, and she'd eyed him sideways, screwing her face up into a squint; they'd still been lying next to each other on the bed.

"His boyfriend said he slept around, sometimes," Marta had said.

"Not with me," Shaw had replied, and gone red behind his moustache.

Halfway down Morris Street, Marta checked her phone again and found two texts from Allan Baird hovering at the top of the screen.

are u coming to the party on sunday night?

And then, sent approximately twelve seconds later: *too good to hang out w/ us now ur not crazy?*

Marta ignored these and was another block along before she caught sight of a house with yellow paint peeling in strips from the siding and a little ironwork fence in front. The ornamentations of the house were white—white cornices around the windows, a white trim below the guttering—but the colour had faded to a dingy alabaster. From where she stood on the opposite side of the street, she could see that there was a little bit of fencing up on the roof as well—a widow's walk, Shaw had said. A lot of the oldest buildings in Halifax had them, relics of the time when sailors' wives would stand looking out over the harbour, waiting for the ships to come in.

Crossing the road, she noticed that there was only a single door out front of the house, only a single number plate beside it. Much of Morris Street had been converted from a residential neighbourhood into a commercial strip, where lower floors were occupied by cafes and bakeries and quaint little shops, but there was no sign of that here. The property hadn't been partitioned, then, and the Zimmerman family had the whole place to themselves. Marta wondered if they were rich. She couldn't remember the last time she'd met anyone in the city who lived in an actual house.

There was a panhandler on the sidewalk outside, sitting crouched with his back to the fence and an empty takeout cup in front of him, held between the toes of his rubber rainboots to stop it from rolling away. He was drinking something dark and frothy out of a plastic bottle—raising it, he caught Marta's eye as she drew nearer. When she was a few yards off, he called out to her, "I've got a question for you," he said, and his voice was thick and hoarse, coming up from deep in his chest. "You always look up to your parents with love and respect?"

Marta stopped on the opposite side of the pavement. He looked very old to her, and sick; his eyes were bloodshot and rimmed with yellow, a pair of poached eggs in his sunken, pitted face. "Yeah," she said. "I try."

The man didn't seem completely satisfied with this. "You gotta do it always, you know, 'cause they're looking out for you. They're like God."

"Yeah?"

"I'm not—I'm not too religious or anything, but I do believe there's somebody up there watching," said the man, abruptly, and pointed one trembling finger upward. Instinctively, Marta tipped her head back and looked up, like she would see God in the grey and smoggy sky above.

"They talk," the man was saying now, tracing a trajectory that Marta couldn't quite follow, "about how the universe is infinite, but we narrowed the Big Bang down to four trillion—" he waved his hand in a vague arc, skittering through the air, sketching the path of history, "—per second. But they say it's infinite."

"Oh," said Marta, and shifted the box to her other hip. Her arm was getting sore. "Yeah."

Looking past him, up at the shuttered windows of Number 27, she wondered how she was ever going to detach herself from him. She recognized the erratic train of thought, ideas overlapping each other in the offbeat rhythm of somebody who had thoroughly disconnected themselves from reality. If they had been sitting in a therapy session together and it was his turn with the ball, Quyen would have been there to gently prod him along. *Really interesting perspective! Thank you for sharing your experience with us! Let's see what everybody else has to say about that, okay?* Experiencing it in the safe and sterilized world of the Barrington Centre was poor preparation for seeing it out in the wild.

"So if you give blood, you go to give blood at a clinic, or at the IWK hospital . . . well, you put a drop of your blood under a microscope, you look at it—you see cells and cells and cells infinitely expanding. Trillions per second."

"Is that right?"

"The whole universe," said the man, his voice rising to an authoritative pitch, "is a drop of God's blood."

"Thanks," said Marta and really meant it. "I'll have to remember that, man. That's pretty good."

"I'm Danny Boy," he told her, the flow coming thicker and faster now, water sluicing down a drain. He was missing teeth, she realized, and it made each word stick on his tongue. "Everybody knows me. Everybody over on Spring Garden Road, everybody who hangs around there. You're talking to the next mayor of Halifax."

"Yeah? You know, I really gotta—"

"I'd be okay," said Danny Boy, "if I could get a tent, you know, if I could get somewhere to live and a way to cope with the post-traumatic stuff. I've been waiting for God to get to me. A lot of people say God has turned his back on them, out here. Not me. Not me."

Abruptly, his leathered face crumpled up and Marta realized, with a sudden horror, that he was going to start crying.

"I should go," she said, but Danny Boy didn't seem to notice at all, too busy rocking back and forth to an internal beat. Other passersby were stopping now, and staring, but Marta was already past him and going quickly up the sagging townhouse stoop. She wouldn't have minded if he'd called her a cunt or something, but she knew she wouldn't have been able to stand him crying.

When she rang the bell, she could hear it faintly, an echoing through the bones of the house—for a moment, nothing happened, and she'd half-raised her hand to ring again when something moved behind the splintered glass pane set into the doorframe. The door opened, just a crack at first, then wider. Through the gap, she could see the sliver of a woman—older, with the same fine floss hair as her son, the same dark eyes.

"Hi there," said Marta, and smiled—she could hear Danny Boy down below on the pavement, snuffling and wheezing to himself, and she raised her voice a notch. "Would you be Mrs. Zimmerman?"

"Can I help you?"

"I'm Marta. I'm a friend of Thomas's. From the counselling centre, you know. Is he in?"

"No. I'm sorry."

She cocked her hip, lifting the box an inch higher. "His ex gave me some of his stuff to give back to him, so I thought I'd just bring it over," she said. The woman reached for the box, but Marta held onto it. "Mind if I come in for a sec? The wind's brutal out here."

"Oh—yes. Yes."

The woman stood aside a little, letting Marta edge past her into the hall. The floor was made from wood, not carpeted, and, following the woman into a cramped front parlour, Marta saw that there was old wallpaper on the walls—everything was shabby, but lovely. "If he's coming back soon," said Marta, "I could just wait for him, maybe. If you that would be all right with you, ma'am, ah—Mrs. Zimmerman."

"Rachel."

"Nice to meet you," said Marta. "You've got a lovely house."

She fidgeted, uncertain—she didn't particularly like the way the woman was staring at her, very intently. The radiator was on full-blast and the air in the parlour was thick and suffocating. Marta wanted to take off her coat, but the woman hadn't invited her to, so she only unzipped it and left it hanging open. She had made the detour on her way to work and was wearing her shapeless janitor's smock underneath. Remembering that, she felt more uncomfortable than ever.

After a moment, when the woman only stared at her, past her, she cleared her throat again. "So, ah—is he coming back soon? I was just kind of hoping to see him, you know. Just to say hi."

"I'll tell him you came," said Rachel Zimmerman, who didn't

seem to have heard. "I'm sure he'll be very glad. I hope you didn't have a long walk, in this cold."

"No, it's—"

"It gets very cold on our street. It comes off the water."

"It's really no big deal," said Marta quickly. "I mean, I just thought he'd want his medicine and phone and stuff back and—" She hesitated for a fraction of a second; the woman's stare was wearing at her badly, sucking at the edges of her words, and she looked away, stooping to put the box down on the floor at her feet. "I was kind of worried about him. He seemed pretty—pretty out of it, last time I saw him. I just wanted to make sure he's okay. Um."

Something switched off behind Rachel Zimmerman's eyes, shutters closing. "I don't know what you mean."

"I was just wondering if he was doing okay."

Shutters behind the eyes, her narrow mouth twisting like a key turned in the lock. "He's fine."

"He just didn't seem that way to me, when I saw him. He was seeming kind of rough and I know he's been having some trouble, so—"

"My son has a disease, that's all," said Rachel Zimmerman. "His condition is the business of his family. I'm sure you can appreciate that."

"Sure," said Marta, "but d'you mind if I wait for him to come back, then? I'd just feel better hearing it from him."

The woman frowned. "It was kind of you to bring his stuff over, but you should go. It's getting late and I have to make supper, and I'm sure *you* have places to be, too."

For a moment, Marta was nonplussed. She'd always prided herself on being well-liked by most people—providing, as a rule, that they weren't directly related to her. Being likeable, or at least generally agreeable, had been one of the few things she *could* pride herself on. Rachel Zimmerman's frank hostility threw her completely.

She cast around for something to say, something to thaw the conversation out a little, and settled at random on the single framed picture hanging on the parlour wall. It was a charcoal sketch of the Halifax harbour done in bold and slightly frantic lines, a chiaroscuro scrawl of light–dark contrasts; squinting at it, she could vaguely distinguish the *black* mound of Georges Island, marked by its *white*-walled lighthouse, rising from the *black* sea, and the sea itself was capped by *white* waves and the *white* sails of little boats hung on *black* masts. The sky over the far Dartmouth shore was black too, but had been done in a mess of spiralling lines—spiral on top of spiral, like the artist had been trying to capture the look of roiling storm clouds.

"That's very pretty," said Marta, nodding to the picture. "I like the sky bit."

Frowning, Rachel Zimmerman followed her gaze. "Oh—yes."

The artist's signature had been scribbled in the bottom lefthand corner of the page, almost hidden by the frame, but still legible: Howard Zimmerman, it said.

"Is your husband an artist, then?" asked Marta.

She only meant it as a harmless bit of chat, something to ingratiate herself and keep from being shooed out of the house. But the question seemed to have the opposite effect: Rachel Zimmerman flinched like she'd been struck. Her eyes widened, then narrowed again. "Why? What do you mean?"

Marta blinked, startled. "Well—the name, there. I just thought, you know . . ."

She trailed off, baffled by the woman's apparent horror at the question. And something was creeping up on her, too—a slow realization that had been dawning since the moment she'd stepped in the door and seen the neat line of coats on their pegs, the ordered row of shoes by the door. Everything was in its place and seemed like it had been that way for a long time, the only sign of disorder a few insects fluttering lazily across the ceiling, smudges of grey lead against the plaster. She looked up at them for a moment, then back at Rachel Zimmerman. "*Is* Thomas staying here?"

"You'd better leave."

"He's not," said Marta. "He's not, is he?"

"I'm asking you to leave."

She looked at the parlour window and the chintz curtains that had been tightly drawn across it, and thought about the rotten food in Thomas Zimmerman's sink.

"So where is he, then?" she asked.

"I'm asking—"

"Do you even know where he is? When was the last time you saw him?"

"I don't know what you're talking about," said Rachel Zimmerman. "But I see my son often. Our family's been through enough with his disease without strangers prying into our business."

"I just want—"

"I won't ask again."

"Fine," Marta said. "I'm going."

She turned toward the door, making to step over the box of Thomas Zimmerman's possessions, but the woman stopped her before she could.

"You can take that with you, too."

"Why," said Marta, unable to keep her voice from rising a little now, "don't *you* keep it? Since you see your son so often and all. You can give it to him yourself."

"We don't need it cluttering up the house. If he wanted those things, I'm sure he would have taken them with him when he moved out. Or he'll be in touch with you, if he wants them back. Anyway, go on."

Marta hesitated a moment longer, then bent to pick up the box again, holding it like a shield between herself and Rachel

Zimmerman's ire. "Thank you for your time, ma'am," she said. "If you do see Thomas, tell him we're all missing him very much at our therapy sessions. Tell him we hope he's all right."

The woman held the door open for her and she went out. Out and down the steps, to where the man who had introduced himself as Danny Boy still stood. He seemed to have calmed down a little; his poached-egg eyes were even redder than before, but he was no longer rocking back and forth. He looked up at her when she stopped beside him with no sign of recognition, as if they'd never spoken before.

"Hey," said Marta, and grinned at him, a little uncertain, scanning his face for any sign that another fit of tears might be coming. She stood for a moment, the box in her arms, and looked at the seagulls on the roof of the house opposite. Their feathers were the same speckled grey as the roof shingles.

Danny Boy was quiet. Whatever vein of talk he'd tapped before, the waters appeared to have run dry.

"You live around here?" she asked him.

"Yeah," he said. "I'm in the hospital parking lot these days. The IWK, you know—the big one, up the road from the university grounds. It's quiet when you want to sleep. I just come here most days when I want to sit and wait for God, you know."

"Shit," said Marta, and blew out her cheeks. "You like it, then? Good place to hang out?"

He shook his head minutely. She was disconcerted by the change in him, the abrupt clamming-up when he'd been so chatty before, but she pushed on anyway, and still in that mild, shoot-the-shit octave. She was starting to shiver in the February chill, but she held the box close against her chest and hunched over it, pressing her lips tightly together. Her face twitched convulsively as she tried to stop her teeth from chattering. "Um—so, I guess you see pretty much everybody come and go on this street, eh?"

For a moment, Danny Boy's protruding eyes were even wider, a pantomime mask of surprise. "Like who?"

"Just, you know, people," she said and then nodded to the peeling paint of Number 27. "The people who live there, even."

He came to life a little at that, and she thought that the opportunity to educate her on something had woken him up—that whatever might have been going on in the mind of Danny Boy, he was a teacher at heart. He stood up straighter. "Jewish, you know."

"Oh," said Marta. "Right. I kind of thought so."

"Zimmerman. Jewish name. You can read it off the mailbox."

"Right," she repeated, and pointedly turned her head away from him, looking out at the passing traffic as if she was nearly indifferent to the entire conversation. She sniffed hard, cleared her throat—she was starting to wonder if it was worth cutting back on the smoking, if only to air her lungs out for a while. "Both of them are, then, I guess. The mom and the son. Both Jewish."

"What son?"

Surprise cut clean through her feigned disinterest; she glanced at him quickly, then pretended that she hadn't. "Hers. I thought he might have moved back in with her lately."

"No," said Danny Boy. "It's only her in there. I don't ever see anybody else coming or going, not ever."

"Really? And no husband, either?"

"Sure, she lives alone," he said and then, with the same abruptness with which he had begun to cry, he laughed. Marta stared at him. He laughed like he was choking, like he was dying, and the sound startled the gulls on the rooftops. It sent them spiralling up into the grey sky, out over the harbourfront, where they swooped and screamed and dived.

"She lives alone," said Danny Boy, the next mayor of Halifax, and laughed. "Can't you just tell?"

The next afternoon, halfway through babysitting duty, Marta called Quyen.

Sitting at the kitchen table again, Nicholas was doing complicated maneuvers with a pair of scissors and a folded piece of paper, trying to make a chain of Valentine's Day hearts. Discarded scraps and flecks of red glitter were spread across the carpet around him, making him look like he was shedding bloodied dandruff. Something for his classroom at school—he'd told her about it earlier, but she'd already forgotten the details. From where she stood, leaning against the counter, Marta watched him absently, automatically, while she dialled the therapist's office number. Even as she did, a new text flashed across the screen—a whole string of them, unanswered, from Allan Baird. First: *what's up?* Then: *how is the sane life treating u?* And: *the party, my place, sunday night. are u coming or not?*

The call clicked through on the second ring. "Barrington Counselling Centre, this is Quyen Richardson speaking. How can I help you today?"

"Hey, it's me, Marta. I'm just calling 'cause I had a question . . ."

There was a sudden alertness in the woman's voice, switching modes, the therapist kicking in. "Yes? What is it? How are you feeling?"

"Oh—great," said Marta. For a moment, she hesitated; she looked down at the pill bottle in her lap, the label peeling and faded, but still wholly legible. She'd gone through the box of Thomas Zimmerman's possessions again and had picked this one out as the most likely clue she had. His mother had talked about his disease, how it was a private affair in their family, but surely it wouldn't *just* be their family who knew about it. She studied the label of the pill bottle and then said, "I've been kind of thinking about that talk we had. Thinking about what I'm going to do now I'm finished at the Centre, you know. It's been really helpful, but I kind of want to keep it going now, keep making progress."

"That's wonderful to hear, Marta. Did you see the email I sent you about the Open Hands organization?"

"Um. Yeah, absolutely. And I was actually also thinking I might want to start seeing a doctor, you know. A psychotherapist or whatever, just seeing someone one-on-one on the regular—yeah?"

Nicholas had put down the scissors. Very deliberately, carefully, he pinched each corner of the folded page between his fingers and slowly drew them apart. Between his hands, the paper unspooled into a string of hearts. He twisted around, holding it up to her— Marta, still cradling the phone to her ear, gave him a thumbs up, pantomiming her approval. *Nice one.*

"Well," said Quyen, "it's great that you feel ready to take that step in your mental wellness journey. But it can be very difficult to get an appointment for regular sessions with a practitioner right now. You might have to go on a waitlist, unless you have the insurance coverage—"

"I think, working at the university, I get that kind of stuff covered. Anyway, I'd really like to get a consultation, at least. Just so I have a path forward, you know?"

"Of course. If you want, I could recommend someone—"

"Actually," said Marta, and held the pill bottle up to the light of the lamp, squinting down at the closely printed text there, "there's somebody I heard about. Um. I think the name's Dr. Simon Greene. I've heard—I've heard he's really good, and I know he treats some pretty serious stuff over there, and I was wondering if you could, maybe, refer me to him."

"Oh. Yes."

Nicholas had started again. A simpler pattern this time, his scissors cutting jagged lines, rising peaks and falling valleys—she couldn't quite make out the whole shape yet.

"Eh. Just if it would be possible, you know."

She thought she could hear the clacking of computer keys on the other end of the line, and then, "Yes. Yes, I can refer you to the psychotherapy office where he works—it's up by Bayer's Road. And I can put a note in the application form, saying that you'd prefer to see Dr. Greene. It might be a week or two before you can get a consultation, depending on his availability. You might still have to go on a list, but—"

"Just a couple weeks, then?"

"They'll give you a call, I'm sure, but it might not be until March. But, Marta—are you sure you're doing all right? Are you keeping busy? If you haven't had a chance to look at the information for the Open Hands foundation and their outreach work, I really think you should consider—"

"I really appreciate it," said Marta quickly.

"But it's not a linear path, you know, nobody expects you to be better instantly, just like that."

The scissors were shards of glass, delicately turning in-out, in-out, and the shapes cut themselves loose and danced in Nicholas's hands. Again, he drew the folded page apart, and this time a row of little paper people spread themselves between his fingers; linked at the hands and feet, all as bloodily red and perfectly uniform as the hearts had been. They danced up and down as he shook them, blank-faced, and their heads bobbed and swung, as if to a tune that only they could hear. Up and up, thought Marta.

"I'm great," she said. "Honestly, I feel great. Really great. Really."

Hanging up, she stared at the shreds of paper on the carpet, wondering what she ought to do next. Nothing, probably—nothing was always the easiest, after all. Nothing was the hole she ended up going down most days. Still, she hadn't realized until Quyen had asked her about it that, in the time since she'd last seen Thomas Zimmerman, thinking about him had been the only distraction she'd had from her own head. And wasn't that what she was meant to be looking for? The key to life in Sanity City was keeping busy, after all. Nobody ever told you how.

It's this or a pottery class. Marta gave the pill bottle one last turn in her hand before tucking it away in her pocket again. The doctor was the one clue to Thomas Zimmerman's life she had, everything else a perfect question mark, punctuating the end of each sentence. Where could he have gone since leaving his apartment? Where had he kept himself? Not with his mother, she was sure of that now—but where then? A normal person would crash at a buddy's place, maybe, but would he? He had lots of friends, Chris had said, but he'd always seemed so quiet at the Centre; she struggled to imagine him casually showing up at somebody's place, barefoot and muddy again, asking if he could sleep on their couch.

Marta looked at Nicholas. He'd gotten bored with the scissors and was doodling on a bit of scrap paper, drawing looping patterns with a Sharpie; the little chain of people lay abandoned on the tiles by his chair. It was pointless, she knew, to think about where a normal person would go when it came to Thomas Zimmerman. Nobody in his way of life—her way, their way—was normal.

Still, there was always one place they could go.

CHAPTER SIX

It was cramped and airless in Jacob Klausner's little two-seater sports car. It had been that way ever since he had bought it, nearly three decades before, back when there had only been two *to* sit. Now, wedged into the passenger's seat, Marta—who was longer and lankier than her father was, taller than her mother had ever been—held the box of Thomas Zimmerman's possessions in her lap and awkwardly folded her limbs around it, her chin sunk down to her chest and her bent knees pressed up against the dashboard. Sideways, head crooked, she looked at the outline of her father's profile, the sagging flesh around the eyes and the corners of his mouth—gravity always seemed to weigh heavier on him than anybody else, and it had made him into a basset hound of a man. His hands, resting on the steering wheel, were lined and knotted, the knuckles swollen and bulging with arthritis. It was quiet in the car, the radio switched off, and his thumbs were tap-tapping in time to nothing at all as he wove them through the morning traffic.

Marta shifted in her seat, the box teetering in her lap; she jogged it from knee to knee. The Doc Marten boots bobbed erratically, threatening to topple out, and she caught them before they could. The leather was soft with wear and—in the heated car—felt uncomfortably warm, as if it had been stitched from breathing skin. In places, it had worn so thin it had started to break; there was a hole in the heel of the left boot, about the size of a nickel. Marta pushed her thumb through it, felt the skin around the edges of the wound pushing *back*.

Her father cleared his throat; hastily, she shoved the hole-heeled boot further into the box.

"Um, thanks—" his hound eyes flicked toward her, and she hesitated, stranded mid-sentence as she wondered why she'd said anything at all—"Thanks for giving me a ride and everything. S'cool of you. I know it's not far, but they're saying the temperature's dropping . . ."

"Well. It's on my way."

"Yeah?"

"To church, you know."

"It's Saturday."

"I *always* go on Saturdays," he said. "We make lunches for the homeless, you know—sandwiches and juice boxes and all."

"Oh," said Marta. "Thanks for driving me, anyway, yeah?"

"It's on my way."

It wasn't. The Abbie J. Lane Memorial Hospital wasn't anywhere near their church—it was on the other side of the downtown strip, past Spring Garden Road and past the public gardens beyond. Marta sank deeper into her seat, turning her face toward the grimy car window. It had snowed in the night and the street was full of a brownish slush of salt and ice, churned up under the wheels. The smell in the car made her a little queasy; the air was thick and clogged with the reek of peppermint and old menthol cigarettes, even though her father had quit smoking years ago—and twice. The first time had only been in quotation marks, "quitting" when she'd been eight and Dina five, but he'd stopped for good just after Nicholas was born.

"So," said Jacob, "is your friend, ah, going to be staying at Abbie J.'s long?"

"I don't know," said Marta. "I don't know if he's there at all. The lady at their reception wouldn't tell me when I called 'cause of patient confidentiality. And he's not really my friend, anyway. He's just a guy I know from therapy and shit—stuff. He's just some guy."

"Abbie J.'s is a pretty long way to go for 'just some guy.'"

She looked at him sharply, but his face had subsided again into doggish indifference, perfectly neutral as he scanned the opposite lane of traffic. "Thomas didn't *ask* me to do it or anything," she told him. "I just wanted to help out, bring him his stuff. If you didn't *want* to drive me, I could have got the bus, Dad. It's not a big deal or anything. I'm not trying to make it a big deal."

"I didn't say you were."

"Yeah—"

"I just said it was a long way."

She wrapped her arms more tightly around the box, feeling it press against her ribs, the thin cardboard bent out of shape, distorted around the lines of Thomas Zimmerman's life. After a few elastic moments of silence, her father cleared his throat wetly, then said, "You and Dee used to like climbing on him."

For a second, Marta didn't know what he meant, until she followed the line of his crooked finger and saw that they had stopped in traffic by the old library building, the one with the once-vandalized Winston Churchill out front. "Oh. Yeah."

"I think I got a photo of you and her either side of him, hanging off his legs. You were doing the peace sign with your fingers. Little hippie. You did that in every picture, even though you didn't know what it meant—you remember that?"

"Maybe."

"Every picture. Your mom thought it was the funniest thing."

She looked at his hands on the wheel, brown and creased and very familiar. The library and Winston Churchill were in the rear-view mirror already, going and going and gone as the lights turned green and the line of cars lurched forward again. She didn't remember playing there at all. She wouldn't have remembered making the peace sign, either, if she hadn't seen it in a handful of photographs, on the rare occasions when Dina had brought out an old photo album to show guests and she hadn't been able to excuse herself quickly enough. *Marta, do you remember the time—? Oh, isn't that just so cute? Isn't that just? Isn't it?*

"I'll take your word for it," she said and reached awkwardly around the box to fiddle with the dial on the radio. "So—what do you think? What are we hearing? Bluegrass, or rock, or a little bit of good old soul?"

When they pulled up in front of the hospital—all severe concrete, a throwback to the nineteen-fifties that reminded Marta of an especially rundown nursing home—she already had her hand on the car door, but Jacob stopped her. "Why don't I take the box in?"

"What? Why?"

He hesitated, seeming to cast around for a moment before answering. "Well—I don't know if you should go inside like that."

She stared at him. "Like what?"

He tipped his head, gestured vaguely, and she looked down at her clothes, surprised. It was the same old Baja sweatshirt she usually wore under her coat when she wasn't at work or doing anything special; her pajama bottoms stuck out from underneath, tartan fabric clashing badly with the pattern of the coarse wool hoodie. "Dad, they won't give a shit what I'm wearing. It's just in and out, ask if he's there, drop the box off at the desk, whatever. It's gonna take three minutes tops, and—"

But he was already setting his jaw decisively, pushing his own door open. "*I'll* go. You wait here."

They tug-of-warred with the box briefly before she let go, smarting with indignation. "Are you serious?"

"It's a hospital."

"It's a *mental* hospital," she said, as the door slammed behind him, sealing her in silence. She remembered that she had forgotten something else, then, and fumbled to roll down her window, calling after him. "Hang on a sec! I've got something else, too."

She took the note from the pocket of her hoodie, unfolding it quickly, scanning the scrawled words one more time to make sure that they rang right. They had been written, written, *over*-written in the technical privacy of her bedroom—she'd sat with her back up against the door, to make sure that Dina didn't come in—and it had taken her six pieces of looseleaf to get them down in a satisfactory order. She had burned up those rejected first drafts later, holding each page to the guttering flame of her lighter and then sweeping the ashy remnants out her window. It had been stupid, but she hadn't been able to stand the idea of Dina going through the trash and finding them.

The sixth and final draft was short, but painstaking, and the words crabbed their way erratic across the page, rising and falling:

TZ, my number is 902-208-8122, call me so i know you're ok or if you need HELP and i will HELP you, any time and any way. we are BOTH crazytown people and that is the ONLY thing that happiness is. stay free. MK.

She folded the page up four times, as tight as it would go, and then—one extra measure—dug the stub of a pencil out of the glove compartment and wrote Thomas Zimmerman's name in block capitals across the outer fold.

Jacob was fidgeting on the sidewalk now; Marta reached out of the car window and wedged the note down into the box, tucking it away into the nest of books and clothes. "Just make sure they know it's for Thomas Zimmerman, okay?"

She watched him go up the hospital steps, a slight figure, slouched and round-shouldered in his coat and heavy work boots, relics of the years he'd spent doing first construction jobs, then basic home repairs, before the arthritic tissue in his hands had finally forced him into retirement. He was uncomfortable, she thought—maybe even a little frightened. She could see it in the way that he walked, with his head bowed down; how he started back suddenly, to let somebody else through the doors ahead of him. She wondered if he thought it was contagious—the whatever-it-was that got treated behind those walls—and that he might become contaminated by it. Or that *she* might, which was maybe why he hadn't wanted her to be the one carrying the box. Like the hospital doors would have shut behind her and she would have been committed, just like that, and never seen again.

She stretched, cracked her neck, felt a knot of muscle in her spine snap. He'd left his wallet there, sitting on the dashboard, and she picked it up, settling back in her seat and thumbing through the few crumpled bills tucked inside. "You should always take fives and tens," Allan Baird had told her once, when they'd been waiting for a therapy session to start, fidgeting in their plastic chairs, their plastic and circular world. *Nothing higher. And if you take a ten, make sure there's another ten in there that you leave behind. People think, if they still have at least one ten left, they must have been imagining having more.*

But Marta left all the bills where they were and looked, instead, at the two little photographs wedged behind the clear plastic pouch of the wallet. One was of her mother, slightly blurred, standing smiling in front of the old clock tower on Citadel Hill, wearing a tartan raincoat and the wind blowing her dark hair all around her face. The other was Nicholas's newest school photo, taken last September.

Marta closed the wallet and put it back on the dash, fiddling with it for a moment to try and get it turned *exactly* the way it had been before. Then she leaned back in her seat and closed her eyes very tightly and didn't open them again until the car door rattled and Jacob was clambering back into the driver's seat. He didn't have the box.

"All good?" she asked.

"Fine," he said. "I gave it to the woman at the desk, there, and told her it was for your friend. Thomas Zimmerman."

"He's a patient? They got him?"

"She checked their system, said he *was* there."

Marta sat up a little straighter in her seat. "Really?"

"Yeah, she said he was there for about two weeks, all the end of January. She said we just missed him. He got checked out on Monday."

"Who checked him out?"

Jacob shrugged. "I don't know. But they left a number, she said—they *have* to leave a number, doing all the paperwork—and she said she could call them, ask them to come pick up the box. Is that all right?"

"Oh," said Marta. "Yeah, sure. Yeah."

"She was very polite, very friendly," he said. "It looked very clean in there."

"Yeah."

He put the car into gear, wheeling them slowly down the hospital drive and back into the road, then asked, "You want to come along to the church, help out making sandwiches? I can drop you off at work after."

"Um . . ." Marta said and then hesitated, gnawing on the rind of her thumb; she'd been planning to drop by Shaw's apartment if he was home, see if he was in the mood to smoke a bowl and watch some cartoons on his laptop, maybe debrief with him on this newest piece in the puzzle that was Thomas Zimmerman, but she couldn't say any of that to her father. Instead, she said, "I don't know."

"You should come. We're down half our volunteers since the pandemic, and they could always use more help. And it wouldn't hurt you to be social."

"I *am* social, Dad. I'm going to a party tomorrow night."

He looked at her sharply. "Where?"

Marta hesitated, then said, "I'll come to church."

"You don't go outside enough, you know. You don't *do* things. You'd feel a lot better *doing* things, getting out there, not just lying around all day and smoking that stuff. The sooner you get back to normal—"

"I *said* I'll come, Dad."

They drove in silence for a while.

"They keep that place very clean," he said. "Everybody was very polite."

"Halle-fucking-lujah," said Marta.

Once, St. Matthew's United Church had served hot breakfasts to the city's homeless population every week, but the pandemic had put an end to this arrangement. Now volunteers packed food in brown paper bags to be distributed afterward at the church door—each with one ham-and-cheese sandwich, one apple, one juice box. Only three other volunteers had shown up this week: a pair of older women with strong Toronto accents and a foreign exchange student from Greece. Marta, standing at the kitchen counter and slathering mayonnaise onto slices of limp white bread, listened while they chatted with her father. One of the Torontonians' nephews had just gotten married, the other had a daughter who'd just been accepted to a grad school in British Columbia.

"Nice weather out there on the west coast," said Jacob Klausner, and seemed to have nothing else to contribute to the conversation.

Marta licked mayonnaise off her thumb and wondered how much longer they'd go for. Her stack of finished sandwiches, she'd noticed, was looking much sloppier than the one in front of the Greek student. Reverend Campbell, their minister, came and stood next to her to work. They'd run out of ham so he slipped a second piece of cheese into each of the sandwiches instead.

"How've you been doing?" he asked her. "We haven't seen you at services in a while. How long's it been, now?"

"About eight years," said Marta, and felt herself start to flush. "I've been working pretty late, you know, so I don't really—"

"It's okay," he said. "I just meant that you've been missed, that's all."

"Oh. Thanks."

Campbell looked over at her wobbling stack of sandwiches, which was shedding crumbs and gobbets of mayonnaise. "Anyway, it's nice of you to volunteer your time like this," he said and then—"Your dad mentioned that you'd been up to the hospital today, looking for a friend of yours."

Marta nodded. "Yeah, just someone I met at therapy. I don't know where he's at."

"You could always ask around the shelters," he said. "Sometimes that's where people end up when there's—there's problems. Shelters have a responsibility to respect privacy, but they could probably let you know if your friend's okay, maybe pass on a message if there's something you want to tell him. It's the Open Hands foundation that does the most, you know, 'in the field' work with people here."

"I could ask," she said, uncertain.

"It speaks very well for you that you're so concerned. Some people wouldn't be."

Marta only shrugged. She ripped open another package of cheese, fiddling with the plastic. Across the kitchen, her father was still talking to the Torontonians, but she noticed that he kept throwing little glances at her. She wondered if he was worried about her, if he thought she might not be behaving herself.

"If you give me a short description of your friend, maybe where he usually spends his time, I can ask around," Campbell was saying now. "We could circulate your phone number to all the shelters. They might not hear anything, of course, but . . ."

"All right," said Marta, and then, suddenly worried he might have the wrong idea about her—"I don't want it to be a big deal, or whatever. It's not, like, a performative thing. I just want to make sure he's okay, just casual."

He laughed. "There's nothing wrong with that."

There was no more bread to be mayonnaise-ed, and so they began to pack the bags, her holding each one open so that he could drop a sandwich inside. Presently, he asked her, "Have you ever considered doing more volunteer work like this? I know the charities around here are always looking for help. You might find it pretty rewarding, performative or not."

"So I've heard," said Marta, and stared down at the bag in her hands, down into its wide and gaping mouth, and wondered what to say. "But that's not really my thing, yeah? I mean, it's very good that people are doing it, people are *called* to do it, but I mostly just want to be easy. Um. Have a good time, good folks, good memories—you know? I don't really know what I'd get out of it."

Again, Campbell laughed, but not at all unkindly. "Well, that's the question, isn't it?" he said. "It sounds clichéd, but the way I always think about it is—you know you're on the right track when it doesn't feel like you're helping them, but like they're helping you."

"It sounds pretty stupid," said Marta. "No offence."

But she still took one of the spare brown paper bags from the stack and wrote her phone number in pen, and then: *Thomas Zimmerman, 30s, tall and dark hair, sheepskin jacket.* She folded it in two and gave it to him. "Any kind of information would be great," she said. "But it's not a big deal, yeah?"

In the end, Marta volunteered to be the one to pass the food bags out, mostly to get away from the general conversation in the kitchen; the Torontonians had an inexhaustible supply of young relatives and each one seemed to be more successful in life than the last. Quietly—sullenly—she thought that if she listened much longer, she'd hear that somebody's grandchild was in the running for prime minister next election.

Like much of Halifax, St. Matthews had been built into the side of a hill, and so the churchyard was set lower than the road, accessed by a set of stairs that led down off the pavement. Marta sat hunkered on the topmost step, the box crammed with food bags beside her, and waited. The wind was picking up, rattling the gates of the Old Burying Ground across the street, where the city's historic dead had been laid to rest and where they'd put the bones of someone very important, she thought, but she couldn't remember who it had been. The guy who burned the White House, maybe, or the one who'd gone to stamp out the Northwest Rebellion.

Her mother must have told her the story.

Her mother had told her *every* story. She'd been a MacLachlan from Mahone Bay and she'd believed in the mythology of Nova Scotia completely, and so Marta had believed in it too. She'd sat on the pier and believed that the tide that lapped at her boots was *all* tides, and the sea that slopped in the harbour was *all* seas. Her mother beside her, pointing out toward the distant mouth of the harbour. *You see?* There was the wreck of the *Teazer* and the *Marie Celeste* and the *Ourang Medan*. The MacLachlan family had chipped the mummified carcasses of polar explorers from the ice and harpooned whales off the coast of Greenland. They'd killed the English at Killiecrankie, the Americans at Fort Oswego, the Germans at El Alamein. These things had been related to her personally—she'd believed them so completely that they'd seemed inevitable; they'd happened before and *would* happen again. Her mother had told her so.

The breathing wind blew low over the grave of the unknown man and sent Marta's hair whipping around her face. She raked it back with her fingers, feeling the ends frayed and frazzled. The bleach was starting to thin it out, she thought, and she wondered if she should let it go natural for a while.

A man was coming down the sidewalk, stopping and starting, eyeing her warily. He was wearing a fungus-green parka and was dragging a little wheeled shopping trolley behind him with one hand. With the other, he held the leash of a dog. He came up and drew level and, for a second, she thought he might walk right past her, but he didn't.

He stopped. "You giving out the food?"

Marta offered him one of the bags. "How's it going, man?"

"Oh, it's going," he said and gave her a thin smile. He talked with a particular lilt that made her think he was a Newfoundlander, or maybe, like Shaw, he had grown up in one of the little towns along the coast. "It sure is going."

He took the bag, opening it a fraction to peer inside. "Wouldn't happen to be any booze in here, huh?"

"I wish."

He'd wrapped the leash around his wrist and the dog took advantage of his distraction to investigate Marta, pressing its wet nose against her knee. It was a wolfish kind of creature, long and lean but quite beautiful; its coat was black and little droplets of melting snow beaded the dark hairs there. Grinning, she held out her hands and the dog mouthed at them gently; she felt its teeth snagging in the wool of her gloves, but it didn't bite.

"What's its name?" she asked.

The man's smile was more animated now. "Theo," he said. "He's a good boy, real clever. He's getting old, now, but he's real clever and he still knows all his tricks."

Marta detached her fingers from Theo's mouth and then dug around in the bags, fishing out another sandwich. "Does he like ham?"

"He likes everything," said the man, and then, twitching the end of the leash—"I've been teaching him how to beg, you know. He can beg, he can *double*-beg." And, to the dog— "Theo, double-beg. Show her how it's done, boy."

Obedient, the dog sat precariously back on his haunches and, wobbling a bit, put first one paw and then the other on Marta's knee. She took the strip of ham from the sandwich and held it out, and he took it delicately from between her fingers. Marta scratched between his ears, feeling tickled and a little guilty, too. It had been quite a small piece of ham and cut very thin—hardly anything.

The man had wrapped his own meal up in its bag and stowed it away in the cart. "Thanks for the food, honey," he said. "We'd better be getting along. I'm after sleeping at the Salvation Army tonight and it always takes us most of the day, just getting uptown. He's a good boy but he doesn't walk fast."

Theo seemed reluctant to go, leaning his flank against Marta's legs and butting his head against her, but the man tugged on the leash and, after a while, he went. The wind moaned in the lofty eaves of the church. Marta watched the man's back until both he and the dog were out of sight, wishing that she'd asked him what *his* name was. She would have felt stupid calling after him now.

She stayed sitting on the step for another forty minutes and gave away twelve more paper bags. The twelfth, to her surprise, went to someone she recognized—Danny Boy, the next mayor of Halifax and the man who knew everybody on Spring Garden Road. He was the last to come by, moving down the sidewalk in a series of birdlike hops and steps, his empty takeout cup gripped in one hand, and he didn't seem at all surprised to see *her*.

"Hello, dear," he said. "D'you have one without any meat in it? I don't like to eat that stuff anymore."

His cheeks and nose were raw with cold and his eyes were weeping a little, something crusted yellowish around the lids. She gave him the sandwich she'd taken apart for Theo and watched him tuck it away into the front of his coat. "Do you want an extra juice box or something? I could get you another apple."

"Naw," said Danny Boy. "I have to be careful what I eat. I've got—in my stomach, you know. Ulcers. I have to be careful or it starts cramping and coming up blood."

"That sounds pretty rough."

"It's the cold," he said. "It gets cold, back of the IWK parking lot. I'd be all right if I had somewhere dry to sleep, that's all."

Marta tried to think of something to say to that, but his attention had already wandered; he looked past her, tipping his head to one side, the wobbling movement making him look more frail and bird-like than ever. "Who's that?"

She looked around. Her father had emerged from the hall and was watching them from under the awning of the door, too far across the churchyard for her to distinguish his expression. Seeing her turn, he made a little jerking motion with one hand, beckoning her back. "Oh—that's just my dad. He's probably wanting to go and let someone else take over, that's all."

Danny Boy seemed to process this for a moment. "You don't look much like him, huh?"

"Guess not," said Marta, and stood up, stiff and shivering as she stooped to pick up the box of food packets. "I don't think I ever took after him, really."

CHAPTER SEVEN

It wasn't until Marta rang the doorbell and was waiting, rocking on her heels on the front porch, that the realization crept slowly over her that something wasn't right. The street was familiar, the street was right, but something was gnawing at the back of her mind. She stared at the door, the dark green paint, and watched transfixed as it swung open. A man, a stranger, stood on the other side, looking at her inquiringly. "Yes?" he asked, and then leaned away from her slightly, his nose wrinkling perceptibly.

Marta looked past him, at a neat front hall and a cozy-looking kitchen beyond it, and then at him again. His hand on the half-open door, the green paint. Only then did she remember that the front door of Shaw's building was red. "Sorry," she told the stranger, and her breath made clouds in the cold evening air. "Wrong house."

She went down off the porch and then wandered along the sidewalk, going two houses closer to the harbour until she caught sight of—for sure this time—the red door of Inglis Lodge, where Shaw boarded. He let her into the front hall, looking skittish and a little distracted, and Marta was struck, as she always was, by the stink of accumulated nicotine, thick and suffocating in the air. It was always warm in the outer halls of Inglis Lodge, the heat cranked up high, and the effect was of someone breathing heavily in your face; the dying gasps of a chain-smoker.

"You're late," he said. He was playing with the sleeves of his over-sized rugby shirt, restless, pulling them down over his hands.

"I got lost."

He sniffed. "Oh."

Following him down the narrow hall, she rolled off the walls, trailing her fingertips along. There was a faint sheen to the wallpaper, as if had been coated in a layer of glue. But it was hard to tell, exactly, because nearly every inch of bare wall was plastered with Christmas decorations, incongruously bright and desperate; reindeers and stars and sleighbells and a dozen cheery, red-cheeked Santa Clauses. They'd been there since the beginning of December and Marta wondered if they'd still be there in August.

"Yeah," she said. "This new stuff's pretty good—it's the leftover Hindu Kush, six bucks for a pre-roll. Mesmerizing shit. I've been feeling like I'm yesterday."

The freezing rain had been coming down on-and-off all evening, making it impossible to keep the bedroom window open. She'd had to resort to using an improvised sploof, binding layers of dryer sheets over the end of discarded toilet paper roll and blowing the smoke down the makeshift tunnel to harmlessly dissipate—it had made her feel like she was in school again, getting stoned in the second-floor bathroom.

"You reek," said Shaw, and sniffed again—pure theatricality, she suspected. There was no chance he could detect the odour of weed here, when everything in the Lodge already smelled foul. "The whole point was coming over so we could smoke together, before the party. I thought we were going to pre-game it."

None of the doors in the Lodge had plates on them. Instead, on most, a single sheet of paper had been affixed to the wood with scotch tape, a number scrawled on it in black marker. On the sheet taped to Shaw's door, an extra word had been added in pen underneath the number six, "FAG."

"Christ," said Marta.

"They've written a lot worse things," said Shaw. "I used to tear the paper off and stick up a new one every time, but that just reminds them I'm here, kind of. Then they start writing more and more. It's better just to leave it alone and pretend it's not there."

"I'm sorry."

He shrugged, fiddling the key in the lock. "That's just the way it goes."

He'd lived in the Lodge the whole five months that she'd known him, but there were still liquor store boxes everywhere in the apartment and a mess of things half-packed, unpacked, overflowing. Some of the boxes were neatly labelled (BOOKS, KITCHEN, WEED STUFF) and others had clearly been taped up and then ripped open again, when Shaw had gone hunting around for something. There were boxes on the floor and stacked in teetering piles next to and on the daybed where Shaw slept; the only spot in the room entirely free of this debris was the coffee table, which was clear of everything except for an ashtray, a cigarette lighter, and a single spoon. The bowl of the spoon was stained black with soot, the metal warped by heat.

"How's the unpacking going?"

"It goes," said Shaw. He was bending over the coffee table, sweeping the lighter and spoon quickly away, tucking them out of sight among the detritus of packing tape and plastic bags on the floor. She sat on the edge of the daybed and watched him, made faintly queasy by the swiftness of his movements. She was conscious of the temporal distance between them; she was still yesterday, cocooned by the Hindu Kush, while he had gone on ahead, into an unkind and unwelcoming future.

"We can still pre-game it," she told him. "We can drink."

He made a face. "I can't. They've got me on a new antidepressant now—one of the SSRI things. I'm not meant to drink."

"What's the point of going to a party, then?"

"Well . . . you're going," he said and smiled at her.

He was standing over her now. Gripped by a sudden anxiety, Marta sensed that he was going to say something important—or maybe he already had, and she just hadn't heard it, because it had fallen between the cracks of yesterday. She didn't think she could stand to hear. With difficulty, she pried her dry tongue from where it had become glued to the roof of her mouth. "Listen," she said, talking as much to herself as to him. "I went to see Zimmerman's mom the other day, like we were talking about."

There was a pause, which Marta—thoroughly disconnected from the run of time—thought might have lasted for days. Shaw's smile had crystallized, frozen. "How come?"

"I thought he might be there, but he's not. Then I checked at the hospital, the psych ward or whatever, and they said he *was* there, and he got checked out by someone. But they don't let anybody check you out, so it was someone in his family, someone he knows, but I don't think it was his mom 'cause—"

"You're rambling," said Shaw. "And I meant, how come you're doing all this?"

"I want to find him, that's all. Nobody seems to know where he is."

"He might want it that way."

She frowned. "Why? Who the fuck wants to vanish off the face of the earth? Who wants to be alone like that?"

"Paranoid schizophrenics," said Shaw, and now his smile was that of a martyr, enduring the coals and the arrows with perfect, virtuous patience. His hand jerked at his side, and she wondered if he was fighting the urge to start rubbing his moustache. "Listen, I don't know that much about what's going on with him these days. He didn't talk that much. I mean, he used to, when he first started coming to sessions, but—"

"Yeah? When was that?"

"Eh, I don't know . . . six years? Seven years? Seven. I think he thought—I mean, everybody thought—he was just depressed. Like, he did his twenty sessions and he left, and he came back, and you could kind of tell there was something weird going on with him, you know? He would talk in the sessions a lot and you could just tell."

Marta nodded. She was remembering Danny Boy and how the words had come spilling out of him, twisting and overlapping themselves, biting at each other, carving living shapes into the air. Crazy talking. "Did he say much about his family?"

"A little bit, I guess. It was usually just about his mother, 'cause he was living with her back then. I always thought that was kind of weird because, you know, he was already twenty-five, twenty-six, and he was still living with her. I mean, no offence or anything, but—"

"None taken," said Marta, who was practising getting the muscles around her mouth to work again, twitching and contorting them, one at a time. "Lived with mom. Weird. Go on."

"He talked about her a lot, but it was never anything consistent. She was great, things were great, or she was out to get him, and she was putting poison in his food. He got really thin after a while—scary thin. I think he stopped eating. I think the centre stepped in, eventually, and he got hospitalized for a while."

"Christ."

"Yeah," said Shaw, and shrugged. "That was his mother, and he still thought she was trying to kill him."

"What about his dad? Was his dad ever in the picture?"

He was starting to look annoyed now. "Not that I know of. My point is, people like that get in their heads, get paranoid about everything. He might not want anybody looking for him, wherever he is. Just forget about it. Don't think about him so much."

"Well, I have to think about something," said Marta. She shifted on the daybed, crossing her arms more tightly over her ribs; the best part of the high had faded, and now she felt dry and wrung out, and the Hindu Kush was sour on her tongue.

Shaw was watching her. "Are you in love with him?" he asked, and she looked at him, startled. He was grinning, but it was all fragile, like he wanted it to be a joke but couldn't quite get the rest of his face to cooperate. Marta looked at him standing there with his long sleeves and receding hairline, surrounded by the detritus of his disassembled life, the glassy smiles and cold eyes of the Santa Clauses and snowmen and reindeer, and couldn't bring herself to lie to him.

"No," she said. "I'm not in love with anybody."

Out on the narrow balcony of Allan Baird's apartment, Marta watched the vodka bottle go around the little knot of partygoers. A cold northwesterly wind was coming in off the harbour; it blew so sharp and biting that, when she drew a breath, she could feel the steel-wool substance of it scouring her lungs from the inside out. A mix of sea brine and engine exhaust, brewed up somewhere away across the water. She coughed and hacked and, turning politely to one side, spat a gob of something white and glistening onto the cement balcony underfoot, missing the toes of her boots by only an inch.

"Ever the lady," said Allan and laughed.

Marta laughed too, a nasal snicker that the wind snatched away immediately, as she wiped a trailing bit of spit away with the sleeve of her coat. "I try, man," she said and then, wincing as she felt the liquor crawling its way down her trachea—"Jesus Christ, that's rough. That is just apocalyptically rough on the pipes."

The vodka bottle continued its trajectory, Allan handing it to Shaw, who passed it on without even a sip. Nat, next, wiped the mouth of the bottle prudently on the edge of her cashmere scarf before drinking. She was the only one of them who had made any apparent effort to dress up for the party; there was a smudge of silver glitter around her eyes and, when she passed the bottle along to Marta, a trace of red lipstick was smeared on the plastic rim.

"Brothers and sisters, here's to one hundred years of happiness," said Marta, and then drank quickly, before she could think twice about it; the vodka hit the back of her throat like a knife, and she fought back the urge to cough again. Her fingers, protruding from the ends of her gloves, were red and raw with cold.

The bottle went around again, close to empty. She took one more gulp, wrinkling her nose as a thread of pain wound its way through her clogged sinuses. She was, generally, an antisocial drinker— liquor usually made her quiet, it sedated her. Still, she felt pretty fine standing there on the balcony, the vodka thinning out her blood as she looked around at their ancient, familiar faces. This was, she thought, the real world. This was life in Sanity City. She drank and then passed the bottle off to Allan.

"Cheers, my dear," he said. "We've been missing you at the sessions, you know. With you gone, and Thomas gone—"

The mention of Thomas Zimmerman sobered her. "So nobody's seen him, then?"

"Nope," said Nat, giggling. "Where *is* he, anyway? We could have had a real reunion, all of us therapy people. Old times for the crazy crowd."

There was a general ripple of laughter at that. The vodka turned sour in the pit of Marta's stomach. Again, the wind seemed to catch at her breath, snatching it clean out of her lungs, and the steel wool was tearing up her throat.

"Do you guys remember," said Allan, "what he did at James Bailey's funeral? Livened that shit up."

Nat pulled her scarf up over her nose to muffle her giggles, and only her eyes showed, bright and very young. Beside her, Shaw was convulsing with stupid, helpless laughter. Looking from one to another, Marta could see that she was on the outside edge of a joke. "Why?" she asked, trying to keep her voice light and easy. "What happened? What did he do?"

Allan was looking sharper than the others, keeping it together, but she could still see the laughter behind his eyes. "It's a long story—before your time."

"C'mon, you can't just tease me like that."

"Tell her," Nat said to Allan, and then, still a little muffled by her scarf as she leaned closer, strands of her hair tickling Marta's cheek, added, "It's not funny, babe, it really isn't. It's absolutely awful. We're awful for laughing, but. . ."

"James Bailey was a guy who used to go to therapy with us, a couple months before you started coming," said Allan, as beside him, Shaw—a mechanical kind of reflex—crossed himself. "He was a suicide case. Went downhill fast when the pandemic started, you know. He drowned at the beginning of last summer, jumping off the pier. Quyen wanted us all to go to the poor son of a bitch's funeral, 'cause basically nobody else was going to, and we brought flowers and stuff for his folks. So, we're lining up to shake hands with them, to say how sorry we were for their loss and our thoughts and prayers were with them and all the conventional shit like that, and Thomas went to shake hands with James's mom—"

"It was so awful, babe."

"—and Thomas shook her hand and said, I swear to God, he actually said: 'The eulogy you gave for James really saved my life, Mrs. Bailey. I was thinking about killing myself until I heard you saying it. I never realized before the effect it would have on my mother, if I died. I never thought about how she'd feel.'"

"Awful."

"Totally serious, totally straight, just like that. He just stood looking at her, shaking her hand, like he was expecting her to smile and thank him for that, or something. Crazy fucker."

"God, yeah," said Marta, and managed to coax the wind-numb muscles of her face into another rictus grin. "Yeah. Crazy."

The bottle emptied, the little circle broke up and dispersed. Nat and Allan both drifted back toward the balcony doors, toward the rest of the party; Shaw lingered uncertainly, looking at Marta with his head tipped to one side. "Shall we?"

Again, she felt the dreadful weight of his expectation pinning her down. *Shall we?* Like they were standing at the edge of some grand ballroom, instead of washed up on the balcony of a shitty student apartment. She was annoyed by his attention, and by his sobriety, and she was annoyed with him, too, for laughing. "I mean, you can do whatever you want, man. It's fucking—" she fumbled for the right word, groping around blindly in the haze "—copacetic. I want to smoke."

"Now?"

"Sure, of course."

He pulled a doubtful face, rubbing his moustache. "You've had a lot to drink already. Are you sure you won't get cross-faded?"

"I'm fine," she said and fumbled in her pockets for a joint. "Have you got a lighter?"

Shaw shook his head, but Marta stuck out her hand, palm-up and insistent. "Come on, you always have one."

She meant it to be funny, or she thought that she had, but she saw him flinch, a twitch in his jaw like she'd feinted to strike him. "What's that supposed to mean?"

"I'm just saying—you always have one, don't you? You don't have to be so fucking weird about it, you know. It's just, eh—it's just a joke and stuff."

But he only gave her a wounded, reproachful look and turned toward the sliding doors, yanking them open. A brief burst of music and laughter escaped into the night air, and then he ducked inside, the door rattling shut behind him. Marta stayed out, although she was shivering with cold now and beginning to feel dizzy. She didn't want him to think that she was following him and so she counted to sixty under her breath, lost track twice, and made it to forty-eight before she couldn't remember what she was doing. Then she went in.

She was barely across the threshold before she nearly tripped over Allan; he was sitting on the rug with a handful of other partygoers ringed around him, a deck of cards scattered around their knees. "Watch out," he told her, pinching her leg playfully. "You're going to get mud all over my carpet. Take off your boots, you uncultured fuck."

Obliging, Marta bent down to untie her laces and found that she was much less dizzy on the floor. She beside him and kicked the boots off, worming her way into their circle. "Did you see where Shaw went?"

"No," said Allan. "But the movements of the guy—his mind—it's all a mystery to me. His taste in women, too."

"I think he's pissed," she said, ignoring his last remark neatly.

"Forget him."

Marta did. After a while, she gave up on remembering anyone or anything at all and concentrated on staying upright. Looking around at them all, blurred around the edges, bright with the residue of vodka, it struck her that they weren't any different from the people who'd come to the group therapy sessions at the Centre; the same faces, the same inward-turned eyes, nobody listening to each other, all just lining up the thoughts inside their own heads. Everywhere, the same. All the same zombies, the reanimated dead, thinking they were alive when they weren't. She was always in circles, always with strangers. And, even if she didn't really like any of them, she was going to miss them when they left her.

Somewhere, off in the apartment, there was the sound of glass shattering. Someone whooped and cheered.

"L'Chaim," said someone else, very close to Marta's ear.

She didn't know what happened first after that—falling down or throwing up.

She remembered her head hitting the wall with a crack, and she remembered the first convulsion tearing through her, but she couldn't put an order to the events; she sat on the bathroom floor, her back to the door and vomit soaking through her sweater. The world was distorted, like someone was playing damaged film through an old projector; everything jumped and tripled; three toilets, three shower curtains, three windows—all blurred and smearing up.

After a while, Marta stood up and made a cursory attempt at cleaning the floor with a wad of toilet paper. Her shirt was a hopeless case—her socks were soaked through, so she took them off, and walked, barefoot, into the hall. She couldn't find her boots in the mess of shoes by the door; after a few seconds of searching, she gave up and seized a pair that looked about the right size, worming her bare feet past the half-knotted laces into them. Somehow, she got through the door and out into the hall before the dark started to close in on her again; she drifted sideways and caught herself, followed the line of the wall with her shoulder, one foot in front of the other. She couldn't remember where the elevators were, but the neon sign for the stairs was hanging in the air above her and she went through the door and into the stairwell.

It was cold and white, greenish floor tiles cast with fluorescent light. She looked down the chute of the stairs and thought for a second that she was on a ship and the ship was sinking. She thought she heard a woman's breathing. She went down the stairs the same way you did in a dream, gripping the railing, not touching the steps but skimming them, throwing herself down and arriving at the bottom in some unknowable way. On the next landing, she started to fade out again, and had to sink down, gripping the cold metal of the banister like a lifeline; through the rails, she could see another set of stairs, then another, down and down. Around and around, and she couldn't see the bottom. How many floors had they gone up in the elevator?

Someone was hanging over her, touching her shoulder; squinting through the fog, she had a vague impression of plastic shopping bags, the hem of a coat. "—okay? Are you okay?"

She gripped the banister more tightly, dragging herself up. "I can't see."

"Is anybody with you? Do you have somebody who can drive you home?"

She shook her head, and the world tilted, tipped—the stairwell was dark and close around her, and the stairs stretched on forever.

"Is there somebody you can call?" the voice was asking. "I think you should call someone to come get you."

"I don't have anybody," said Marta, "so that's not going to happen."

She took one step and then another, and in the stairwell the dark opened up to take her. Ready, grateful, she went down.

CHAPTER EIGHT

When the cold world came back into focus, she was kneeling in front of a toilet. It was morning and she was in front of a toilet. In a bathroom again. For a moment, Marta wondered if it was the *same* bathroom, if time had looped up on itself and she was still in Allan's apartment, if the rest of her existence would be spent crawling in circles across white tiles. Then she saw the wallpaper with the rose-patterned strip that ran around the baseboard, and she knew that she was home. A wave of nausea hit her and she hunched over the toilet bowl; she stuck her fingers in her mouth as far as they would go and she couldn't make herself vomit. Spitting and gagging, kneading the spongy flesh behind her tonsils, but all that came out were a few lung-wrenching coughs.

The sound, echoing off the porcelain, crashed around the bathroom like thunder—it would wake the others up, if they weren't up already. She could hear the general clatter of someone moving around in Dina and Nicholas's bedroom, the creak-slap of feet hitting the floorboards. It was still early, then; Dina liked to be up by seven on Mondays, so that she could have the coffee in the pot and the porridge on the stove by the time their father rolled out of bed around eight.

Marta spat a knot of mucous into the toilet bowl and then wiped her hands on the knees of her jeans. Her legs were numb, and she had to pull herself up with her back pressed against the bathroom door, both hands gripping the edge of the sink. She was still wearing her coat, but her feet were bare again. Mascara had made dark and watery tracks down her cheeks.

Wobbling out of the bathroom, Marta was disconcerted to see that Allan was sitting at their kitchen table, picking at an open package of Saltine crackers. She stared at him, blinking hard in case that might make him vanish, but he gave her a grin and bright little wave. Salt-crusted crumbs sprayed across the tabletop and went down the front of his shirt. "Morning. Looking good, there, sunshine."

She blinked again. "You didn't come home with me, did you?"

"You wish," he said and winked at her. He was looking much too cheerful, she thought, and not the least bit hungover.

"No, I just meant—" She broke off, gripping the bathroom door-frame for balance; she'd thought for a moment that he might be the voice she'd heard on the stairs, the last thing she could remember before the waters had risen over her head. "I mean, why are you here?"

"You said I could come over later. I came over."

"But why?"

He made a sour face, exhaling a mouthful of crumbs. "You all did a number on that apartment. Landlord's sent a glazer to fix the window."

The floor tilted under her as she crossed the room to join him, dropping heavily into a chair and propping herself up against the table, her head in her hands.

"How did you get in?"

"You let me in."

"Oh."

"You told me there was going to be breakfast."

Her phone was on the table, powered off. She switched it on and saw that she had two missed calls from Dina and two from a number she didn't know. There was a string of texts, too—they flashed across the screen so quickly that her head swam trying to decipher them, another wave of nausea tightening her throat, making saliva well up under her tongue. She closed her eyes tightly and only opened them in time to read the very last message.

We should talk.

It was signed "Christopher." It took her a few moments, the name bouncing sluggishly around her aching head, to realize that this had to be Chris, the man she'd met in Thomas Zimmerman's apartment.

Pointedly, Allan cleared his throat. "Breakfast," he repeated.

"Fuck off," said Marta. "You're eating our crackers, aren't you? Isn't that breakfast? Anyway, I don't remember saying you could have shit."

He snickered. "Feels like just about the least you could do. You drank about a fifth of my best vodka last night, you know."

Marta ignored him, leaning over her phone again and swallowing hard. Her tongue crawled up her throat, carried along on a tide of saliva and stomach acids, and threatened to choke her. She tried to focus on Chris's texts instead. He'd sent them all at nearly two in the morning, three neat sets of three words and all fired off in quick succession, each sent within a minute of the next.

More to say.

About T.

We should talk.

It took her three tries to type a response, clumsy fingers slipping every which way across the grease-printed screen. Eventually, she managed to punch in a short response—*yes pls today?*—and had just hit send when Dina appeared in the doorway of her and Nicholas's bedroom, wearing her dressing gown and blinking owlishly in the morning light. She looked from Marta to Allan.

"Morning," he said and treated her to the same airy wave and grin with which he'd greeted Marta. As if it was his kitchen and they were the ones intruding in it. "You must be Dina, right?"

Dina gave him an economical portion of a smile and then looked back at Marta again. "I didn't know you were having anybody over.

I tried calling last night to see when you'd be home, but you didn't pick up."

"Sorry."

"What time did you get in?"

Her phone buzzed in her hand, an answering text from Chris: *Could do before work. 10am @ the McDonalds on Spring Garden Rd?*

"Um," she said, "I don't actually remember. Late, early. Anyway, it's all right—we'll be heading out pretty soon. We'll go and get some food or something, get out of your hair."

"We don't have to," said Allan, piping up from the sidelines with his mouth jammed full of crackers, dribbling fragments on the tabletop. "I don't have class 'til noon today."

"Well, *I* have to."

She stood up quickly, too quickly, and had to lean on the back of her chair for a moment. It felt suddenly much too hot in the apartment and she wanted more than anything to be out in the fresh air, where she could breathe and—even better—where Dina wouldn't be looking at her. She inhaled desperately. "Christ, it smells rank in here."

"It's you," said Allan. "I think you have dried puke on the back of your coat."

"Oh, for fuck's sake," said Marta. She tore the coat off and balled it up, ignoring the look of horror on her sister's face. "Don't worry, Dee, I'll do the laundry this time. Just leave the hamper in my room and I'll do it after my shift tonight."

She went to dig up some clean clothes and, when she emerged from her room, Allan and Dina were chatting together by the stove, her sister asking him politely about his pharmacy program as she filled the coffee pot. They were *still* talking when she ducked into the bathroom to take a shower, *still* talking when she came out, her bleached hair hanging in bedraggled rattails down her back. Another wave of nausea had hit her as she'd stepped into the shower and she'd thrown up again; she'd washed the mess away and sluiced water down the drain until the odour of bile had dissipated.

"—been really hard, of course," Allan was saying now, and it took her a second to realize he was still talking about his program. His round face was contorted into an expression of pained earnestness and, with a creeping kind of alarm, she noticed that his voice had shifted, sounding just a fraction deeper than it usually was. "But you just know the work's going to be so rewarding. I'd rather be doing that, doing something that can really make a difference for people, than just going the easy route."

"Well, of course," said Dina. "I think that's incredibly admirable."

"Come on," said Marta, cutting in quickly before Allan could open his mouth. "I'll buy you breakfast, yeah? Let's just get out of here."

It took her a long time to find another jacket, rummaging around in the back of the hall closet, and even longer to find her boots; one was by the fridge and one in the spare room, shoved under her cot. It was only then, picking them up, that she noticed something was wrong with them. Something was different. She held them up to the kitchen light, squinting as her head spun—she turned them over in her hands and looked at the rubber soles, then at the knotted laces, then at scuffed leather of each toe.

"What is it?" asked Allan. He was waiting by the door now. She supposed that the last of the crackers had been secreted into his pockets, and probably several of their tea bags and packets of sugar and whatever else he'd been able to find. He was a pathological mooch, his determination to cadge and wheedle and *take* completely out of proportion to his actual circumstances in life. He got a monthly allowance from his parents in Ottawa that was nearly double Marta's pay cheque, but she'd seen him steal pens from the receptionist's desk at the Barrington Centre.

"These aren't mine," she said. "These aren't my boots."

They weren't. They were too large, for one, and too old as well;

her boots had been shiny and new, bright out of the box just last Christmas, and these were scratched and pitted, the leather bleached around the stitched seams by salt. And they were the wrong brand, too—the tag said they were Doc Martens, which hers certainly hadn't been.

"What are you talking about?"

"I've stolen somebody's boots," said Marta. "I must have left mine at your apartment."

She held the boots up to show him. Dina had vanished back into her room and, through the half-open door, Marta could hear the sound of her voice—Nicholas was being gently cajoled out of bed.

Allan made an impatient noise in the back of his throat. "Well, I can look for them later, then. Come on, just wear those for now—they do fit, don't they?"

Marta shrugged. She bent down and untangled the laces, teasing out the knots, starting with the left boot. When she slipped her foot in, the leather closed up around her. It felt warm and soft like skin. It felt familiar. Crouching, ignoring the swift surge of nausea, Marta ran her fingertips over the back seam and knew, even before she felt it, that there would be a hole there.

A hole in the heel the size of a nickel.

There was a woman in a red anorak sitting on a cardboard pallet on the corner of Spring Garden Road, an empty cup on the sidewalk in front of her. The light switched to red just as Marta and Allan drew level with her and they were forced to stand waiting on the curb, watching the line of traffic advance; the woman held her cup toward them, but they both ignored her—they were too busy arguing. They'd been arguing in the queue at the Tim Hortons, too, and all the time they'd been waiting to collect their coffees and bagels, and they'd argued sitting on a bench by the pier to eat.

"But did you *know* he was at the party last night?" asked Marta. It was the fifth or sixth time she'd asked some variation of the question. He had a knack for leading her off down tangents, evading the point.

He said, "Well, I saw him, yeah."

"What do you mean? It was *your* party."

"I mean, I texted him about it when I texted you, but just to give him the invite. He never answered. I didn't know he was going to come."

"Why didn't you tell me?"

"I didn't think you'd care—Christ, I don't even care. Am I my schizo's keeper?"

"Excuse me," said the woman.

Marta rocked on her heels, feeling the leather of Thomas Zimmerman's boots rubbing at her ankles. She'd had to stuff an extra sock into each toe to keep from stepping right out of them, but once she'd gotten used to the odd fleshiness of them, they'd started to feel comfortable enough.

So he *had* gotten the box she'd left at the hospital, then.

"I've been looking for the guy all over," she said. "Ever since he quit coming to the meetings. I think he's having some kind of psychotic break."

"News at eleven."

He'd gotten his boots and his phone and the note she'd written to him, but he hadn't called her.

"But did he look okay to you? Did you talk to him at all?"

"Of course not," said Allan. "I was busy watching you puke on the rug. Anyway, he looked like he always looks, crazy, and everybody's saying *he's* the one who freaked out and broke my fucking window, too."

"Are you—"

"Excuse me," said the woman in the red anorak again, more loudly this time. "Do you have any change?"

They both looked down at her.

"Um, sorry," said Marta, and spread her hands helplessly. "Got nothing."

"It's just," said the woman, "that my house is being renovated because they found mould in the walls, black mould, and so I can't stay there anymore, and I need to be able to pay for the renovations, the fixing, because I have two kids, they're three and six, real young, and we can't stay in the house with the mould there, because the health effects—"

The light turned green and Allan plunged out into the road immediately, Marta following hastily in his wake. She heard the woman's voice trailing after them, high and plaintive, but she was too sick to feel guilty and too guilty to look back. On the opposite pavement, Allan laughed. "Bet she doesn't even have any children," he said and then, thoughtfully, "You know, when you said you had a nephew, I figured your sister would be a lot older. She looks pretty young to be a mom."

"She was. Is. She was fifteen when it happened."

"The way you talked, I thought she'd be older than you."

"She is," said Marta, "on the inside."

"You made her sound like a real bitch, the way you were talking about her in sessions. She seems okay to me."

She shot him a wary look. "Dina wouldn't be interested in you— she wouldn't be interested in *any* of my friends—so don't . . ."

"Please," said Allan, and grinned. "Anyway, I figured she was taken already. You know, the kid and all. Dad's not around these days?"

"Not as far as I know."

"Oh?"

Marta swallowed hard, a fresh bout of nausea churning in her gut, and wished that she hadn't run across the street so quickly. "Well, Dina never really told us who it was, or anything about it 'til she was about fourteen weeks in," she said and pressed her hand flat against her stomach, like she could hold herself together or hold the honesty of it back. "I remember wishing that she'd come to me for help and shit, and I could've taken her to get an abortion or something." Then, flushing and sick, she went on, "I mean, I just had this fantasy, back then. Before he was born. I don't know why—I guess it sounds kind of fucked up."

"Maybe," said Allan, and shrugged. "Who cares?"

"I mean, I guess I just wanted her to *ask* me, yeah? It could have brought us closer together or whatever. I don't know."

He laughed. "You two really don't get along, huh?"

"Not for as long as I can remember," said Marta with perfect truthfulness, and saw, ahead of them, the golden arches of the McDonald's sign. Gratefully, she seized on it, fishing out her phone and double-checking the time. "Look, I'm stopping here—I've got to meet somebody. I'll see you around, all right?"

Chris was waiting for her at the table nearest the window, turning a takeout cup full of steaming coffee around and around in his hands. He looked a little wan and thin around the edges but much less wound-up than when she'd last seen him, and miles better than Marta herself felt when she sat down across from him. "Are you all right?" he asked her, and she was surprised to hear a note of genuine concern in his voice. "You look kind of sick."

"It's just drinking," said Marta. "I'm sorry to say I'll probably live."

He didn't say anything to that, only looked at her carefully, and she wondered if he was seeing her now as he'd seen Thomas Zimmerman. The Second Coming of Crazy. When the silence got to be so awkward that she couldn't stand it, she cleared her throat. "So, you wanted to talk about something?"

He nodded. "I heard you visited Thomas's mom. She called me and said you'd been there. You'd been looking for him and stuff. She thought maybe I'd sent you."

"Really?"

"I think the exact word might have been 'spy.'"

"Jesus Christ."

For the first time since they'd met, she heard him laugh. "For what it's worth," he said, "she never liked me, either. I don't think she ever got over Thomas wanting to move in with me in the first place, and he only ever did it 'cause he had some crazy idea that she was poisoning him. She hated that, the poison thing. She thought I was the one who came up with it, just to lure him out or something."

"Did you?"

"Of course not," said Chris and seemed to sober immediately, looking down into the depths of his coffee cup. "So, you think he might be in trouble, then?"

Marta shrugged.

"I mean, it's not like it matters much to me anymore. Like I said, we're broke up, and I'm done riding that crazy train, I'm done with him, but—" he hesitated, turning his cup first one way and then the other to make a perfect ring on the tabletop—"if she told you she had nothing to do with him running off, she's a fucking liar. That's all."

"What do you mean?"

"Well, the last thing he did before he flipped out was call her. He came back from his doctor's appointment that afternoon and he called her right away—they were talking for, like, an hour before he lost it. That's when all this stuff went down and we got in a fight, and the place got smashed up."

"The shepherdess," said Marta.

"The what?"

"The little shepherdess you had on the windowsill in your kitchen. I saw her that first time I was there, with Thomas."

"Right, that," said Chris, and frowned, as if he still wasn't entirely sure he remembered. "That was just one of his bullshit little trinkets,

I think, something he got when he was a kid. Well, anyway, he smashed it all up and that's when he left."

"But," said Marta, "you didn't hear what they were talking about? Nothing?"

He shrugged. "Never told me. He didn't tell me where he was going, either."

"Well, he was in the hospital for a while," she said. "Were you the one who came and checked him out on Monday?"

"Not me," said Chris. And then, with an odd kind of anxiety, as if worried that he might have unbent himself too much toward her and lost whatever ground he'd once had, "Look, I'm only telling you any of this so the record's straight. Just in case she's been saying stuff about me, making things up, whatever the fuck. I just want the record straight. Whatever's wrong with him, it's nothing to do with me. That's all."

"So what do you think it was, then?"

"I don't know," he said and shrugged again, anxiety fading quickly into a fresh and jagged irritation. "I don't know shit about shit. Ask somebody who does."

Late that afternoon and on her way up to the university for her shift, Marta stopped by Inglis Lodge to see Shaw. She found him out on the front porch, sitting in the single rusted old lawn chair that all the Lodge's residents seemed to share and thumbing fragments of weed into the bowl of a pipe. He looked tired but not overly hungover, and not overly glad to see her, either. "I didn't know you were coming around. You should have texted."

"Well, I wanted to be spontaneous," said Marta, and gave him a sickly grin. She'd gone directly from the McDonald's to the drugstore across the street to buy Alka-Seltzer and ibuprofen, but she still felt loose and watery around the edges.

Shaw made an indistinct noise in the back of his throat and bent over the pipe again. She watched him smoke up, holding his lighter to the bowl and waiting for it to catch. When he lifted the pipe to take a drag, the sleeve of his jacket slipped down an inch, and—just for a moment—she saw the broken skin of his forearm, crisscrossed with peeling scabs.

"Was I an asshole last night?" she asked.

He turned his head away from her, blowing a stream of smoke out across the snowy yard, then coughed quietly. "Not really."

"I'm sorry," said Marta. "I don't remember what I said, but I'm sure it was just some bullshit. You know how it is."

He nodded and took another drag. She waited for him to speak, hands jammed in her jacket pockets and shivering, wishing that she hadn't puked on her warmest coat and wishing, too, that he'd offer her the pipe. She looked down at the toes of Thomas Zimmerman's boots. She wanted to tell Shaw everything she'd found out from Chris, but there was faraway look to his face—closed off, like the shutters had come down.

"Are you pissed at me?" she asked.

A faint crease appeared in his forehead, like it was a question that he had to consider quite carefully. "No," he said and then, "I guess I stopped feeling angry about most stuff a while ago. I don't feel that much about anything on a day-to-day basis."

Marta looked at him worriedly. It was the kind of remark that Quyen would have called "a cause for concern," the kind of thing people said before they went to run a bath and you didn't see them again. Like Kelsie McDonald, who'd attended the therapy group for a few sessions in November until the chemicals in her brain had worked themselves up into a lather. According to the rumour that had gone around, she'd slit her wrist and played with a vein there for twenty minutes, until her parents had noticed and called an ambulance.

Shaw coughed again, then went on, still with the same tone

of contemplative calm. "Sometimes I just feel like less of a whole person than I used to be, you know? There's less of me inside, like I've deteriorated or degenerated."

"Yeah?"

"I think the word in French is *déchirer*."

"Torn up," said Marta.

"Yeah," he said. "I feel all torn up."

The pipe had burnt itself out, smouldered into nothing, and the conversation lapsed again while he repacked it. Out on the sidewalk, a woman was walking slowly, dragging a shopping cart behind her. The cart was filled to the brim with a collection of empty cans and bottles, and every time the wheels hit a crack in the pavement, it rattled like thunder. When she'd drawn level, she stopped and called out to them across the yard. "Do either of you guys have a couple of bucks? I just wanna buy some cigarettes."

It was the woman in the red anorak again.

Irritated, Marta held up her empty hands, but Shaw put the pipe down gingerly on the porch and got to his feet, starting slowly off across the lawn. He dug through his coat pockets and found a crumpled five-dollar bill for the woman. "There's a gas station just a couple minutes down the road, if you want to go there."

The woman gave him a tight nod, pocketing the money, then continued her slow and rattling progress. Marta looked longingly at the pipe but didn't touch it. She waited until Shaw had trudged back to his seat before saying, a little sullenly, "She's lying like a motherfucker, that one. She told me'n Allan earlier she had black mould in her house and her kids were having their little lungs rotted out."

"So? It's all the same to me."

He sounded colder than ever now.

"Eugene, listen," she said. "I don't know if you're pissed or not, but I *told* you I don't remember what I said last night, whatever I said."

It was the first time she'd ever called him that, Eugene, and the pettiness of it was bitter on her tongue. There seemed to be something bitter in *his* mouth, too; he pressed his lips together tightly, turning them bloodless. He'd told her once how badly he hated his name and why, but the exact reason escaped her now—something to do with his father back in Yarmouth, maybe.

"You don't have amnesia," he said.

"I never—"

"Don't remember this, remember that, forget this and that and the other fucking thing. You always talk like you've got some kind of retro-antero-amnesia thing, but you don't. You just forget the stuff you don't want to remember, that's all."

"Why are you giving me such a hard time? Isn't it enough I've been sick all day?"

"You'll be sick next time, too," he said. "At least I can admit that I'm wrong, I'm fucked, what's going on with me. At least I know it's a cry for help."

Marta looked down. "Your pipe's gone out again," she said and laughed. It was a hoarse sound, hanging like smoke in the air between them, but she forced herself to ignore it. There was an itch of guilt-like mould in the back of her throat. She ignored that, too.

CHAPTER NINE

It was the third week of February before she got the call to say she was off the doctor's waiting list and into his calendar. The Tuesday after that, Marta rode the 29 bus out to a fancy office block by Bayers Road, where she had only been once before in her life and couldn't, now, remember the exact occasion—it had been a radiologist or an oncologist, maybe, but she'd only sat in the waiting room, holding her mother's coat and purse in her lap. She had read magazines with Dina. They had both read a lot of magazines back then.

Today, she didn't mind the ride much, because it gave her a chance to jot down more thoughts in her notebook. Not thoughts—facts. A list of uncontestable, inarguable facts, aligned neatly down the left side of the page, and Thomas Zimmerman's initials at the top. She wrote everything with initials and abbreviations, in case Dina went snooping around her bedroom again. The facts, abbreviated and initialed, were these:

7th Jan, TZ is UPSET – man in sink?

9th of Jan, TZ has dr appt, is UPSET. Mom called. No therapy. Fight w/ C and leaves

? of Jan, checks into mental ward at hospital

7th of Feb, he's checked out by somebody—who?

13th of Feb, TZ attends party, (freaks out & smashes window?) and loses his boots

???

It wasn't a long list and, if it hadn't been a very small notebook, the shortness of it might have been upsetting—the facts swallowed up by an expanse of empty page. As it was, Marta still wasn't entirely confident with them. She turned the page and began a list of questions, instead. It made for a markedly longer list.

Where did TZ go?
Why upset after dr appointment?
Why leave therapy?
Why not ask Quy et al for help?
Why call mom if he doesn't trust? (poison, food, etc)
Where now?

When the bus deposited her at Bayers Road, she wandered around the ground-floor shopping complex for a while, picking things up aimlessly and then putting them back on the shelves, and then rode the glass-walled elevator up to the floor where the psychotherapist's practice was. It was much fancier than the utilitarian brutalism of the Barrington Centre downtown; the walls were all a slick mirrored black, the fixtures brass and glass, and there was no overworked and harried receptionist to greet her. She only pressed a call button on the wall and told the metallic voice who answered what her name was and what time her appointment was meant to be. Dr. Simon Greene would see her soon, the voice told her—she should take a seat and fill out a form on her phone in the meantime.

There were no magazines in this waiting room, only a coat rack and two padded leather couches and a shiny black coffee machine in the corner. Curious, Marta spent a few minutes experimenting with the different flavours of coffee you could get with the pull of a lever. Sweet, caramelized nectars, more like liquid candy than anything else, and night and day from the dishwater-thin stuff they had every morning at home—she drank half a cup before she remembered that she didn't really like coffee at all and poured the remainder out into the wastepaper basket.

The form was all the standard stuff, and she rattled through the familiar formula she'd supplied a dozen times before. First her details and personal information, then the concerns she hoped to see addressed, and then a series of statements to either agree or disagree with.

I've been having trouble sleeping.

I've experienced suicidal thoughts.

Marta made a series of check marks—mostly in the "agree" column—and had just slipped her phone back into her pocket when the office door opened.

A man leaned out. "Hi," he said. "Marta Klausner?"

"The one and only," said Marta, and brushed off the knees of her jeans as she stood to shake his hand. She had made a conscious effort to dress nicely for the occasion, but that had only meant teasing the worst knots out of her hair with a comb and picking out one of her few T-shirts without a jokey stoner slogan on it.

"I'm Simon. Please—come in."

He was younger than she'd been expecting and good-looking in the most direct way. Everything from the decisive grip of his handshake to the cut of his jaw made him seem like a man travelling a hundred miles an hour in his own direction. And, looking at him, Marta thought she could see straight away why he was working out of such a slick operation, why his waiting list might be particularly long. A firm hand went a long way when you thought you were drowning.

With that same hand, he propelled her to a plush chair in the corner of the room. "Before we start, do you want any coffee? Tea? Juice?"

"Eh, no. No, thanks, I'm okay."

Simon Greene glanced briefly at her completed intake form when it flashed across the screen of his desk computer, then sat down opposite her, back-to-front in the chair with his chin resting on his folded arms. If it had been somebody else, she might have thought it was a little funny—the studied casualness of it, the pose so reminiscent of the therapists she'd always mentally classified as the "approachable teacher" type—but he sold it pretty well. And there was nothing funny about the way he looked at her, narrow and intent like he was trying to read something written small across her soul. He waited until she was starting to squirm, shrinking from his scrutiny, then said, "So. What's on your mind today, Marta?"

She looked at him, at the desk behind him where a sleek laptop still sat open, and then down at her knotted fingers in her lap. It was all too easy to fall into the regular routine of things. "I've been—I've been struggling sometimes," she told him, meaning to spin out a lie but finding that the truth came much more quickly; the old vein opened very easily under the knife. "I keep having thoughts, you know, about bad things happening. I think about it a lot at night and I'm having trouble sleeping. I feel like it's keeping me apart from the people I care about the most."

Greene didn't make a note of anything, only kept looking at her with the same startling attentiveness. Marta didn't consider herself to be any kind of qualified judge on the issue, but she thought that this was probably what so many people found attractive, why every other patient she'd ever met seemed to be half in love with their therapist. The sensation of being the subject of somebody's complete and perfect attention was addictive for a person who'd been starved of it for years.

"What do you think is behind these thoughts?"

"I don't know," said Marta. "I guess I'm . . . I mean, I get pretty scared sometimes. It's like I keep going down a path in my head, over and over, down, and I don't know how to get out of it."

He tipped his head to one side, frowned—again, the pantomime of paying attention struck Marta as much less cartoonish than it had any right to, much more disconcerting. "How long has this been going on?" he asked.

"It's hard to remember," said Marta, and then continued, gnawing on her thumbnail as she struggled to find the right words. "I just don't remember, yeah? I mean, I've been having trouble remembering things that happened to me, you know, things that happened when I was younger. And I can't really visualize the future anymore, I can't see it, so . . ."

That seemed to catch his interest; the chair creaked as he leaned forward. "Have you undergone any kind of trauma in the past?"

"Like what?"

"Childhood trauma, say. A traumatic event in your life, something that might have disrupted things for you. I only ask because memory issues—lost time, fuzzy patches, whole years missing—are often symptomatic of that kind of experience."

Marta looked down at the bloody rind of her cuticle. She was starting to wish that she hadn't come. It had been a stupid idea, half-formed, a desire to walk in Thomas Zimmerman's muddied footsteps for a while, like that would bring her closer to him somehow. "I don't remember anything," she said and then stopped, thinking about what Shaw had said. *You just forget the stuff you don't want to remember.* Just about the last words he'd said to her; they hadn't spoken since and he hadn't answered a single one of her texts.

She hesitated, then tried again, "The only thing that ever happened was my mom died, but I was older, then."

"How old?"

"About fourteen when they diagnosed her," said Marta. "Eighteen when she died. The cancer spread to her liver, you know, and they didn't realize at first. She didn't want to eat after a while, and then—yeah. She didn't. I stopped remembering things after that."

"Is it that you stopped remembering," he asked, "or you stopped thinking about it?"

She frowned, bit her cuticle again. "Both, I guess. I feel her coming up in my head sometimes and I just turn away from her, yeah? I go left instead of right, or whatever. I don't like to remember her straight on."

"And do you think that was the start of it for you? Your mother's passing?"

"Yes," said Marta, and then almost immediately shook her head. She looked at the reddened tips of her fingers and saw, through them, the cracked asphalt of the parking lot behind Fairview Lawn Cemetery, where she'd walked around and around, and where Dina had come to find her on the afternoon of the funeral. "No. That was when I got diagnosed with clinical depression, but it wasn't the start. It was just when I stopped caring. I stopped pretending I was any better than I was."

Dina had come to find her in the parking lot. She'd been wearing one of their mother's dresses, and so had Marta, because neither of them had owned any black clothes that were suitable, because neither of them had ever been to a funeral before. In another six months, she'd be wearing nothing but maternity dresses. Dina, dirt on her fingers, catching Marta's arm, stopping her in her orbit as she tried to go around, around. *What's wrong with you? Can't you just keep it together, for Dad?*

"Can you tell me a little more about that?"

Can't you?

"No," said Marta. "I'm not really interested in going over that stuff. The grief thing. I just want to go up and up, yeah? Gotta get down with the moving on already, take the troubles to the river and throw them away. You know."

"Please understand, I'm not asking you this because I'm trying to make you uncomfortable. If there's anything you'd rather not disclose, that's completely—"

"It's cool," said Marta. "I just don't have anything to say about her anymore, you know? I've said it all already. I'm twenty-six years old, I gotta just get over it and . . ." but the words trailed off, curling in on themselves, turning shrivelled-up and small as she saw him smile; she faltered, blinked, prick of needles tenting the skin as the blush crept over her. "What? What's so funny about that?"

"Well—you say 'twenty-six' like you're already a senior citizen, but most of the patients I see regularly are decades older than you. And, quite often, we end up going over the childhood years, high school years, all of it. In many cases, the pattern is set early on."

Up. Up. Simon Greene was looking at her expectantly now, but Marta only clasped her hands tightly between her knees and looked at him, through him, to the office window where the February sky was grey and clouded, domed like an eggshell. Before, when she'd been younger, the sky over Halifax had always been the arched roof of a cathedral, dizzyingly high and far away from her. Now, she thought that she could touch it if she tried—she would stand up straight one day and her head would brush against the clouds. She wondered vaguely what Thomas Zimmerman's pattern was and how it had been set. And where were his footprints now? Where was he?

The chair creaked again as Greene leaned back. "I can see you're going through a lot. Do you think you deserve this?"

"Yes," said Marta. It wasn't something that she had to think about.

"Why?"

"I'm a bad person," she said and then, seeing his eyebrows raise a fraction, added quickly, "I feel like I'm a bad person."

"What makes you a bad person?"

She hesitated—how could she explain it to him if he didn't already know? In all his training, his certification courses, had nobody ever told him that sometimes bad wasn't an entity in itself, just the absence of anything good? Still, in her silence, he carried on easily. "Do you think you've made mistakes?"

"Yes, a lot."

He laughed, and the sound was so sudden and sharp that Marta looked at him quickly, startled, and saw that he was grinning. "Welcome to being an adult," he told her. "Welcome to adulthood, where you fuck up and torture yourself over it. Of course you've made mistakes—everybody has."

She stared at him for a moment, dazed, and then she began to laugh, too. Her discomfort was fading a little, now that he seemed to have put the subject of childhood experiences aside, and she permitted herself—just for a moment—to enjoy the intensity of his attention. Deep down, she suspected that she was just as much of a sucker as any patient who ever fell in love with a therapist. She was just as starved, and drowning, too.

"I'm going to show you something," he said and reached back to take a book from his desk, leafing through the pages until he came to one that had been marked with a bright blue sticky-note. "You might have seen it before—I don't know. Have you ever heard about the Window of Tolerance?"

"I don't think so."

He held the book open to a page, showing her the large diagram printed there; a flat line drawn straight across, and a second wavey line curving through it. Above the straight line, the blank expanse of the page was labelled in big blocky capitals: ZONE OF HYPERAROUSAL. "That's where you are when you're all wound up," said Greene, punctuating each word with a tap of his pen. "Your mind's going a mile a minute, your heart, everything is in overdrive. You're primed for something, some kind of adrenal rush, and you're just flying from second to second. That's where people sometimes get into a lot of destructive behaviours—they start looking for sensation-seeking stuff, when they're just trying to keep going. That's where addictions start."

Marta wasn't sure what he expected from her—she nodded, leaning forward to rest her chin in her hands, trying to look attentive.

Down below the straight line was ZONE OF HYPOAROUSAL,

stretching across the bottom of the page. "This," said Greene, "is the opposite end of the scale. You're lethargic, you're unmotivated, you're numb—there's just this sense of disconnect between you and the rest of the world. Everyone around you. Maybe you feel too tired to get out of bed, maybe you aren't interested in doing anything anymore. Does that make sense?"

Marta nodded.

"It's only when we're between the two states that we're in the Window of Tolerance, as it were. We're safe, we're comfortable—we can cope with whatever life's throwing our way."

"Sure."

He guided the tip of his pen along the page. "If you had to guess where your head is at, where your body is at, whenever you're having these thoughts . . . would you say it was here—" his pen tapped the low curve of the wave, then swerved up to the top of the page "—or up here?"

She studied the diagram for a moment. "Down there, I think," she said and tipped her head. "There, in the, ah—the zone of hypoarousal."

That seemed to be the right answer, or at least the one that Greene had been expecting. He threw himself back again, the movement so violent that the legs of his chair scraped an inch across the polished tiles, and nodded. Then he asked, "Have you ever taken medication?"

"No. People have talked about it, but I never . . ."

"The reason I ask is, the way you come off to me, just having this conversation, I think you would benefit from it."

"I always—I've just heard it can kind of . . ."

"Fuck you up? It can, absolutely. You're right to be cautious. But with a doctor monitoring you closely, taking a controlled dose, the side effects would be reversible—you might not even notice them at all. I wouldn't recommend them to just anyone. I'm not a pill-pusher, especially with someone your age. But I think you're a very intelligent, articulate person, and I think you're describing a pretty serious situation. I think medication could help get rid of some of those highs and lows. It could keep you in the window."

"All right," said Marta, and then glanced at the clock; she knew that she had been allotted thirty minutes for her appointment, and that time was now half-gone. It wasn't until Greene went around his desk and began to consult his laptop again that an idea struck her.

"I'm going to recommend they start you on something called fluoxetine," he said. "It's essentially the same thing as Prozac—it's meant to boost the levels of serotonin in your brain, and it might even you out a bit."

She nodded. "All right, yeah. For sure."

"The process isn't as simple as it used to be, before the pandemic, but it shouldn't be that hard, either. I can send the prescription to your pharmacist and you can talk over the details with them. Since it's your first time, they'll probably want to have a consultation with you—even just a quick chat over the phone, if you like—and then you'll be all set."

"Great," said Marta. "Thank you. And—" She hesitated, mind racing; she looked at the book, still open on the desk. "And would it be possible for me to get a photocopy of that diagram? The different zones? I think it would be really helpful to have it, just to refer to, when I feel myself kind of slipping out of that window."

"Sure," he said and smiled at her. "It'll just take a minute . . ."

"No worries."

The moment that the office door closed behind him, Marta stood and quickly crossed to the desk, turning the laptop around toward her to see the screen. There were a few tabs open—her patient file, a page on fluoxetine, a memo from another doctor. Quickly, fingers slipping on the trackpad, she clicked on the search bar and typed: THOMAS ZIMMERMAN. At once, a document popped up, labelled

"Patient File: T. Zimmerman." Marta clicked on it, scanning it briefly. She thought that she could hear the sound of a copier humming, a mechanical whirr.

Hastily, fumbling, she fished her phone out of her jacket pocket and snapped a photo of the file. The copier had stopped making noise now, and all she could hear was the click-clack of nearing footsteps. Quickly, she closed the tab, spun the laptop around to face away, and was barely back into the chair before the door opened again and Greene came in. He beamed serenely at her, handing over a pristine photocopy of the diagram.

"Thanks," said Marta. "This has all been really helpful."

When the appointment was done, he walked her to the door and shook hands with her again briskly. "Keep an open mind about the medication," he told her. "It's not a miracle cure, of course, but you'll be surprised by how much difference it can make."

Marta gripped his hand tightly. "I'll do anything I can to beat this thing," she said. "Anything at all. I swear to God I will."

When she waited for the bus, it didn't come. She walked all the way back to the South End, keeping her head down to stop it from brushing against the sky.

Figures were moving behind the fogged glass of the door again, darting quickly back and forth between kitchen and bathroom, dark shapes in the water. Sitting cross-legged on her bed, Marta watched them idly. She thought she knew, even without seeing them clearly, exactly what they were doing in the fog. It was always the same: Nicholas with his toothbrush sticking out of his mouth, dribbling toothpaste as he dragged his half-empty backpack behind him, Dina buttoning up her blouse as she stuck pins in her hair, and her father standing at the stove to stir the oatmeal, the only point of calm in the morning rush. He'd turned the radio on while he cooked, cranking the volume up as far as it would go, and the closed bedroom door did nothing to block out the voice of the weatherman. Her ancient laptop, propped open on the comforter beside her, was starting to overheat, the hum rising alarmingly high.

Marta held the phone closer, jamming her fingers hard into her other ear to blot the sound out. "Sorry, can you repeat that? It's getting kind of noisy on my end. Sorry."

There was a slight pause, and then the voice of the pharmacist broke through the static again, a little louder than before. "I said, do you take any other drugs regularly? Prescription drugs, party drugs, marijuana—anything like that?"

"I smoke weed sometimes."

"What about alcohol?"

"Yeah, I drink alcohol," said Marta, and stretched, arching her back as a yawn picked her throat apart. She was still wearing her janitor's uniform—she'd been too tired to change after her shift the night before, too tired to do anything except drag a spoon around the bowl of congealed baked beans that Dina had left out for her, spit mouthwash down the sink, fall into bed. The rumpled fabric reeked of ozone cleaning spray. The seams had left lines like ugly stitch-marks on her arms and stomach. Frankenstein monster, raised from the dead with lightning in her brain.

"Okay," said the pharmacist, "I'd recommend that you keep your alcohol consumption as minimal as possible while you're taking the fluoxetine, because it *is* a depressant. There can be some pretty drastic side effects. I'd stay away from marijuana, too."

"Right," said Marta, and leaned down to adjust her laptop, tilting it up to rest on her knee—the hum faltered, faded, as the mechanism began to cool again. She had transferred the blurred and panicked photograph that she had taken at the doctor's office to her computer, and now she looked at it, blown up across the screen, stretching into a pixelated mess. It was nearly impossible to decipher the text, her hands had been shaking so badly as she'd taken the photo, but she could just make out Thomas Zimmerman's name and addresses printed at the top, followed by a long stream of incomprehensible medical jargon and abbreviations of words she didn't know at all. Underneath that were his emergency contacts: his mother was the first, which didn't surprise Marta at all, but the second was a name that she didn't know. John Zimmerman, it said and then in brackets beside that: cousin.

"—nausea or vomiting," the pharmacist was saying now. "Or fatigue, headaches, heart palpitations, joint pain, fever, flu symptoms, insomnia, or tremors. You understand?"

"Right, yes."

One-handed, Marta typed the name "John Zimmerman" and "Halifax" into the search bar of her computer and scrolled through the results. There were only a smattering of hits, most of them announcements for local concerts and music events; John Zimmerman, the first link told her, was the singer for a Nova Scotian blues group. No social media page for him, but she kept going until she found a Facebook account for the band, a string of upcoming events listed.

"—loose or bloody stool, blurred vision, difficulty balancing. Got it?"

With her free hand, Marta groped around on the windowsill, found the shrivelled remains of a half-smoked joint, and wedged it in her mouth as she went hunting for a lighter. "Yep," she told the pharmacist on the other end of the phone, her voice muffled around the joint. "I've got it."

CHAPTER TEN

"Nice makeup," said Allan Baird, and his nicotine-tainted breath hung in a haze, clogging the close air between them. "You look like the girl who fucked the band."

Marta wrinkled her nose and felt the stuff crawl on her skin— blue wavy lines down her cheeks like tears, glossed with a sheen of glitter. Dina had done them for her. She didn't usually wear much makeup, and the layers of foundation and glitter made her skin feel itchy, sticky. Whenever she blinked, the coating of mascara daubed across her lashes made them cling together and get gummed up. "Thanks," she said and primped for him, turning her head left and right so that he could admire her tears. "I'm laughing like hell on the inside."

Teasing, grinning, he tugged on the end of one of her loose, uneven braids. "Washing your hair does wonders, you know."

"Funny, man."

"Swear to God, you're the prettiest rat-faced little hippy in the whole bar," he said and took a hank of hair in each fist, one on each side of her head, bunching them up to make a matching pair of ram's horns.

Marta shoved him away, giggling, but she couldn't shove him very far. They were in the women's bathroom of the House of Blues, sandwiched into the approximate twelve inches of free space between the sinks and the cubicle doors. "Hurry up," she said, "or somebody's gonna come in."

123

Déjà vu tickled the back of her mind as he produced the pills from his jacket pocket, a plastic bottle of the over-the-counter anti-nausea stuff. Her own freshly prescribed fluoxetine tablets were in her coat pocket, still unopened; she'd picked them up that afternoon. He twisted the lid off the bottle and shook a pill out onto her palm. It was white and flattish, its surface faintly granulated, and it was cut down the middle by a faint line. This dividing groove made her think of an amoeba, splitting in two, going on forever. Squinting, she could see that there were two numbers stamped onto the pill: 44 above the line and 198 under it. "How many do you have to take to feel something?"

He shrugged. "I don't know. A bunch."

"You said you knew people who did it."

"Not with pills. They got the little gel capsules, put them in disposables syringes, and then shot up like that. They needed a lot of capsules to get something going, and you need even more when you're just taking it orally."

He tipped the bottle again, and a little landslide of pills came rattling out into her hand. They didn't look like anything special and, again, she squinted at the little printed numbers. Forty-four over a hundred-and-ninety-eight. Allan was watching her. "What does this stuff mean?" she asked him, rolling the pills around her palm, and then—nothing ventured—popping one into her mouth. "The numbers. What's up with that?"

He shook a few out into his own palm. "I don't know. Probably the minimum toxic dose, or the lethal dose, or whatever."

Marta stopped, the pill still sticking on her tongue. It tasted horrible, liquefying grainy and sour, but she didn't swallow it down. Instead, she stared at him for a moment, and then, rolling the pill into her cheek, said, "What?"

"Well—that's just pharmaceutical policy, isn't it? We had to do a whole unit on it. If the drug's potentially lethal, toxic, whatever, then they have to say what the lethal dosage is. You know, forty-four milligrams, hundred-and-ninety-eight milligrams."

She looked at the pill bottle again, then at him. "If it's lethal . . ."

"Everything is lethal. You can overdose on marijuana, caffeine, anything—you can overdose on potassium if you eat enough bananas. Come on, don't chicken out on me. I'm giving you a good tip on this stuff. You're going to like it."

She didn't, already. The pill under her tongue was a rotten seed; she swallowed it down dry and then another seven, one after another, gulping quickly, gagging—they tasted even worse now, chalky and thick, and they made her throat close up. Allan had done the same, although she noticed that he'd counted out a full dozen pills for himself. When he put the bottle down on the edge of the sink between them, it rattled hollow, nearly empty. "We'll get more," he said.

For a few moments, they stood together, listening to the dull thump of music from the bar stereo and the murmur of voices that rose and then receded like a tide. Marta's stomach twisted suddenly, a clammy feeling beginning to rise. Quickly, she turned on the taps and leaned over the sink to scoop up water in her cupped hands, gulping it down, washing away all remnants of the sticky, bitter powder. She spat, wiped her mouth—too late, she remembered her lipstick. A red smear ran down her chin. In the mirror, she saw that Allan was grinning at her again.

"What is it?"

"Nothing," he said and grinned, broad and cagey, but she thought she saw something strange behind his split-open eyes. Her stomach turned again, spit welling up in her mouth and an uncomfortable tightness under her jaw—quickly, she pushed past him and into one of the narrow cubicles, pushing the door shut with her boot as she leaned over the toilet. She tried to retch, but nothing came out except pearly strings of spit, flecked with gobs of white powder.

Outside, Allan was laughing. "Pussy," he said, and the cubicle shook, echoing thunder—he'd kicked the door, she thought. Then she heard his footsteps going, the washroom door creaking and swinging as he left. Alone, she sat back on her heels, kneeling, resting her head in her hands and her elbows on the toilet bowl. Saliva made an oil slick on the surface of the water. Marta looked at the graffiti on the stall walls, layers on layers of Sharpie scrawl. *Whoever taught me that my emotions were a burden did not understand what a priveledge it was to look into my psyche.* This was directly above the toilet tank, and beside it: *Show hole for a cigarette.* Slowly, she dragged her gaze up—slowly, she went up the wall. *Goodbye to a great guy.* And, above that, in careful block capitals: *I LOVE YOUR SWEET FACE AND YOUR DEAR SMILING EYES.*

She stood, and her head spun, the world teetering skewed around her. Squinting, she focused with difficulty on the words scrawled directly at eye-level to her, a meandering string of words that wound and danced across the green-painted wall. *The heart asks more than life can give. When that is learned, then all is learned.*

"Amen," said Marta softly, and dug her pen out of her pocket—propping herself against the wall, she uncapped it and began to write, in straggling, teetering letters. She wrote: *a girl still stands with dirt in her hands and a hole in the back of her head.* Then she capped the pen and pushed the cubicle door open again.

Allan was waiting for her in the hall. His face was bathed in reddish light from the bar, the shadows making his head look—to Marta—swollen and distorted, a funhouse mirror man with bulging eyes and bee-stung, hypoxic cheeks. "Can't handle your dimenhydrinate, eh?"

She didn't answer. The washrooms and the swing-door through to the kitchens behind them, the bar in front, they were hanging in the between-space. It was early in the evening but the House of Blues had amassed a fair crowd already, more than half the tables full with the usual collection of older types, blues musicians, aging groupies, all gathered around talking and laughing and swilling their liquor. It was deafening, and the whole bar was lit with a reddish glow. Squinting in the churning dark, Marta could see all the familiar bits of memorabilia strung around ceiling, piled up in the corners, all exactly the way she remembered: the taxidermized bear's head mounted on one wall, with its beaded eyes and patchy pelt, the rows of vintage album covers, the carved totem pole. They found a corner table, facing the stage, where a couple of roadies Marta didn't know were setting up the sound equipment for the show.

Marta offered to get their drinks, hoping that she would know somebody behind the counter—that it would be Emma or Sal or Torrie, the collection of kind older women who had always given her free drinks while she was working and, sometimes, had the kitchen send out a blooming onion for her to have for supper. But it was a harried young girl who mixed the drinks, her face unfamiliar, and all the other servers were the same. A little disconcerted, she carried two White Russians back to their table. She wanted to sit drinking, thinking of what she would say to Thomas Zimmerman's cousin, but Allan was watching her intently—she could see the question hanging off his tongue and, putting her glass down, she surrendered to it.

"Yeah? What's up?"

"I," said Allan, "have something I want to ask you."

"Fire away."

"You used to work here, right? Setting up amps and making drinks and shit?"

"Is that the question?"

"No," he said. "It's this—how come you're a janitor now?"

Marta ran her thumb around the rim of the glass, scraping the sugar away and then licking it off her thumbnail; she was still making a concerted effort to speak lightly, airily, matching his matter-of-fact tone as closely as she could manage. "Well, the pandemic happened. They let go of a lot of people, when they stopped doing live concerts for a while. And they always need more people to mop floors and clean toilets."

A server was passing by their table, and Allan sketched silent motions in the air for her to bring them the same again. "Sure," he said, and his smile didn't as much as flicker. He spread his hands and looked at her, expectant and easy. "Your turn."

Marta hesitated for a second, scraping the granules of sugar out from under her nails and studying him; she had meant to ask him something about Thomas Zimmerman—if he knew anything about the man's family, where he might be now, anything, but now he had gotten her off-balance, unsure of herself and of him. "You seem like you've got it all figured out sometimes," she said. "Why were you in therapy?"

"It was recommended to me."

"Who recommended it?"

"My family doctor."

"Why? For what?"

"I don't know," said Allan. "I'm not really an unhappy person. Things don't bother me so much anymore—they don't touch me. I don't get down about too much."

"So why did you go to the sessions at all?"

He shrugged. "It seemed like fun."

Marta opened her mouth, but her next question was interrupted by a sudden surge of applause and cheers from around the room. The band had appeared and were settling themselves on the stage and, front and centre under the scarlet lights of the bar, was the man that Marta recognized from the internet search she'd done. He was a dark, slight figure, with a narrow and fine-boned face, and considerably older than his cousin, she thought. He was wearing a dark suit striped with grey and an old-fashioned brimmed hat. Up on the stage, he looked like a spectre from a long-gone age of blues.

Like one of the real greats. He grinned at the crowd, ducked his head in a funny kind of bow, and then—putting his harmonica to his lips—launched into the first notes of the song, the rest of the band following along.

Listening, Marta was struck with the awful melancholy of it, how the twang and scream of the harmonica was so penetratingly loud, cutting clean through the guitar and saxophone. John Zimmerman played with his eyes closed. He seemed to be caught up in a kind of rapture—he turned, he spun, he kicked and danced, and the harmonica was silver and light in his hands.

Allan leaned across the table. "One more question."

"Yeah?"

"How come you were a roadie, if you only worked at the bar? Don't roadies have to, y'know, go on the road?"

Reluctantly, Marta tore her eyes away from the stage. The tempo of the song had dropped and John was singing now, his voice a bullfrog croak. It was a tune she vaguely recognized—*Seeing all the faces of the girls I knew before, think I'll wait 'til the last moment I can't take an-y-more* . . .

"Uh, well—I was technically just a techie, you know, but I slung amps and shit. I did the heavy stuff."

"Here?"

She scowled at him. "Yes, here. Shush, I'm trying to listen."

. . . *singing HEY, honey, honey, where's the summertime gone?*

"The guy at the door didn't seem to know you," said Allan.

. . . *honey, where's the summertime gone?*

Marta turned her head away and pretended that she hadn't heard him. Gradually, she was becoming aware of something else going on—a stir in the crowd, another burst of applause that seemed to be directed somewhere else besides the little stage. Looking around, she saw that a man and woman, both very old, white-haired, had gotten up from their table and started to dance. They danced very well, very lightly, swinging back and forth to the music—they moved through the steps of a dance that had come and gone decades ago. Somebody up on the balcony started to clap again, more rhythmically, keeping time for them.

But I saw you in the morning, and you were lying in bed, saying HEY, honey, honey, where's the summertime gone? Where's the summertime gone?

On stage, the musicians were still playing, but they were all watching the dancers. All except for John Zimmerman, who was still caught up in his own music, shuffling a strange little dance of his own across the stage. The couple, too, appeared entirely absorbed by the rhythm—they didn't seem to notice the attention they were getting at all.

Marta, watching them, felt her ribcage contract, a prickling at the back of her throat that she couldn't blame on the drink or the pills. She was going to cry. She was. Quickly, she stood up and, ignoring Allan's inquisitive stare, picked her way around the edge of the room, past the dancers, the bar, the bouncer by the door. *Honey, honey*—? She went out and into the night, and stood, swinging her arms back and forth, turning her face toward the sky. There were only ever one or two stars over Halifax, pinpricks in the muddy night, and tonight there were none at all.

She stood under the rusting old awning and fogged-over windows, papered with their tattered posters and flyers; she could hear the music still playing inside, and see the shapes drifting in the mist behind the glass. She had hung up some of those posters, she remembered—she had been to some of those shows. There was nobody who would remember that now, she knew, except for her. Five whole years of her life, the only ones she could retain with any kind of accuracy, and it didn't make a difference to anybody.

There was a cluster of men standing smoking on the sidewalk a few yards away, shuffling their feet and talking quietly—after a while, one called out to Marta, "You want a cigarette while you're waiting?"

She looked at them, startled, then over her shoulder. She sniffed hard. "Thanks," she said and drifted closer—she'd quit smoking tobacco years ago, considering herself to be a one-drug addict, monogamous in her bad habits, but she wasn't in the habit of turning down anything free. No harm. She fell into orbit with them, and took the cigarette when it was offered, leaning in close to let the man light it for her. "Thanks," she said again, and held the cigarette awkwardly between her finger and thumb to take a drag. The nicotine was raw, but so was the night air.

"You meeting somebody out here?" said the man, as the little group opened up, letting Marta in. He was young—they all were—and looked to be about Dina's age, in his early twenties. His hand, still turning the lighter over and over, was stained with ink, tattoos Marta couldn't quite make out the shape of in the dark.

"No," said Marta, and felt something awkward in her isolation. "I was just thinking, you know, if I was going to go back in or not."

"You should," said the man. "It's a pretty good vibe in there."

"Doing karaoke later on," said one of the others.

The first man grinned at Marta, blue smoke leaking from between his teeth. "Hey, weird question, but do you, like—d'you speak French and stuff?"

"Um, yeah. Some."

"Great," said the man, beaming. "Great. Can you say—" he hesitated, taking a pull on the cigarette and screwing his face up, thoughtful—"Can you tell me how to say something? Tell me how you say: 'We're all going to die.'"

Marta hesitated, glanced at the other men, unsure if she was getting made fun of, but they were all smiling at their friend with an amiable kind of bemusement, looking as lost as she felt. "*Nous allons tous mourir*," she said. "I think."

"How do you say that? Like, in English, how do you pronounce it?"

"*Nous allons tous mourir.*"

"Too-mur-ear."

" Moo-rir. Moo, like a cow."

The aspiring linguist seemed tickled by this; he repeated it several times to himself, beaming, and one by one the others joined in, echoing him. New-all-on-too-moo-rear. New-all-on-too-moo-rear. "Why do you want to know that, anyway?" said one of them, stubbing out his cigarette on the sidewalk and grinding it under his boot.

"It's 'cause I lived in Quebec for three months," said the linguist, and then, glancing briefly at Marta with an apologetic grimace, "No offence, babe, you're not from Quebec. You're okay. But they're all assholes up there. You say *salut*, 'hi', they don't say shit. Hold doors open, they don't say thank you. They don't say shit."

"So?"

"I want something I can say back to them. Just, like, when I hold a door open and they don't say thank you, I'll just say . . ."

"*Nous allons tous mourir,*" said Marta.

"Exactly."

They all laughed a little, their cigarettes burned down to smouldering embers, and then the group began to drift back toward the bar. "You're welcome to hang out with us if you end up coming in," one of them told Marta. "We got a table in the corner. You can come hang out."

Then they were gone and Marta was alone on the sidewalk again, her cigarette charring her fingertips and feeling cold down to her bones. The door, swinging shut behind them, flew suddenly open again and she glanced around to see that someone else had come out of the bar. She braced herself for it to be Allan, coming to pester her with a dozen more of his questions, but it wasn't—it was John

Zimmerman. He nodded to her, thumbing a cigarette out of the breast pocket of his suit jacket. "Hey, there."

"Hey," said Marta, and realized that she had been staring. "I . . . I thought you were playing."

"Short gig," he said indistinctly, the cigarette wedged between his teeth as he lit up. "They want the stage for karaoke."

"You sounded really good. The real deal."

"Thanks, baby. What's your name?"

"Marta."

"That's pretty," he said and grinned at her. Looking at him in the light that shone dimly through the layers of flyers and pamphlets, she wasn't sure if he was handsome or not—more than anything, she thought that he looked preserved. There was something about the fine bones of his face, his narrow fingers, that made her think of things kept in formaldehyde, or trapped behind glass, skewered with pins.

"You got a boyfriend, Marta? Husband?"

"Yeah," said Marta. "A boyfriend."

" Course you do, course you do. Every beautiful woman's got a boyfriend."

Marta grinned. She figured she knew pretty well when somebody was using recycled material on her and didn't take it too personally. "Yeah, they sure do."

"Is he working?"

"No," she said, automatically. She'd only been thinking about Thomas Zimmerman, about how he was most likely unemployed and therefore not working, but she realized as soon as she said it that John had meant the question in a different way.

"So, what? He doesn't come out to bars with you?"

"Oh," said Marta. "Naw. Not tonight."

"Really? He doesn't want to show you off? Men nowadays—" He broke off, laughed, tapping the ash off his cigarette. "I don't know. If it was me, I'd be all over you, honey."

Marta's grin was starting to get sore on her face. "Your name sounded so familiar, when I read it on the poster," she said, unable to stomach any more of the snail's-pace small-talking. Better to get it done, better to get it *over*. "You're not related to a guy named Thomas, are you? Thomas Zimmerman?"

For a second, she thought she saw something shift and turn in his eyes, a mental landscape reconfiguring itself as he looked at her. "I guess I might be," he said. "You know Thomas?"

"Sure, he's a friend of mine. He's not here tonight, is he?"

"Not really his scene," said John and laughed like it was a joke. With an abrupt little flick of the wrist, he threw out his cigarette and turned toward the door again. "You coming in?"

"Maybe," said Marta. She felt around in her jacket pockets for change that she knew wasn't there; she didn't particularly want to go back into the bar, but she wanted to stick near to him all the same—wanted to keep working the conversation around to Thomas Zimmerman. "I don't have too much money left. Maybe one drink."

"You want some money?"

"Yeah. You got two bucks?"

He thumbed a five-dollar bill out of his pocket and held it out to her. Numbly, she took it.

"You like to smoke dope?"

"Yeah, I do," said Marta.

"Good, good. C'mon," he said and drew her down to the street corner, fishing a plastic baggie out of his pocket. "Good shit—family connection. You got something to put it in?"

"Naw, sorry."

She held out her gloved hand and he dropped the furled-up green into it; nonplussed, she slipped the bud into her coat pocket, loose and all. John gave her some papers, too, then—with a wink—made to go past her and back into the bar.

"Wait," said Marta, and was faintly surprised when he did. She'd

CHAPTER ELEVEN

The apartment that belonged to John Zimmerman was, it turned out, just over a twenty-minute walk away. It was in a towering complex on Barrington Street, only a few blocks up from the counselling centre. One of the newer constructions in the downtown area, its smooth white façade was illuminated by a line of bright exterior lights, making it stand out sharply among the shabbier concrete edifices. Marta was surprised—it was a central location, prime property in a city where housing prices were constantly going up. She couldn't imagine how much the rent would be, with a view of the harbour on one side and the main artery of Spring Garden Road on the other—it was already bad enough where her family lived, way out on the edge of the South End. "You live here?"

"Wait 'til you see the inside," said John.

The moment they were through the main entryway, she knew exactly what he meant. Looking past the glass interior doors, she could see a spacious lobby, with marbled tiles and brass furnishings. There was a fireplace against one wall with armchairs arranged around it and a synthetic fire flickering behind the grate. "God," she said quietly, automatically dropping her voice, an awed hush. "It looks like the Park Plaza or something, doesn't it?"

Allan whistled. "It's not bad."

There was a keypad set into the wall; John pressed numbers and the interior doors unlocked with a loud click. They followed him through the lobby and into an elevator, where he pressed a button for the ninth floor. The elevator's walls were mirrored and Marta studied her reflection, very grey and wrung-out beneath her makeup, colourless and shabby against the splendour of her surroundings. She smiled at herself, sucked in her cheeks, smiled again.

Allan was watching her again. "Why do you keep doing that?" he asked quietly.

"What?"

"Smiling like that. You do it a lot."

"It makes you feel happier. It releases chemicals into your brain—makes you happy."

"Does it?"

Before she could answer, the elevator chimed crystalline, and the doors slid open. The apartment was 904, and John had called it his, but he didn't open the door himself, only knocked. After a minute, it was opened by a woman who wore a silk kimono and a quantity of burnished makeup caked around her eyes.

"This is Roz," John said and then, jerking his thumb in their general direction, "These are my good friends, my new friends, ah—"

"Marta," said Marta.

"Charlie," said Allan, for no discernable reason, and started to giggle.

"They were at the show, you know. Thought we could keep the party going back here."

Roz smiled. She was tall, more than a whole head taller than Marta, and the effect was accentuated by the fact that she wore her hair piled up on her head in an auburn frizz. When she stepped aside to let them through into the apartment, Marta caught a gust of eye-wateringly floral perfume seeping from the folds of her kimono. The place was lovely, but everything was in slight disarray: some of the Japanese paintings on the walls were hung askew, the tapestries stained, the deep couches piled incongruously with silk pillows and foamy plush throws. Perched on the low coffee table was an ashtray in the shape of a man's head, his mouth hanging grotesquely open, so that any ashes tapped out on his lip would run down his throat.

"You can make yourselves at home anywhere you like," said Roz.

Allan needed no further invitation, throwing himself down on the couch, but Marta hesitated a moment longer. "We're not imposing, yeah?"

"Of course not. John *always* has people come over after a show."

Marta went around the other side of the coffee table, meaning to join Allan, and then faltered as she felt something crunch under the sole of her boot. Thomas Zimmerman's boot. She lifted her foot gingerly up again and saw, on the carpet, splintered fragments of blue willow patterned porcelain. "Shit, I'm really sorry, did I—?"

Briskly, Roz bent down, sweeping the shards into her palm. "Don't worry about it, honey," she said and carried the handful of porcelain very carefully into the kitchen. Over her shoulder, dropping the pieces with a rattle down into the trash can, she went on, "We had a vase get broken the other day. I thought I'd cleaned it all up, but I guess I must have missed a piece. Good thing you had those boots on, eh?"

Bemused, Marta sank down on the cushions next to Allan, slotting herself tight against his side. Something of the melancholy she'd felt in the bar still lingered and she thought that even he would be better than nothing, just to get close with. She turned her ankle, checking the underside of the boot—there were still a few tiny shards of porcelain embedded in the rubber sole.

"Should we wait?" she asked.

Roz was wiping her hands delicately on her kimono. "For what?"

"Well—for Thomas. I thought he was going to be here, too."

The effect of the words was instantaneous. She heard—or felt—the slightest catch in Allan's breath, a trembling in his ribcage like he was holding a breath in. Trying not to laugh, she thought. And just as brief, a look that passed between Roz and John, something silent and indecipherable.

"I thought he'd be around," said Marta, directing the remark mostly toward the latter, as she looked up at him plaintively. "I thought that's what you meant, when you asked us to come over. That he might be coming."

There was a momentary pause, and then John smiled, treating her to yet another little wink. "Hold that thought, honey."

Reluctantly, Marta subsided again, sinking back into the cushions and feeling the vibrations of Allan's laughter. They sat on the couch, a bottle of wine between them, as Roz fussed around with a record player in the corner.

"Why do you have one?" Marta asked, meaning the record player. "Isn't it a lot of work to keep changing the albums?"

"Some inconvenience," said Roz, shrugging her immaculate shoulders. "Such is life, you know? But the sound."

"The sound's real good," said John quickly.

She wondered, too, where everyone else was—not just Thomas Zimmerman, but the rest of the band, too. She had been expecting a party, but it seemed to only be the four of them. The record was old, something reedy and repetitive. Marta didn't like it much, but she took care to nod appreciatively, like she was hanging on every note. Whenever she caught John watching her, she smiled. Whenever he looked away, she stole little glances at the front door, like the simple act of looking could make Thomas Zimmerman appear. She felt somehow that she was witnessing an elaborate performance, that everything—from the artwork to the wine to the music—was all an intricate bit of showmanship staged for their benefit.

When the record finally stuttered its way to a stop, John left for a moment and then came back carrying a tray of weed paraphernalia and a tall glass bong. They smoked up and Marta, who never used a bong if she could help it, followed the others' lead. "I usually just smoke joints," she said.

John laughed. "It's a waste of weed, honey. All the smoke gets away from you. Any breath you're not taking is a waste."

Marta decided it wasn't worth arguing—it would be pointless to explain that she didn't smoke joints because it was an efficient use of cannabis; that if her sole aim was getting as fucked up as possible, she would have popped a few gummies or bought a vape, or something equally cheating. It was about the high, sure, but it was also about the sensation of infinity she got, propped up on the radiator with her feet out the window, and about the easy feeling she'd have, passing a joint back and forth with Shaw. And she thought about the day she'd felt such a monstrous tightening in her chest, thought her ribcage was caving in and her heart was seizing up, and Shaw had put his hand on her back, fingers spread wide between her shoulder blades . . . *Just breathe, Marta. Open up.*

"Open up," said Allan, a short eternity later, and put another pill in her mouth.

It felt bulkier, more slippery than the other pills had been, and sat on her cotton-thick tongue like a lump of lead. "What is it?" Marta asked him, the words coming out indistinct, and blew spit out her mouth in shining wet that dribbled down her chin.

Someone laughed, but she wasn't sure if it was John or Roz—in the warm light of the lamps, they both had taken on the same face, perfectly indistinguishable from each other. A pair of clay masks, with leathery burnished skin and lovely matching smiles.

They laughed, the masks, and Marta laughed too. "Oh, God, man," she said.

"Go on, then," said Allan.

Laughing wetly, Marta nodded, and swallowed the pill down. She was sinking fast, as she usually did, into an easy kind of introspection, and into a hazy quiet. She looked around the room, and at her own hands, and at the lamplight fermenting in the wine bottle.

"Thomas," she said, pronouncing the name thickly, a smack of saliva on the S that dragged it out much too long. The hiss of an adder on her tongue. "You texted him, then? He's—he's coming here?"

Again, John's finger was at his lips. "Soon," he said.

Marta wanted to ask when, wanted desperately to know, but she thought if she opened her mouth she might drown. She bit down hard, tasted the adder's blood—she held the thought, like he'd told her to. After a while, she was aware of a change in the tenor of the conversation between the two hosts. John was getting up, moving with purpose toward a door—ajar—that Marta thought must lead to the bedroom. Roz had vanished into the kitchen, clearing away the glasses and wine bottle.

"Look," said Allan suddenly, and it took Marta a second to realize that he actually wanted her to look. Obliging, she complied, turning toward the hall, the coat rack, and the front door beyond.

"Look," he said, "what's on the other side of that door? What's there? Nothing."

"The hallway."

"Where? There's nothing. What really exists if you don't see it? Nothing."

"I could open the door," said Marta. "See the hallway. It's still there."

"So what? That's just changing the game—you'd see the hall, but you wouldn't see what was in the elevators, or outside the building. Nothing else. You keep the door closed and it doesn't really matter, does it?"

She looked at the door, then at him, thrown by the perfect sincerity in his voice, the conviction. He was watching her intently, and his eyes were very bright and wet, like he was gripped by some overpowering feeling. She looked at the door again. "I can see the light," she said and traced it in the air with the tip of her finger. "Around the edge of the door. I can see the light coming underneath. So."

"What? So what?"

"I know it's coming from somewhere, you know?"

He was grinning, already shaking his head, dismissive. "The

light's here. You can see it. If you couldn't, you wouldn't know it was there at all."

"I guess."

"It's the same way with the whole world," he said. "To me. What else is there, if I don't see it? Nothing. Nobody. I'm the only real person, there's nothing beyond the limits of me, because I don't see it—I don't feel it. The same thing, dying. Nothing's going to be left when I'm gone. I go, so goes the world. You get it?"

"Yeah."

"You get it now?"

"I don't know," said Marta thickly. "It just seems like kind of a selfish perspective. Self-centred, you know?"

"How? It's the same way for everybody, even if they don't realize it. We're all the only person in our heads. Who else?"

"Feels like it would be pretty lonely, if you were the only real person on Earth."

"It's not too bad."

"I think I'd be lonely."

"Sure," said Allan, "if you thought you were missing out on something. But if you were the only person who ever existed, you wouldn't imagine any other way. You wouldn't care so much about Thomas, because he wouldn't be there to care *about*. Nobody else in the world. What are you missing?"

Looking at him, Marta had a sudden vision of something bubbling up, liquid and shining, fountaining into the air—like champagne foaming out of an uncorked bottle. That was his life, then. The only man on Earth. She saw herself there, at the very edge, the pure white run-off streaming away around her and nothing ahead. Higher and higher. She shivered and drew her knees up closer to her chest—she laughed again, wetter and more frenzied than before. "Fuck me, man," she said. "Man, I haven't been this high since—"

He grinned. "Yeah? Since when?"

"Since my mom's funeral," said Marta, and clamped her hands over her mouth to stop herself from giggling.

She felt a sudden stutter in her chest, her heart pitching and yawing, a sickening roll behind her ribcage—she pressed her hand to her breastbone, feeling the butterfly pulse against the skin. She wondered if it was the drink or the drugs or something else entirely, if Allan Baird's philosophy might be poisoning her. With some difficulty, she stood up, lurching to her feet and then holding her arms out like a tightrope walker as the world started to smear itself across the inner part of her eyes. Somewhere, quite far away, Allan was laughing at her, but she ignored him. She gouged her fingernails into her palms, trying to jolt herself awake and sober. When that didn't work, she thought about Thomas Zimmerman. She thought about the shards of porcelain on the floor.

Marta didn't make a conscious decision to move, but somehow she seemed to go anyway because one moment, she was standing by the coffee table, and the next she was in the bathroom. In between, she'd been nowhere; the water had closed over her head again. She stood leaning against the sink and tried to think about Thomas Zimmerman some more, in case it sobered her up, but she found that she couldn't sustain it—whenever she tried to make the connection in her head between him and the broken porcelain on the floor, what Allan had told her kept getting in the way. She kept looking toward the closed bathroom door and wondering if the world might have disappeared from the other side of it. She wouldn't have minded if it had, she thought.

She glanced away from the door, down at the sink, and was surprised to see her bottle of antidepressants sitting by the taps—she couldn't remember taking them out of her pocket at all. But she had. With difficulty, she managed to twist the safety-proofed top of the bottle off and pour a jumble of capsules into her palm. They were prettier than Allan's medicine had been and much more appetizing, each one a light and shiny teal, waxy like soap. Marta looked at them for a long time, trying to remember why they were in her hand at all.

The living room had changed by the time that she got back. It had rearranged itself, everything contorting into a different sequence, and someone had turned off the lights, too. Everything was a blueish kind of dark, furniture looming pale out of the shadows like a drifting field of icebergs. She hit her shin on something and saw that it was the frame of a bed. Only then did it dimly occur to her that she had gone into the bedroom instead.

"You better sit down," said John Zimmerman. "You're looking pretty out of it, honey."

Marta hadn't seen him before—she couldn't even see him now, not really. His mask-stiff face hovered at the corner of her eye, a crackle of movement in the dark, getting closer. She sat on the edge of the bed and he sat beside her; she slid herself back along the mattress until her back was pressed against the wall and her heart beating itself against the plaster. Her whole body felt porous and insubstantial, suddenly; she could feel her mind sloughing away, sloshing out through the sieve of her body. Thickly, painfully, she asked, "Isn't Thomas coming?"

"Don't worry about him now. It's just the two of us. And you don't have to worry about Roz, either, she's—"

"But he's been here. He *has* been here, hasn't here?"

"Why, honey?"

The lights were still off but, even peering through the dark, she could see that there were no curtains on the bedroom windows. Through the glass, fogged with flecks of snow, she could see the lights of the next apartment building.

"He's been here," she said. "He's been here recently—he's been . . ."

"He's gone."

She couldn't make sense of it. "What do you mean?"

"He was crashing with us for a couple weeks," he said and looked around, as if searching for the clue to Thomas Zimmerman's existence. "But he's gone, now. You don't have to worry about him—you don't have to *think* about him."

Vaguely, Marta wished that this was true. She tipped her head back against the wall and wondered why she hadn't died yet, when it felt like her heart was forcing itself out of her body, from between her shoulder blades.

"You look beat," he said.

"I am," said a voice that Marta supposed to be hers.

"You've been going pretty hard all night."

"Yes," she said. "It's the hyp. . . the hyper—" She saw the word in her mind's eye, just the way that Dr. Simon Greene had showed it to her that day in his office, but she couldn't get her mouth around it, somehow. She broke it up into thirds, portioned it like the pills, "—the hyp'rarousal."

The zone of hyperarousal. She knew it pretty well. She'd spent nearly every night there, back when she'd first worked at the House of Blues—skinny little Marta Klausner, no mom, no chance, no problem. Skinny little Marta Klausner with her rat's face and dandelion-fluff hair, who talked like she was one of the boys until they mostly started believing it, bad for a fuck but always ready to do molly out back behind the dumpsters.

"The what?"

"The hyp'sal," she said and then, giving up, "The up, the up."

And that was all it was, of course. Because when you were up, you were pretty fucking *up*, and there was no knowing where you'd be when you came back down again. You'd fallen off the tightrope and, defiant of all gravity, gone flying up into sky, where you were only a hunger, a mouth, a hole, a cavity in the ground that got wider and wider until it was a grave in Fairview Lawn Cemetery. Marta's heart stuttered again and she put a hand over it to keep it from crawling up her throat. It was at that moment that John kissed her. He kissed her cheek first and then, putting his hand under her chin, tried to turn her head to kiss her properly. She let him, only because she couldn't feel her mouth anymore.

Marta stayed very still, pinned against the plaster by her own paralysis, and when he stopped kissing her, he put his hand between her legs instead. For the briefest second, she felt a red worm of pain in her cunt, but the sensation was quickly drowned out by her heartbeat. She could *hear* that heartbeat now—a high vibrato note like the twang of a sawblade, over and over, reverberating through the bedroom.

"It's okay," John Zimmerman told her, and then crooked his fingers so that the worm writhed again. "You can relax. Like I said, it's just you and me here, that's all."

But it wasn't. There was someone else, too. She could see them out of the corner of her eye now, a figure who crawled across the bedsheets toward her, who was screaming words in her ear with a voice of smashed porcelain. She listened and couldn't understand—she thought it might be Thomas at first, that he'd come after all, but it couldn't be him. *Crashing with us a couple weeks, but he's gone now.* The figure crawled across the bed, and the bed rolled and pitched under it.

And Marta said, "Mom?"

John was talking to her again, but she couldn't hear him over the ground-glass voice of whatever was in the bed, and she couldn't hear that over her own heart, and she couldn't hear her heart because she was feeling it stop, and she couldn't feel anything anymore—not even her stomach when, very quiet and easy, she leaned over the edge of the bed and vomited a gutful of pills and liquor onto the floor.

CHAPTER TWELVE

Above her head, the blinds were drawn, and fingers of sunlight pried them apart. Marta turned her face into the pillows and her stomach turned too, vertigo hitting her like the bed wasn't there at all. The mattress under her smelled of mothballs and, worse, of vomit—that was her, and her clothes too. Still reeking. She sat up and had to brace herself quickly, the world skewing sideways; the pixelated haze resolved itself finally into a cluttered room, the threadbare carpet littered with crumpled magazines and overflowing ashtrays. The walls had a strange sheen to them, sticky like flypaper in the sunlight.

"Hey," said Shaw. He was sitting on a cardboard box, eating noodles out of a mug.

Something was crusted in her hair. Gripped with a sudden disgust, she pulled her shirt off over her head and stood, stripped and shivering, wondering if she was going to throw up again.

Shaw looked at her bare chest, then at her face, all with the same detachment, like she was something under a microscope. He'd shaved sometime since she'd last seen him, the first time she'd ever seen him without his moustache. It should have made him look younger, but it didn't—instead, all his shrunk-in skin was exposed, and his bare lip, sucked inward, gave him the look of an ancient chimpanzee. "Rough night?"

She balled the ruined shirt up, holding it away from her body. "Did I get here on my own?"

"Allan brought you."

The words conjured up a few tattered shreds of memory; Allan's hand gripping her elbow to help her into the taxi, his fingers skimming her stomach as he'd pulled her shirt straight, done up the front of her jeans. She shivered. "Did he tell you anything about what happened?"

"No," said Shaw. "I got some clean clothes you can wear, if you want."

Marta nodded. She ran her fingers through her hair, teasing out the crumbling fragments of vomit, and tried to breathe shallowly through her mouth. In the light, she felt more sober, but the world was still dark and shrunk down minutely, like she was looking at it through the wrong end of a telescope.

"Communal laundry machine's out there, down at the end of the hall," said Shaw, tipping his head toward the door. "Room with the shitty old toilet and sink in it."

She nodded again, and it made dots swim in front of her eyes. Spit welled up under her tongue, a clammy contracting of the skin around her Adam's apple. "Sorry," she said and went quickly past him and into the little closet of a bathroom. She leaned over the sink, her hair hanging down over her bare chest, and spat, gagged. Nothing came up, only a clear and frothing stream of saliva. She stayed there, hanging over the sink, until she felt marginally better. Then she washed her hands and splashed water over her face. Clumps of disintegrating mascara got caught in her eyelashes, ran in dark rivulets down to her chin.

Chills were setting in, and she shivered badly as she went back to Shaw. He was sitting on the daybed now, white, worm-like noodles unspooling from the end of his fork. He was watching her through his lashes and pretending that he wasn't. Sometimes there was a spasm around his mouth, like he was going to say something, but he didn't. The force of his patience drilled into Marta's ears until she couldn't stand it. "Did I say anything stupid?"

He shook his head. "You don't remember?"

"It's all blackout now. I don't know what I said, what I did . . ."

"Oh."

"Guess it's the amnesia," she said and cracked a smile that didn't stick. She wished that Shaw would go away, but he wouldn't—it was his apartment. And if she went, it would mean finding somewhere to go, might even mean going home, and she couldn't contemplate that. "*Real* amnesia, not the fake kind this time."

"Well, you were pretty out of it. You said some stuff about Thomas Zimmerman, I think—none of it made much sense to me." There was a fractional pause, and his fingernails picked and pulled at the loose skin of the scab. "Still haven't found him, huh?"

She drained the last of the water from the glass and swilled it down, the metal on her tongue; when the glass touched the carpet again, the sound seemed very loud in the apartment, ringing like a bell in the deadened air. "I don't know," she said, "what it's going to take."

"What?"

But she wasn't really listening, lost in the dark tunnel that had opened up around her, the walls that contracted and pressed in on every side, intestinal stewing, suffocating in the stomach of something great and beyond her. "I was trying. I don't know. I don't know what it takes. Eight years of trying to die, and I never got closer than that, and I still fucked it up."

"Laundry's down the hall," he said.

In the communal laundry room of Inglis Lodge, there was a toilet with its lid fastened shut with duct tape, a Sharpie-scrawled sign fixed over it: NOT WORKING. Marta sat leaning against the washing machine door, feeling it hum against her spine, and held her phone to her ear, listening to the instructions of a robotic little voice. It told her that none of the volunteers employed by the suicide hotline were currently available, that she'd been placed in a queue, and that she should wait and stay on the line. She had time to put her clothes through the spin cycle and then bundle them into the dryer before the phone clicked and crackled, a brief blast of static signalling that she'd been put through to an operator. Not too bad: she'd heard stories around the Barrington Centre of people who'd been kept on hold for whole hours.

"Hello, this is the Suicide Crisis Helpline," said a voice. It was a girl and she sounded very young—she sounded like she could have been in high school. "What's going on with you today?"

"I tried to kill myself last night," said Marta.

There was a fractional pause, and then, "I can tell from your voice that you must be in a lot of pain. It sounds like this is very hard for you."

Marta opened her mouth to answer, although she wasn't quite sure how she could, but she needn't have bothered—the girl was already going on. "There's just a few questions I need to ask you, okay? And then we can see about getting you some help. Is that okay with you?"

"Um. Yeah."

"Do you think you or anyone else around you is in immediate danger?"

"Not really. It was just some pills and I puked them up last night. My head feels kind of funny, but—"

"So you aren't in immediate danger?"

Marta blinked. "No. I'm just calling because I tried to do it last—I mean, I almost did, and I'm feeling kind of fucked up about it."

"Yes," said the girl. "I can tell from your voice that you must be in a lot of pain. It sounds like this is very hard for you."

"Thanks," said Marta. She'd never heard that particular line before—she wondered if it was a recent addition to whatever flow-chart the hotline provided its operators with. In her mind's eye, she could picture it quite clearly; the girl sitting with her headset on at a desk in some anonymous call centre, one of a hundred unqualified and unpaid and unknowing volunteers, a big instructional binder open in front of her.

"Now, the second question I have to ask is, do you have any plan to harm yourself in the immediate future?"

"Not immediately, no."

"Good," said the girl. "You're doing really great. I know this is very hard for you."

"It is," said Marta. "I feel so fucked up, I don't know what I'm going to do or—"

"The third question I have to ask is: do you have a support system right now? Anyone you can talk to about this?"

"Well, there's *you*. That's why I called you."

"Yes, and you're doing really well. I can tell this is very hard for you. But do you have a support network where you are—any family, any friends, any coworkers who could help you right now?"

In the privacy of the laundry room, Marta made faces at the far wall. She could feel her temper starting to fray. "If I was the kind of person with a support network, I probably wouldn't be calling a suicide hotline."

There was a huff of staticky breath down the line, as if the operator had let out a particularly piercing sigh. "Are you saying that no, you don't have a support system in place?"

"Listen," Marta told the girl. "I tried to kill myself because I wanted to do it, because I couldn't think of a good reason not to do it, and it felt like—it feels like it's the right thing to do. It feels like it would be the best thing that could happen to me, now, and the longer I keep dragging it out, the longer I keep kicking the can down the road, the more I'm going to fuck it up for everybody. Not just me. The stuff I loved, the people I loved—I'm taking it apart with my hands, now, and I don't know why. I don't know why I can't stop. I've fucked my life away for nothing. There isn't a reason why. It just feels like it's the right thing to do. I can't stop. I just want somebody to tell me to stop."

There was a slight pause. "Ma'am," said the girl. "I know this is very hard for you and I can tell from your voice that you must be in a lot of pain, but I'm required by law to keep going through this checklist of questions."

Marta hung up.

When she got back to the apartment, her clothes still slightly damp and rumpled from the dryer but clean again, Shaw was crouching by his coffee table rolling a joint. The sight made her nauseated and she turned her head away; even the smell was more cloying and terrible than it had been before. "You remember that poster they used to have on the wall at the centre?" she asked. "It said, um, 'sadness is temporary, suicide is forever' or whatever."

He nodded. "'Permanent.' It was, 'Suicide is permanent'."

"I used to look at that and just think—yeah, it had *better* be. I used to think it'd be a real drag if you had to do it twice."

"Yeah."

She threw herself down on the daybed, tilting her head back to stare up at the stains on the plaster ceiling, mapping them like clouds on a summer day; one that looked like the mast of a sailboat, another that puffed out like the dead head of a dandelion. "I guess," she said, "that I can't even do it *once*. And it felt real shitty while I was doing it, too. I always figured overdosing would be peaceful, but I thought my heart was going to blow. Total failure."

He put out the tip of tongue to lick down the paper, folding it neatly into place, then tucked the finished joint away behind his ear. "Well, it's not easy."

"They should have a hotline for that too," she said, picking up her glass of water.

"For what? For how to commit suicide?"

"Yeah, you could call and be like—'I've got the pills, I've got the razorblades, so what's the next step?'"

He giggled, reaching down to pick at a scab on his wrist. "Christ, that's so fucked up."

"I know," said Marta, and swallowed again, cold tap water sore on her teeth, tasting of chlorine; all the water in the city tasted like shit. Worse in old buildings, where the pipes were clogged with rust. Dina had bought a filter. She said, "I'm sorry for being a dick."

He'd gone too far, picking at the scab—she could tell from how he frowned, a flutter of pain, and pulled his sleeve down again. Between his nails, a piece of bloodied skin. "Don't worry about it," he said. "Water under the bridge."

"No, but I don't want you to just be cool with it because you don't care," she said. "Or because you're too depressed to care or too fucked up to care or whatever. You're my friend, yeah? I should treat you better, even if you're down—shit, *especially* if you're down. Yeah?"

"Yeah," said Shaw, and pulled himself up to sit on the daybed beside her. He put his arms around her shoulders very loosely, giving her the gentlest of jostles, but she noticed that he'd run his hand quickly over the cushions first. He'd wiped the blood off his fingertips before he touched her. He hesitated, then said, "You can stay, if you need some time to get your head together. If you aren't ready to go home yet."

Marta blanched. "Fuck, man, I wasn't even thinking about that. What day is it now—Tuesday?"

"Wednesday. It's Wednesday afternoon."

"Fuck," she said, and her stomach pitched and sank again. Saliva, still laced with the powder of pills uncountable, pills unnameable, was crawling its way up her throat again, and she hunched forward to put her head down on her knees. *How much more? What does it take?* "I should've called to say I was going to be out all night," she said. "I should have—don't touch me, man, or I'm gonna puke on you—I should have called. Christ, I was supposed to take Nicky to school and everything."

"I'm sure if you just explain what happened, say you're sorry and all, they'll understand. I mean, what's done is done, you know?"

"And done, and done, and done," said Marta, voice muffled as she rested her head against her knees. She sucked back the gob of spit that threatened to choke her, winced, sniffed hard. "Over and over again, man. Eight years, doing it—nearly a third of my whole life. They don't deserve that shit."

He was quite for a moment, and she felt his hand resting on her shoulder, not quite clasping it—the fingers twitched convulsively, brushed her very lightly, but didn't hold her. He said, "I don't even call my parents back in Yarmouth anymore."

"Oh," she said and straightened up a little, wiping first her mouth and then her nose and then her eyes with the back of her hand. "You don't get along with either of them, then?"

"I do sometimes," said Shaw. "I did. But they don't feel like *my* parents anymore, you know? Like, when I think about them, they belong to somebody else. And that's just the way that everything is these days, the way I've been—all the people I know, I *knew*, and what I felt, what I did. I don't feel it."

"Christ, Shaw, I'm really sorry—"

"I'm not telling you as a bid for sympathy. I'm just saying, you shouldn't get like this if you can help it—you don't want it to hollow you out, tear you up. *Déchirer*, you know." His hand slipped from her shoulder as he interlaced his fingers, held them close together and linked at the knuckles; the gesture reminded Marta of the nursery game she'd sometimes played with Nicholas when he was a toddler, trying to coax a giggle out of him. *Here is the church and here is the steeple, open the doors and—*

"You don't want to feel like nothing all the time."

"Hypoarousal," said Marta, the word coming back to her on a tide of memory. "The hypozone."

Wasn't that what it was? The diametric opposite of hyperarousal, the flip side of whatever madness had gripped her the night before; the zone of hypoarousal, the cold world where grey tides swept up a pebbled shore, and people lay among the stones and became stones themselves, ossified from the inside out.

"Yeah," said Shaw. "So if there's anything in the world that can keep you out of that, can make you feel all right. . ."

Marta thought about it for a moment, then realized that she didn't really need to, anyway. There was only one thing that had kept her from straying into the hypozone. "I want to find Thomas Zimmerman," she said. "I want to keep looking for him."

He hesitated. Then he nodded. "All right," he said. "Then that's what we'll do."

Her father helped her pack. It didn't take long. He sat on the bed and watched while she piled the last of her clothes into the duffle bag, and it dawned on her that it was the first time that she could remember having seen him in the bedroom since she had moved back in. The light seemed to hit him differently; it rounded off the years and made him a much younger man. "Don't know what we're going to do with the space," he said.

Crouching, she felt around under the bed, fishing out her stash tin to tuck away in her pocket. "Nicholas can have it. Maybe put the computer in here and get him a little desk, and he could do his school stuff. Or you could have a real dining room."

He grunted, noncommittal, and then, "What's the rent like at Inglis Lodge?"

"About four hundred each, Shaw says, if we split it between us. It's a real flophouse kind of place, but the electric and water's included, and he says the landlord gets the snow shovelled out most days."

Another grunt, no more enthusiastic than the first. "Your manager at the university called our landline last night. She says you missed your shift again."

"Yep."

Standing over the duffle, she did a quick inventory—clothes, old CDs, laptop, smoking gear, the novelty pint glass she'd once stolen from the House of Blues, the stuffed highland cow toy that her mother had bought her on a trip to Cape Breton. Nothing else. She'd sold most of her other possessions when she'd moved out of her apartment, or given them away to the friends she never saw anymore.

"She said that was the third shift in a row."

"Yep," she said, "I guess maybe it was. Don't worry about it."

He stared at her. "Don't *worry?* Marta, how're you going to make rent if they fire you?"

"I'll be all right," she said. "Shaw says he can put me in touch with the manager at his supermarket and maybe get me a cashier gig. They don't usually hire you for that unless you have prior experience working the cash machine thing, but he'll give me some pointers. We'll figure something out." She stood, swinging the duffel bag over her shoulder, giving him a little turn. "So—all good?"

"Fine," he said and then pressed his lips together, as if he was on the verge of saying something more, but Marta didn't wait to hear what it was. She shouldered the bag and went past him, out and through to the kitchen, where Dina and Nicholas stood waiting.

"Ready to go?" said Dina, bright and falsely cheerful. She was holding a bulging plastic bag, which she pressed into Marta's hands. "There's some leftovers in there—mash and meatloaf and some of the tomato salad. And I can come by Sunday afternoon, if you want, and bring some more. You can just call."

Marta stowed the bag in her duffel. "Thanks," she said and stepped forward to give Dina a hug, pretending that she couldn't feel the weight of the accumulated earth between them.

Pressed up against his mother's side, Nicholas was watching her solemnly.

"See you," said Marta, and brushed his chin with her fingertips, tickling him—he leaned away from her, scowling, and she let her hand drop. "You can come visit me, you know. We can hang out any time."

But he only nodded, sharp and jerky, and looked down at his toes. "Bye," he said.

Her father had come out into the kitchen to join them—he raised his hand, then lowered it again, a fitful uncertain little wave. "You look after yourself."

"You bet," she said and gave him little salute. She grinned at him, at them, and kept grinning until the door was shut between them, between her and the place that had been her home. It shouldn't have made any real difference, she knew. She shouldn't have cared. It had only been a single bed and a radiator that sounded like a woman breathing in the night. Even when she'd been there, she hadn't ever really been there, and now she was neither.

It got cold in Inglis Lodge at night. Shaw said it was because the heating didn't work—the pipes just made rattling noises and spat clouds of steam—so most of the tenants kept the thermostats turned down. Marta thought it had to be even colder inside the lodge than out in the snow, but she wasn't inclined to complain. She wore her coat and gloves, and Shaw wrapped himself up in an old housecoat, and the electric kettle boiled while they set the chessboard up on the coffee table between them. With most of his belongings still taped up in boxes and her duffel, the inside of the apartment looked more like the baggage handlers' room at an airport than an actual home. It was in one of these boxes that Shaw had found the chessboard.

"I haven't actually played in years," he said.

"I never learned," said Marta. "Dad tried teaching me the rules one time, but I couldn't get the hang of it—the thinking-two-moves-ahead thing, yeah? I couldn't anticipate. Nicky's been getting pretty good, though."

"Some of the pawns are probably missing and I don't have a fucking clue where the black bishop is, but . . ."

"It'll do fine."

Shaw poured them each a mug of anemically weak mint tea, and Marta began to arrange the board. In the first row, left-hand square, she put the white king down. "Okay, that's A1, that's square one, day one, whatever. That's back in January, the day he came to therapy without his shoes."

"Yep."

"So he's feeling—he's feeling not well, fucked up, and he calls his doctor, Simon Greene, and they talk."

"Should we put one down for the doctor, too?"

Marta shook her head impatiently, blowing the steam off her mug and then risking a single, scorching sip. "Man, I'm not gonna be able to keep it straight if we do days *and* people. Let's just do it like a calendar, yeah? So, Thomas Zimmerman is going through a rough patch anyway, mental health up and down shit. So he goes to the doctor about it and the doctor's kind of a tell-it-like-it-is doc, kind of a look-you-in-the-eye-and-give-it-to-you-straight type of guy, and he says something that Thomas Zimmerman doesn't like. You follow me?"

"Yeah."

"Then he calls his mom after to—I don't know, get comforted?"

Now it was Shaw's turn to shake his head. "No, he was too paranoid about her. He wouldn't go to *her* for comfort."

"Right, fair point. So he calls his mom, weird old bitch, and they argue, and whatever she says, it freaks him out even more. So he gets in a fight with his boyfriend and he leaves, and he ends up in the mental ward at Abbie J. Lane Hospital. So the hospital's next, yeah?"

He dug around in the baggie of pieces and drew out the black rook; Marta put it on a square two rows up. "He's there for about two weeks," she said. "That's a pretty long stay, isn't it? Given the state of the hospitals around here, don't they cycle through patients kinda quick?"

"Usually, yeah—they don't have a lot of beds to go around in there. *I've* only ever been in for a couple days at a time."

"So they must have thought it was a real crisis," said Marta, and then put two pawns down on the board, one beside the rook, one another six squares along. "Then his cousin comes and checks him out and lets him crash for a couple weeks. And he gets the box of stuff I left for him at the hospital, and he sees the text from Allan inviting him to the party, and he shows up."

Shaw mimed swinging his fist into something invisible. "Yeah. Broken window."

"Right, broken window. Now, I didn't see him that night, 'cause I was busy being drunk and kind of a dick—"

"You weren't that bad," he said.

"—but we can assume that, you know, not all was well with him, then. He's still in kind of a strange place. And I take his boots, and he goes back to his cousin's place, and then a while later—" she held out her hand, grasping impatiently at the air, and he handed her another rook "—he starts causing problems for his cousin, breaking vases and shit, and maybe he gets kicked out. And *that*—" she put the rook down another two rows along "—was only a few days ago, 'cause they still had bits of porcelain on their carpet the night I was there. You follow me?"

"I think so," said Shaw. "I don't know where you're going from here, though."

Together, they sat sipping their tea, looking down at the erratic trail of pieces as it wound across the chessboard. Marta said, "I don't know where *anybody* would go from here."

CHAPTER THIRTEEN

There was a man sitting in the atrium of the bank, across from the row of bank machines. When the automatic door swung open, letting in Marta and Shaw, he stubbed out his cigarette and looked at them curiously. They brought with them the reek of weed, which—mixing with the clouds of nicotine still hanging stale in the air—was suffocating. They stood at the machine farthest from the man; Marta withdrew sixty dollars, punching the buttons quickly so that she wouldn't have to see her remaining bank balance flash across the screen and then declining to take a receipt. "I'm probably getting pretty close to the red," she remarked, tucking the bills into her coat pocket. "The university's gonna send me the last pay cheque at the beginning of the month, but it won't be much. They're probably subtracting the shit out of it."

"Well, one of the guys who stocks the shelves for us just gave his two-week notice. You might be able to snap his job up, if I talk to. . ."

Across the room, the man leaned forward slightly. "Hi," he said.

Shaw blinked. "Hey."

"Twenty bucks?" the man asked. He was looking at Marta.

She stared at him mutely for a moment, then took the joint out of her mouth and handed it off to Shaw. "I'm sorry?"

"I said twenty bucks?"

"I don't have twenty bucks," said Marta. "I don't have any money."

He shook his head impatiently. "No, I said, you. You come over here."

"We don't have twenty bucks," Marta repeated, and turned to Shaw for support; he nodded, wreathed in smoke from the smouldering joint, and spread his hands. The man looked at them with real contempt and then settled back in his seat. Mutely, they went past him and out into the street again, where the rain had slackened off; a fog was settling in over the city now, and everything was smudged around the edges. A car wheeled by in the road and its headlights were like halos, streaks of gold extending in all directions and so blindingly beautiful that Marta could only stare, mesmerized, and wait for it to pass.

"What the hell just happened?" she asked after a moment, tipping her head back toward the bank. "Did he want money or what?"

She put her hand into her pocket, felt the bills wrapped up cold and silky, curled like a living thing in her pocket; she felt guilty now for lying—they could have given him something. "We could have asked if he's seen Thomas."

"I think," said Shaw, "he wanted you to do something."

"Oh. Fuck that."

Instead, they made their first attempt outside the little Tim Horton's on Spring Garden Road, where there were always one or two panhandlers hanging around even on the coldest mornings. Today it was a young woman, sitting on the sidewalk in a stiff pose that reminded Marta vaguely of one of Dina's old dolls—legs splayed out straight, back rigid. There was a takeout cup at her feet and a piece of cardboard propped up in her lap, a few words written across it in marker. Marta could just about make out the message—"passing thru so please be kind"—from where she and Shaw stood, loitering under the awning of a boutique gift shop, pretending to admire the range of shawls and pottery in its window.

"She's more likely to talk to you than me," said Shaw, who was staring fixedly at a tortoiseshell vase.

"Why?"

"Well, she's a girl and so are you," he said and then, with a rare grin, "Even if you don't always want to be one."

Marta stopped pretending to examine an arrangement of model ships, turning to frown at him. "Fuck's that mean?"

"I'm just saying, you *are* a woman underneath it all and it's going to come off less creepy if it's you. Go on."

"Fine," said Marta. "And while I'm doing that, *you* can go talk to the guy outside the drug store who always smells like Alka-Seltzer and zit cream."

Giving him one last warning scowl, she ambled down the sidewalk and approached the woman with what she hoped was her friendliest and most casual grin, reaching up to brush her hair from her eyes; it was growing long and dark again, and she'd taken to keeping it in a mess of little plaits and pigtails. "Hey," she said and fished out one of the twenties she'd gotten from the bank, stooping to tuck it into the empty cup.

The woman beamed. "Bless you, honey," she said and then, with a sudden look of anxiety, "Are you sure you meant to give so much?"

"Yeah, no worries," said Marta, and stayed hunkered down there, gnawing on her lip as she tried to remember how they'd agreed to phrase the question. She regretted getting high now. She was going to have to cut back if she wanted to keep her train of thought from derailing itself on every turn. "Um, look, you don't know a guy called Thomas Zimmerman, do you? He might be living around here, sleeping kind of rough."

The woman hesitated, then tapped the sign. "I'm sorry, dear. I'm just passing through."

"Right," said Marta, and wished that she'd thought to split the bills into tens or fives. She stood up, brushing off the knees of her jeans. "Well, no worries," and then, hesitating a moment longer, unable to resist asking, "Listen, I know this is a weird question, so you don't have to answer, but have you ever used a paper bag instead of a tampon when you're menstruating? I saw a statistic about it on a poster, once."

The woman looked at her curiously for a moment. "No, I don't usually worry about the blood so much," she said. "Vaginal discharge is worse."

"Really?"

"Blood dries pretty fast," said the woman. "If you get wet, you're going to be wet all night, and it's bad this time of year. You start feeling cold and gross, like someone poured egg whites into your pussy. You get sick, sometimes."

"Christ," said Marta, and shivered. She pressed her thighs tight together in sympathy.

That night, her thighs were still together as she perched on the windowsill of Inglis Lodge with the chessboard balanced on her lap. She watched as, sitting on the edge of the bed, Shaw was going to work on himself.

"Sorry," he said, before he started, with an odd, frail kind of self-deprecation. "I have to. I can't think until I do it, you know? I have to wake up."

Marta nodded. It was the first time she'd actually seen him do it, although she knew that he'd done it at least twice since she'd moved in with him. The first time had been with the bathroom door closed, and she'd listened very hard to the conspicuous silence, broken only by a few rapid little breaths, a sigh; the second time, he'd left the door ajar, and she'd watched just the thinnest sliver of it. She'd suspected, then, that he might *want* her to see.

Now she saw.

In one hand, he held his lighter, and in the other, the bread knife he'd taken from the drawer—he flicked the wheel, then held the knife blade over the flame. Then he moved the lighter slowly back and forth, the metal turning black and burnished in the heat. A dark thread of smoke rose up, uncurling from around the blade's edge, and a carcinogenic chemical smell began to fill the room. Marta turned her face away. "Smells like poison," she said and then, when he didn't answer, drummed her heels against the wall. "It's gonna set the smoke alarm off."

"It won't. I took the batteries out."

"It smells like death, man."

"You can open the window, if you want to."

She did, wrenching it open with some difficulty—the wood was swollen with damp and she had to grip it with both hands, levering it up one screeching inch at a time. On the bed, Shaw had put the lighter down and begun to roll up his left sleeve to the elbow. As she watched, he hesitated for a moment, then pressed the flat of the knife blade down against the bare skin of his forearm; he did it slowly, flinching when the metal first touched his flesh, then harder—he doubled over, pressing down harder and harder. When he took the knife away again, Marta could see that the skin was very red, and stained with dark smears of charcoal. There was charcoal on his hands too; his fingertips were black as, again, he picked up the lighter and began to flick the wheel.

"Have you ever—" Marta began and then hesitated, making a vague seesawing gesture over her own forearm. "You know. Cut out the middleman. Cut."

"I don't like blood," said Shaw.

He repeated the process with the lighter three more times, heating the blade and then laying it against his skin with ritualistic care. Each time, he flinched; the knife bobbed and shook. Marta thought she could smell something else in the air now, frying meat, but maybe that was only her imagination. When he began to flick the lighter for the fourth time, she couldn't stand it anymore. "Give it a break, okay? You got it, you feel it. You're awake. Give it some time for the feeling to sink in before you do it again."

For a second, he hesitated, but then he complied, putting the lighter and the blackened knife down on the table. He sat back on the couch, holding his arm out at a stiff angle—from the crook of his elbow down to his wrist, cross-hatched lines of black streaked the swollen skin, making his forearm look like seared steak on a grill. His eyes were very wet, but there was an awful serenity in his face. He looked at the burn marks and not at her.

She glanced down at the chessboard, turning it around on her knees so that the squares pinwheeled into an optical spin. "Do you think we're doing this the wrong way?"

With his unburnt hand, he made a vague gesture to the room—the tangle of blankets piled up at one end of the daybed, the boxes on the floor, the stack of dirty dishes in the sink that was swiftly becoming a wonder of architectural ingenuity.

"Naw, I mean, we doing the search the wrong way? The people down on Spring Garden Road, the ones asking for money—they won't really want to talk to us 'cause they're working. Like they're on the clock, yeah? We're, ah, cutting into their business margins or whatever. So it's kind of like if someone came up to you while you were bagging groceries and started asking you weird questions about whatever-the-fuck."

"Happens more often than you'd think," said Shaw and, though his voice was still hoarse and distinctly tearful, he managed the sliver of a grin.

"But you're not exactly receptive to that shit, yeah? Nobody would be."

"So?"

"So we should be looking for people to talk to who'll *want* to talk, who *aren't* panhandling or soaping down car windows or gathering bottles for the recycling plant. Just hanging around."

In her lap, she turned the chessboard around into a diamond, matching each corner to a point of the compass. She liked the sense of exactness it gave her, to lay it all out across the sixty-four squares. It didn't matter if she forgot—she could map reality onto the board. The chess pieces themselves had long since vanished, absorbed one by one into the mass of clothes heaped up on the floor, but there was a small collection of used bottle caps on the windowsill and she used these instead. "If you put the city in quarters, right, there's only so many places people hang out. So, only so many places we can look, yeah?" She had to prompt him again; he was busy nursing his arm against his chest, pressing gingerly down on the raw skin, the same tentative taps as someone feeling for thin ice on a frozen pond. "Yeah, Shaw?"

"Yeah."

"There's always somebody out on the Commons," she said and put the red cap of a Smirnoff bottle in the western corner of the board, then another beside it, "—and I've heard people sometimes hang around Citadel Hill, sucking dick for cash."

"Not this early in the year," said Shaw. "Too cold. We should be looking at all the libraries, instead—they'll be going there to get out of the cold weather."

Two more caps down, one rum and one gin, and then another. "And the Salvation Army, uptown. There's always like, five or six people just sitting around outside. Or in the North End around Gottingen Street, where they got all the methadone clinics and the crack houses."

He blanched. "I'm not going down there."

"Aw, man, it isn't *that*—"

"I'm not," he said. "Not after dark, not to go asking people questions. They don't fuck around. It's a bad vibe, Marta, seriously."

"Suit yourself," she said and looked back down at the chessboard, balanced precariously on her knees. Five bottle caps and five new places to try, but she couldn't help but feel unsatisfied, still. "I wish we knew where they're all going at night," she said.

"I think there's a couple tents set up in Victoria Park. And that little scrubby park on Quinpool, too, the one where we set off the firecrackers on New Year's."

"I know," said Marta. "But d'you remember how many there used to be, before the police came and shut them down? That summer when there were all those protests outside the old library? There were dozens and dozens of tents, all over, and now it's just five or six. They got to have gone *someplace*, yeah?"

"Someplace out of the city?"

Marta shrugged and the chessboard wobbled, the cap marking the Salvation Army rolling down to bounce, gently, between the two of the public libraries. "Maybe," she said, righting the makeshift pieces again. "Anyway, I guess we've got enough to go along for a while, yeah?"

Marta wanted to try the Salvation Army men's shelter first, and it was far enough along Gottingen Street and into the shabbier parts of the city that Shaw insisted she wait until after his shift was done at the supermarket, so that they could go together. The snow was coming down heavy as they went up through the city, skirting the edge of Citadel Hill. "Blowjob hill," quipped Marta, trying to make Shaw laugh, but—for once—the wind had died down to nearly nothing. The snow fell in soft fat flakes that stuck like dandruff in her hair, and she picked them out with her fingertips.

"It looks nice," said Shaw.

"Yes, very picturesque. It'll all be brown as shit and slushy tomorrow morning, though—this fucking province, it never stays good for long. Not in March."

"Your hair," he said, "looks nice. I'll like the way your roots come through, like it's moving all the time, running down like water. It's pretty."

"Oh—thanks," said Marta, and then didn't know what else to say.

She wondered if this was something he'd written out in his head, turning it over and over the same way they'd sometimes prepared their little speeches prior to therapy sessions. He'd stared at her for a long time that morning while she'd been brushing out her braids. Ducking her chin, she sniffed and then jammed her thumb to the side of her nostril, blowing a dob of snot out her nose and into the sharp evening air. She said, "Pretty fucking cold."

It felt even colder by the time they got onto Gottingen Street, the snow starting to pile up in drifts on the sidewalk. Maybe that was why there were only two people outside the doors of the men's shelter where, in finer weather, you could sometimes find a group of six or seven. One stood smoking a cigarette under the lit awning, directly below the crimson shield of the Salvation Army. He was tightly wrapped in layers of coats and fleeces and scarves, only a thin wedge of his face unobscured, and his eyes, which watched Marta and Shaw intently as they trudged up. The other man was sitting slumped against one of the cement planters by the doors, a little farther off.

Marta looked to the smoker first. "Hey, man. Cold evening, eh?"

It was hard to tell, but the visible part of his face appeared to contort with an incredulous disdain. "Yes," he said, the words mumbled through his scarf. "It sure is."

"You staying here tonight, then?"

"I guess."

"Have they still got any beds free in the dorm?" asked Shaw.

"Did the last time I checked," said the man, and then, hooking his nicotine-stained fingers into his scarf and drawing it down to expose his mouth, added more clearly, "It's a men-only shelter, though. Girls don't come in. Sorry."

He was looking at Marta.

"Great, thanks," said Shaw, and then, quietly in her ear, "I'll go in, take a quick look, eh? Ask around for Thomas?"

She nodded and watched him edge past the man and up to the front door, pausing briefly to read the list of regulations and warnings taped to the glass, then slipping quietly inside. The smoker took another pull on his cigarette and eyed her with frosty indifference.

Marta turned her attention to the second man.

He was still sitting in the shadow of the planters, chin propped up on his hand and apparently occupied with studying the dimensions of each snowflake that landed on his coat sleeve. The asphalt was slanted slightly and something wet and dark had gone spilling down it, a slow-spreading puddle that swept up all the grit and grime and old cigarette butts in its path, carrying them out toward the street. The snow, falling more heavily now, was turning it to sludge. Marta was looking at the liquid, wondering if it had come *from* the man or if he just happened to be sitting near it, and it was in doing this that she realized she recognized him.

"Hey," she said and took a step toward him, skirting the edge of the spill. "Hey, didn't you come by our church a couple weeks back? You came by St. Matthews, yeah?"

He raised his head, squinting at her vaguely in the light of the red sign, and she saw it *was* him—the first man to have taken a bagged sandwich from her, the man who'd brought his dog and showed her tricks. It felt like a long time ago, now. "Oh," he said and then nodded just once, a single up-down swing of the head.

"Where's Theo?" asked Marta.

He stared at her and didn't answer, and it dawned on her suddenly that he was very drunk. The skin high around his cheeks had a raw look to it, and his lips were red too, but everything else was the sickly grey of wet cement.

"Your dog," she repeated, sounding out the words more distinctly. "You brought him to the church, you said his name was Theo. Isn't he here?"

For a moment, the man only stared at her as if he was trying to make sense of her entire existence. Then, the lilt of his accent thickened almost beyond the point of deciphering, the words grotesquely slurred, "Shelter. He got took away." His voice quavered, as if he was unsure of this fact. He licked his red lips then tried again, with a degree more conviction, "He got—yeah."

The words themselves barely registered to Marta. A particular kind of unease was creeping over her, looking down at him. "Are you feeling all right?" she asked. "You've had a bit to drink, yeah? You feeling kind of sick, maybe?"

Again, he gave a jerky nod. "I feel," he said, in that same tone of trembling uncertainty, "a pain, I think, in my. . ."

"Yeah? Whereabouts, man?'

Vaguely, he waved one hand in the approximate area of his clavicle. His hands were bare and that, too, worried Marta; it wasn't the kind of evening to be out in the snow without much on, especially wasted. She held out her hands to him. "Here, why don't I help you up? You might feel better if you go inside and sit down in the warm a while."

"They won't take him," said the smoker by the door. She hadn't known that he was listening, but he had turned to watch them, sucking on the last remnants of his roll-up. "You gotta be sober or they won't let you in," he said and then, with an odd kind of triumph, "And they don't let women come in, either."

Marta ignored him, crouching down and clasping one of the man's hands tightly in hers, hooking the other under his elbow. He wasn't much taller than her and felt considerably lighter, but it was still a challenge to get him standing, his legs swaying like reeds. The reek of liquor was eye-wateringly strong and edged with something else, too—a cloying, citrusy kind of smell. In the end, she got him sitting propped up on the edge of the planter, her arm around his shoulders to keep him from slipping.

"Christ, man, how much have you been drinking?"

"Not much," he said thickly.

"Ask him," said the smoker, "*what* he's been drinking. Go on."

Marta looked around, meaning to tell him to fuck off, but he caught her eye and then tipped his head meaningfully. With the smouldering end of his cigarette, he pointed at something level with their feet. Frowning, she looked down at the ground. She thought he was pointing at the puddle of whatever-it-was, but he frowned and waggled his cigarette again, and she looked again.

This time, she saw it—a single bottle, half-hidden in the shadows at the base of the planter.

Marta used the toe of her boot to kick it over, turning it so the label faced up. It was a seventeen-ounce bottle, made from an opaque plastic, and one she recognized just as quickly as she'd recognized the drinker; she'd seen a bottle just like it in most of the shops and restaurants she'd gone into, since the start of the pandemic. It was hand sanitizer.

"Christ," she said. "Did you really drink all of that?"

Under her hand, she felt the muscles in his back twitch, convulse—he retched and spat, a spattering of dark holes sunk in the snow at their feet. "I tried it and threw up some blood," he said. "So I mixed the rest with water."

"And you drank it all?"

"Yes," he said and threw up again, the soft pulp of his insides sizzling red in the snow.

Petrified, Marta looked from him to the blood; she felt a sudden insane urge to stir the snow with her boot and stamp out the blood, make everything clean and good as new again, but that would have been worse than useless. She turned to look at the smoker. "What the fuck are *you* doing, just standing there? Why don't you go in there and get someone to help?"

He stamped out his cigarette butt; he'd readjusted his scarf to hide his mouth and cheeks, but she could see his eyes glitter below the brim of his hat. "Who's gonna help?"

"*Anyone*," said Marta. "Christ, aren't there staff around?"

He hesitated for a moment, glancing toward the doors.

"Go on," she told him. "Or stay here and look after him, and *I'll* go in and get help."

That seemed to do it. "They don't let women in," said the smoker, and cast one more contemptuous look at her, before yanking the door open and sloping inside.

Marta kept her arm around the man's shoulders; she didn't know what else to do but hold him and feel the mad spasms of his heart. He was shaking badly, little convulsive twitches of the shoulders and spine, and when he opened his mouth to try and talk, a frothy bubble of blood ballooned out, popped, clung to his lips in a stringy tangle of gore. "Sorry."

"Don't say that," Marta told him. "It's nothing, yeah? Tomorrow, you're gonna be fine and it's not even going to feel like anything."

"I'm sorry."

"It's going to be fine," she said and then went on, not knowing quite why, except that she wanted him to know it, "I really liked you, when I met you at the church. You were the first guy to come get a sandwich and you were sweet to me, and so was your dog. I really liked you. It's going to be fine. Everything is."

It was only after the ambulance had come and gone that Marta remembered she still didn't know his name.

There was still a little dried blood under her fingernails that night as she filled the electric kettle for tea and ramen. As she set it down to boil, she heard the drawer open behind her and a rattle of cutlery. Turning, she saw that Shaw had taken a knife from the drawer. She stared at him. "What are you doing?"

He only looked at her. There was nothing of shame there, nothing of defiance, only a flat serenity—she could tell that he expected her to understand, and she did. She listened to the kettle boiling, and watched as, sitting on the bed, Shaw heated the knife. She made the tea and, when it was ready, stood leaning against the windowsill and cradling the mug in her hands, feeling the warmth spread through her fingers and up into her chest.

When Shaw had finished, he looked up at her. "It's gone now," he said.

"Yes," she said, thinking that he meant the evening itself. "It's gone."

She'd felt it go too.

She thought about Allan and his vanishing world, the king of his lonely little reality—time was the same way, when you got this low. It disappeared around you one bit at a time. Where was I last night? Where was I this morning? You got out of sync with everybody else. Somebody spoke and you didn't hear them, you were left standing there minutes later, wondering why the memory of it was echoing around your head.

But she remembered the blood that had burned in the snow. She remembered that, and she remembered the pieces on the chessboard, and she knew it was too late to forget now.

They stayed there quietly for a while, while the heat seeped into her hands and the tea turned cold, and then Marta went to fill the kettle again. Later, curled up beside him on the bed, listening to the soft noises that he made, she stared up at the shaft of light from the street above and remembered it all over again. She remembered standing there and watching him burn himself again, and she remembered how she'd felt no pain at all, and she wished that she could forget it.

And she couldn't.

CHAPTER FOURTEEN

The next morning, the burns on Shaw's arms had turned bad—sickly yellow blisters, swollen and distended. The largest one was the size of an egg, ballooning out a good two inches from his skin. He sat on the couch with his arm held rigidly out from his side, his face taut and pale, head turned away like he was trying very hard not to look at the burns. There were deep hollows around his eyes. He hadn't slept all that night—his arm had been hurt too badly. "Listen," said Marta, who was thoroughly disconcerted by the sight of the blisters. "You really need to go to the hospital, man. The emergency room at the IWK. We can go this morning—I'll come with you . . ."

Mutely, he shook his head.

"You don't have to tell them what happened. We had some fireworks left over from New Year's Eve, we were fucking around trying to set them off, you got some burns—we'll just make something up."

Again, he shook his head.

"You're really hurt, man. You really did a number."

"I need to wake up," he told her. He started to cry. "I just need to wake up, you know?"

She looked at him for a moment, at his wan and wrung-out face, and the swollen mass of blisters. Then she crossed the room and pried out one of the thumbtacks holding up an old Pink Floyd poster. The corner peeled away from the wall, flapping loose. She took the lighter from the coffee table and flicked a flame to life, then held the end of the thumbtack to it until had turned black. They

went into the bathroom, and Shaw held his arm over the sink—
Marta found an old towel and put it down folded beside the sink.
She found a box of assorted Band-Aids in the bathroom cupboard
and a few rolls of gauze, and arranged those beside the sink. Then,
holding the tack carefully between finger and thumb, she looked at
Shaw. "You ready?"

He nodded. She drove the tack into the first blister, puncturing it.
A bead of amber-coloured liquid appeared, but no more. She drove
the tack in again, twisting it back and forth, and then picked up
the towel, wadding it into a ball. Gingerly, she pressed down on the
blister and more liquid began to leak out, yellow like wax, running
down Shaw's wrist and dripping off the ends of his fingers, down
into the basin. She pressed and kept pressing, until the towel was
soaked through and the blister was flat to his skin and pale.

"You awake now?" she asked Shaw, and he nodded. "Good. You
stay awake. You remember this next time you pick up the lighter."

By the time they were done, Shaw was pale and shaking; the sink
was a mess and his arm was, too. He turned the taps on and washed
the stuff away down the drain, and then held his arm under the
stream, his brow furrowed, twitching with pain. Marta covered the
drained blisters with folded pieces of gauze and taped them down as
neatly as she could with the mismatched Band-Aids.

In bed, she held him, and—when he put his arms around her—she
felt the cloth of the bandage rasp against her skin, rough and sickening. She curled herself around him, hip to hip; beyond the curve of
his shoulder, she could see the darkened room and, directly opposite,
the apartment door. What was beyond it? What else was there? She
thought about Allan again, and all his rotting, bitter philosophy. Ego
death, she thought. Whatever people thought they found on a trip—
take enough shrooms, high enough dose, and the psilocybin dissolved
your entire self, and all you could know was the whole universe. Ego
death, but in reverse; the world went away and only you were left.

She drifted in and out for a while, listening to the ragged drag of Shaw's breath, and woke up in the early hours of the afternoon, dizzy. She rolled her head into the pillows, keeping her eyes shut—the mattress pitched under her, seesawing up and down. Shaw was still asleep beside her—he had turned onto his side and was lying with his bandaged arm stretched out awkwardly. Carefully, Marta detached herself from him and sat up. Something turned in her stomach and she had to scramble for the sink again; she threw up with an easy efficiency and, wiping her mouth on her sleeve, felt immediately better.

There was an open can on the floor beside the sink; the cider was flat but still cold. Most things kept cold in Inglis Lodge, where the radiators had been on the fritz for weeks. She finished it and then cracked open the second can. The garbage bag was overflowing with soiled paper towels, all stained with that thick, yellowish pus—she stuffed them down, then knotted the bag, dragging it out and across to the door; she wanted it gone before Shaw could wake up and see it.

She heaved it down to the street and then sat down beside it on the curb to smoke. Tapping the ashes of the joint, she balanced her phone on her knees and, for the first time in weeks, checked her inbox. She went backwards through the unopened emails—a severance notice from the university for her job, an email from Allan asking why she hadn't answered any of his texts—scrolling until she found the last email that Quyen had sent her. The one about working for the charity, Open Hands. She read the email twice, then clicked the link. Her joint burned down to an ashy stub and heat nipped at her fingertips.

There was a young man singing on the corner of Spring Garden Road and South Park Street. He had a good voice, light and clear, but he broke off when he saw Marta coming and so she only caught a few words. "And King David had red hair, red hair, red hair—" Then, speaking quite normally, "You got any money? Anything to fix my teeth?"

Bracing herself for whatever might be coming next, she spread her hands, contorting her face into an apologetic grimace. "Sorry. I wish I had some, I'd give it to you. I'm sorry."

To her surprise, he only nodded, as if this was entirely irrelevant to him. "That's all right. You have a good day."

"You too."

She made to go past him, to cross the street, but he caught her eye again and asked, "You got a passport?"

Marta shook her head.

"See about getting one," he told her. "When you start noticing people's hairlines rising, that's a sign. It's time for you to dig up your dead and go to Israel."

"I'd love to," said Marta, who didn't know what else to say.

"Remember, Abraham had blue eyes," he said. His nose was running badly and looked oddly flat, like it had been broken and set wrong. He went on, "Me, I'm just waiting for money, but it's hard, 'cause I don't have a fixed address. If I had somewhere to live, if I was living with somebody, I could figure shit out. I could give them seventy, eighty percent—eighty percent of what I make every month . . ."

Too late, she saw where he was going with it; she felt sick in her stomach, but not with him, with herself. It felt somehow demeaning to him that he should be asking her. "I can't help you," she said. "I'm sorry."

"Are you psychic?"

"What?"

"Can you read minds? Are you psychic?"

"No, I don't think so."

"Do you want to learn how? I could teach you."

"I wouldn't want to read minds."

"You should," he said. "It would make you a better person."

She shrugged. "I'd better go. I'm late."

She edged past him and walked quickly down the sidewalk, feeling giddy and weightless and beyond herself—on a whim, she turned and saw that he was staring after her. "Hey," she said, pulling her scarf down away from her mouth and raising her voice to be heard over the roar of traffic. "Do you know a guy named Thomas? Thomas Zimmerman?"

He frowned. "I know a Thomas," he said. "I don't know the other name. It was just Thomas."

"Where did you see him?"

But he only smiled at her and began to sing, quietly first and then louder and louder until people began to stare, and still his voice went seesawing wildly up through the octaves. "King David had blue eyes, blue eyes, blue eyes—"

Marta turned her back on him quickly, hurrying across the street and on, but she could still hear him singing all the way down the block. Blue eyes, blue eyes, sang the prophet of Spring Garden Road, fainter now, keeping rhythm with the beat of her pulse, and he was still singing when she got to the apartment building where her family lived. She still had her key, but it felt strange to just walk in now that she didn't live there anymore, somehow. She settled for a compromise, letting herself in the front and then knocking on the unit door, waiting. Dina let her in with a finger on her lips—their father was asleep in his recliner. "I was just on my way out," said Dina softly, and Marta saw that she was wearing her coat, had one glove on, one off. "I have to pick Nicky up from hockey practice."

"Oh—right."

"You can stay and have some coffee, if you want—he'll probably be up soon, if you want to wait a little."

"Actually, I was hoping to talk to you."

Dina looked a little taken aback for a moment, then frowned. "Why? What's wrong?"

"Nothing," said Marta. "Nothing's wrong. I just wanted to ask you for a favour."

"What?"

The surprise was gone now, replaced with a brisk disinterest. She hurried around Marta, sweeping things into her purse, knotting her scarf around her neck, stooping to check her reflection in the mirrored metal of the toaster.

"Do you think you could lend me some money? It would only be about seventy dollars and I could probably pay you back by the end of the month."

"Why?"

"Well—guess I figured you'd want it back pretty soon and all."

Dina was tucking a stray wisp of hair back into her ponytail. "I mean," she said, "why do you need the money?"

"It's for a job," said Marta, and then, when Dina only made a little noise in her throat, "A job application thing."

"What kind of job needs you to *pay* to apply? Are you sure it's not a scam?"

"It's not. It's for a charity—for helping the homeless. They need to run a background check on every applicant with the police, just so they know your criminal record and stuff, and it costs about sixty-five, seventy bucks to get that done with the RCMP. I'd be paying it myself, if I could, but I'm already in the red."

"Oh."

"I'll pay you back as soon as I can."

"Can we talk about it later? I've really got to go."

But Marta followed her out into the hall. "Listen, I'm not just asking for money to do whatever-the-fuck, buy drugs or something. I really want this job. I'm serious."

"You've never been interested in charity work before."

"I know. That's why I want to do it now."

"And you're *sure* it's not a scam?"

"I *know* it's not," said Marta, and held out her phone, where she'd kept the Open Hands web page up. "They call it being an 'outreach specialist,' but it just means you help out running the shelters and getting people medical care and shit. They're saying it's 'part of our citywide effort to engage individuals experiencing homelessness, encourage them to accept services and safe housing' and they don't care if you never got a college degree."

"Well, you're still not even qualified. The only thing you've ever done before is be a janitor, be a dishwasher. They'll want people with experience and CPR training and things, working with vulnerable populations and—why do you want to do it so much, anyway?"

She thought about Shaw's face, his liquid skin running down the drain like wax. She thought, she thought. "Because it's what I want to do," she said. "And I have to do *something*. And I'm tired of pretending like I don't care about stuff, like it doesn't really matter to me. I mean—fuck it, you know? I have to get some kind of work, make some kind of money, and I'd rather be helping people than scrubbing toilets or washing dishes at the House of Blues. I mean, Christ, I want to do something, Dee. I want to. Isn't that good enough, if nobody's hurting?"

"Fine," said Dina.

"Really?"

They were out in the street now and she was conscious of the difference between them: of Dina's smart felted coat, her jaunty red scarf and gloves, and of the fact that she herself hadn't even brushed her hair that morning, looked considerably shabbier.

"Yes, all right—fine. You can have the money. Do you want it in cash or cheque?"

"Uh, um. Cash would be better, I guess."

"We can stop at the bank on the way, then. Come on."

"Thanks," said Marta. "Really, Dee—thank you."

But Dina only shrugged. "We'd better hurry. Nicky'll be waiting for me."

They walked down the street together, and Marta realized that she couldn't remember the last time they'd been out in the city together. She tried to think of something to say—she felt that something needed to be said, that they couldn't just walk on opposite sides of the pavement like perfect strangers—but couldn't. At the bank on the corner, they stopped and Marta waited, fidgeting and looking at the passing snowplows, while Dina withdrew eighty dollars from the bank and then presented her with the four crisp twenties. Marta rolled them up tightly, tucked them into the pocket of her coat. "Thank you," she said. "I really do mean it."

"Get the job," said Dina, and then smiled a little. "You should come around the apartment more often, you know—even if you're not living with us, I think it'd mean a lot to Nicky if you came around. Dad, too. We'd all like to see you."

"Yeah, I will. I just need to get things figured out, get my head straight. I'm working on it."

"Right," said Dina. She looked away for a moment, looked pained—she gnawed on the rind of her thumb, and Marta was interested to notice that this, too, was something they both did, worrying at the raw flesh around the cuticle. Genetic tick. Then, "Was it always that bad for you?"

Marta blinked; it wasn't what she'd been expecting. "Was what bad?"

In the parking lot, Dina's hand, fingers too caked in dirt to tell if she'd been gnawing on them, and Marta had looked down at those fingers, spread wide and grasp, and thought: Grave dirt. It's grave dirt.

"Living with us," said Dina. "I mean, not just lately, not just the last couple years, or the funeral, but all of it. When we were growing up—" She saw Marta open her mouth and pushed on quickly, before her sister could say anything. "The way you talk about it sometimes, you make it sound like it was awful, like it was traumatic. I mean, you talk about repressing things, like it was all so bad you can't even think about it, ever. But I was there too, you know, and I remember what it was like. It wasn't bad."

"No," said Marta. "It wasn't."

It was her sister's hand on her arm, fingers caked in the grave dirt. Can't you just keep it together? Just today?

"Dad's always done his best. So did Mom, when she was—"

"Yeah. I know."

"It wasn't ever that bad."

"I know," said Marta.

"It just makes us feel like shit, you know, when you talk like that. How bad you feel all the time. They didn't always understand, but they did everything they could. Even when Dad was on his own, when it was just him—he nearly killed himself looking after us, making sure we were all right. He did all that so you could keep hanging around with your friends and never go to college, smoking and messing around and doing nothing all the time. So I could have Nicky, so we could all stay together. Do you know how lucky we were?"

"I know. I know we were lucky. I know it was good."

"Then why do you always—?"

"It was really good, while it was happening," said Marta. "While it lasted, while it was all of us together. That's why I don't ever want to think about it, you know—that's why I can't think about it anymore. It was the best part of my life, and it's over, and I can't think about it now. I can't have it in my head, when everything's fucked."

"Marta . . ."

"Because what happens," she went on, "is that it tells you lies. It tells you things were bad, when they weren't, because you need a reason why everything's bad now. And I loved her, you know. And it's just taking her away from me, all the time. I mean, that's what it feels like."

"I'm sorry."

"Me too," said Marta. "I mean, I'm really sorry, you know. The way things get. How they got, after she died. I think I wanted to be somebody, then, but you were already being her—you were being Mom—so I just had to be myself instead, and I tried to be myself very hard. And I think maybe that wasn't always a good person to be, you know?"

"Yes."

"Or a happy person, either, I guess."

"Yes," said Dina, and then, quiet and a little abruptly, "I used to wish you'd come to me about it, you know. Before the funeral, before it—it happened like that. I wished you'd talked to me. I don't know, it's stupid."

"A bit," said Marta. "But I do know what you mean."

The bus was pulling up to the curb, the other waiting passengers shuffling into a queue, fumbling around in their pockets for tickets and passes and ID cards. Marta sniffed hard, rubbed her nose; Dina twitched at the collar of her coat. "Well—good luck with the job application. Let us know how it goes."

"I will."

"You going back to Inglis?"

"Not yet," said Marta. "I want to visit somebody first."

Danny Boy, the next mayor of Halifax, was at his station outside the Zimmerman house again. To the passersby, he kept up a steady refrain of questions, peppered with the occasional plaintive remark—"Got any change, please? It's a cold day out here, awful cold March we've been having. Got any money for the bus ticket home? It's awful cold. Any change for the bus home?"—but he broke off abruptly when he saw Marta coming. His leathered face, creased deep around the mouth, walnut-flesh contorting into a cheerful grin. "Oh, it's you. You don't have any change for the bus, do you, dear?"

"Sorry," she said and touched her hand to the bills in her pocket, guilty. "Why do you have to take a bus, anyway? I thought you just lived up in the IWK parking lot."

He sniffed. "Better when you ask for something small. People don't care to listen to the angels much around here."

"Oh. Well, sorry. Might have a bit of weed, though, if you want any."

"I don't like that stuff, dear. It makes your brain turn to shit."

"You might be right about that," said Marta, and then, tipping him a little salute, "If you'll excuse me, just a second—"

Dipping his grey head, he shuffled aside and let her go past him, up the ice-slick steps to the door of the Zimmerman home. She knocked twice and then, standing on the doorstep, brushed at the knees of her jeans. She tried to see her reflection in the fogged pane of the door and, while she was squinting hopelessly at the blurred haze of her uncombed hair, something moved behind the glass. Briefly, Rachel Zimmerman's face appeared superimposed over hers; she peered out at Marta through the pane, then drew back quickly, shaking her head. Her lips moved, framing silent words—*Go away*.

"Please," said Marta, and leaned up against the glass, speaking loudly and slowly with her mouth to the crack of the door. "Please, can you let me in, just for a second?"

Another shake of the head. *Go away.*

"Please, just for a couple minutes! Just to talk!"

"You won't have any luck with that one," remarked Danny Boy, from his place down on the sidewalk. "Blood from a stone's heart. Stone deaf. She doesn't hear the angels at all."

Marta ignored him. "Listen," she said. "I'd just like to talk for a couple minutes, that's all. It won't take long. It's just about Thomas."

There was the sound of a bolt turning and then the door drawn slowly open; Marta went in quickly, before the woman could change her mind, and slipped past her into the front parlour. It was all as she'd remembered it, perfectly neat and well-ordered. The house was, but Rachel Zimmerman was not—her grey hair was escaping its loose bun in wisps and her eyes were very dark, very wet, the skin underneath puffy. She looked at Marta and through her, and her hands were knotted at her ribs.

"Hey," said Marta, and then, nodding to the couch, "Is it okay if I sit down for a minute? I've been walking all over today and I'm pretty wrung out."

Mutely, the woman shook her head.

But Marta had been expecting it. "I wanted to say sorry," she said, "for how I acted when I was here before. I was worried about Thomas, but I guess you must be, too. And I wasn't really thinking about that—about how you must be feeling in all this."

"It's been difficult," said Rachel. "For everyone."

"I mean, I know it's gotta be hard. I know you think I don't understand, but I think I do. I get it. From the other side of it, from the other end, I do." She hesitated, looking at her. "I mean, I know how it was with me, so I think I might know how it was with Thomas, too."

"Do you?"

"I think so," said Marta. "I was diagnosed with clinical depression when I was about eighteen, you know. It was just after my mom passed, and my dad was worried about us—me and my sister, how we were dealing with it—so we ended up at the doctor's a lot."

She hesitated, eyeing the woman cautiously, probing for a reaction, but Rachel Zimmerman wasn't even looking at her; her attention seemed to have slipped from Marta to the picture on the wall, the stormy charcoal sketch of the harbour.

Undaunted, Marta plunged on. "So he diagnosed me, you know, and he said it was a stress thing. Grief thing. I was overwhelmed with losing her, and my sister getting pregnant pretty soon after, and everything that was going on in the family. He said that might've set it all off. And I wanted that to be true, but I knew deep down it wasn't, because I knew I'd always been that way. Almost as long as I could remember, I knew I'd been feeling down and low. And that was the thing that made it so hard, yeah? With my family. They were always good, it was always good when we were together, and it drove me crazy that I couldn't be happy. They loved me, and I couldn't stand to be around them, and it never made sense. There wasn't ever a reason. That was the hardest thing to accept, you know, because I wanted there to be a reason. But they loved me, and they couldn't make me better, and they couldn't make me worse. So it wasn't their fault."

Already, she'd said more to Rachel than she ever had at the Barrington Centre, in all the therapy sessions she'd ever attended. But it was too late to stop now and so she went on, pushing desperately, persistently forward. "I just mean, I don't think what's happening to Thomas is your fault, either. I don't think you need to feel that way, or blame yourself, or anything like that. You could have loved him, and done everything you thought was right, and it wouldn't have made any difference. These things just get into your head sometimes, and they bend the whole world around to fit the shape of whatever's wrong with you, and nobody can stop it."

Rachel didn't say anything. Trying to string her thoughts together, fidgeting, Marta had crossed her legs, and the scuffed toe of one boot—of Thomas's boot—bobbed and jerked in the air. It was there that Rachel was looking.

"I just mean," said Marta, "that there doesn't need to be a reason. I think sometimes that's the hardest thing."

She stopped, then, because she thought if she didn't she might start to cry, and that would have been the real point of no return.

After a moment, Rachel said, "He called me."

"When?"

"The night that he . . ." She broke off, gesturing vaguely to the air between them, where Thomas Zimmerman was not. "He called me."

Marta didn't know whether she ought to interject or not. It felt silly, almost, but the woman spoke so haltingly, and she was afraid that, without prompting, the talk might all dry up. Gently, she tried. "What did he say?"

"He was very upset. He was asking questions about me, his father, our family. He wanted to know if he was . . . if he was the only one, or if he wasn't. He kept asking, you know, what was wrong with him. Was it genetic. Did I know what was wrong with him. He was very upset."

"You'd never told him?"

Rachel shook her head. "His father—my husband—he left a long time ago. We never talked about it. We never called it what it was."

"So Thomas found out from the doctor," said Marta. "That it was genetic, that both of them had it, and he never knew. And that's what sent him off."

There was quiet in the room, cloying and sickly, while Rachel Zimmerman bent her head and looked down at her knotted fingers. The living room window had been opened an inch, just to let in the cold seaward breeze, and it made the curtains flutter gently. Looking at them, Marta imagined that she could see a hand reaching through, trying to touch her. "I'm going to find him," she said aloud. "I promise."

Snow was falling by the time that she left the house and Danny Boy was gone from his spot outside. For a single panicked moment, she thought that he might have left, but he had only retreated off the sidewalk, sheltering from the cold in the little alcove below the stairs. She leaned over the railing and looked down at him, crouched on the pavement with his head low, his shoulders hunched forward. "Hey," she said. "You said you knew everybody around here, right?"

He looked up. Snow was sticking to the tufts of his eyebrows, making a white thatch over his split-veined eyes. "Sure," he said "I'm the next mayor, you know. Everybody knows me."

CHAPTER FIFTEEN

A boy went into the McDonald's. He walked very quickly, holding himself stiff-backed and rigid, passing the line of customers waiting for their morning coffees without a glance. Past the scattering of tables, past the pick-up counter—he disappeared into the men's washroom. Marta watched him go from where she stood, second in line and waiting for the pair of construction workers ahead of her to finish ordering their breakfast sandwiches. He was young, maybe only a few years older than Nicholas, but the years hung around him very raw.

"Can I help you?"

She flinched. The construction workers had moved along down the counter and the server was looking at her expectantly, fingers hovering over the screen of his tablet. Vaguely, she looked up at the fluorescent menu. "Uh, yeah," she said and sniffed hard, her nose running badly. "I'll have two black coffees, two bacon and egg sandwiches, and hash-browns, and hotcakes. Large, thanks. Everything large."

Stifling a jaw-cracking yawn, she patted her pockets, remembered belatedly that all she had left were the bills that Dina had given her. She hesitated for a moment, but the customers behind her were getting restless and the server was watching her. She extracted a twenty from the roll and gave it to him, tucking the remaining bills back into her coat pocket. As long as she had the sixty-five left over, it wouldn't matter.

Waiting for the food, faintly nauseated as the grease-reek heat of the fryers rolled over her, she saw the boy reappear again. Again, he walked past the customers without looking at them and straight back out into the street. Marta felt a fresh wave of discomfort grip her, not entirely physical now, but a cloying and creeping sadness under the skin—she'd gotten a better look at his face this time. He was young, very young, but she thought she recognized the single-minded focus of a perennial user chasing a high. She'd experienced it often enough herself.

She found Danny Boy waiting for her under the awning when she came out, the paper takeout bags awkwardly heaped up in her arms as she tried to balance the coffees. He'd been talking with a man panhandling on the curb, stooping low and conferring in soft voices, but the conversation seemed to have ended. "Here you go," she said, letting him take the bags from her. "Nothing but Mickey D's best for you, man."

"Thanks," he said, tucking most of the food away into his battered duffel bag, and then ripping open the bag of hashbrowns.

"Knock yourself out," said Marta, and blew a gust of steam off her coffee, taking a scorching sip as she turned to study the nearby panhandler. His face and hands were very red and cracked in the cold. She dropped the handful of change left over from the twenty into his empty cup and, looking down, saw that there was a cat curled up at his feet, next to a little cardboard sign that read: NOT A BAD PERSON, JUST HUNGRY.

Danny Boy was nearly done with the hashbrowns, his whole face contorting, stretching, a look of intense concentration on his weathered face as he chewed. She wondered if his teeth hurt him, or if he was used to it, now, and no longer noticed. He took the second coffee cup from her when she offered it, screwing up his face as he took a gulp. "Nobody's seen your guy for a while," he remarked. "It's a competitive spot, working this strip, and a lot of people coming and going. But he—" he tipped his cup in a vague gesture toward the hunched-up form of the panhandler "—saw him just this last Monday, hanging around at the public library."

Another week gone, then. Marta frowned. "The library? Really?"

"A lot of people go when it's cold, 'cause they have comfy chairs and they keep the heat on, and you can stay all day."

"And it was him for sure? It was Thomas Zimmerman?"

"Sure. Says he's been living in a house on South Park."

"Whose house?"

"Nobody's," said Danny Boy. "It's just an old house, all boarded up—someplace to get out of the cold. That's what everybody needs, you know. Just four walls and a roof, or at least a tent to get under, when the winter gets bad in the city."

"Could you take me there?"

For a moment, she saw the red threads of veins that laced the edges of his eyes as they widened, then narrowed, gummed and crusted with stuff unnameable. "Well—you don't want to go now, do you?"

Marta looked away down the street and, scanning the bustling passersby, caught sight of the boy she had seen before, moving less stiffly now but still caught up in a daze as he came down the street. Watching, she saw him approach the panhandler on the curb—they didn't speak, but the panhandler gave the boy a fractional nod. Slowly, the boy crouched down. He kept himself angled away from the panhandler, as seemingly indifferent to him as he had been to the customers lined up in the McDonald's, but he reached out and offered his hand to the cat. The animal stretched, looked at him through slitted eyes, then delicately sniffed at his fingers. Bending lower, the boy began to pet its matted fur, scratching it behind the ears and letting it rub its head against his bony wrist. Marta felt a soreness in her ribs again, but a different sadness now—the same hollow feeling that had gripped her at the House of Blues, when she had seen the old couple dance.

She took a sip of coffee. "Sure," she told Danny Boy. "Why not? I got nowhere to be in a hurry—do you?"

The house was very old. From the sidewalk, Marta studied it, with its peeling white paint walls and boarded-up windows, the front porch half collapsed and nearly covered by the snow that had drifted up over it. On one side of the property was a bed-and-breakfast, with a sign pinned to the door saying it was closed for the winter, and on the other was the gated Holy Cross Cemetery, where the tops of the headstones protruded from the snow and the white-walled chapel on its little hill all but blended into the polar landscape. Beside her, Danny Boy was shifting from foot to foot, skittish—he had followed the line of her sight, was looking at the graves.

"Somebody was telling me I gotta dig up my dead," she remarked. "He said I should take 'em to Israel or something."

He blew out his cheeks. "Jesus, I wouldn't know where to start."

"Me neither," she said. Her mother wasn't in Holy Cross, but buried up in Fairview Lawn Cemetery, with soldiers and pensioners and Protestants, and—somewhere—the mass grave they'd made for those who had died in the Halifax Explosion. Strata built up in layers to make a perfect cross-section of the city. In her mind's eye, Marta saw her mother's coffin down under the earth and, in it, nothing except the tumour that had killed her—a shrivelled flesh thing, a little larger than a peach pit, that remained after everything else had gone. She could dig it up and hold it in the palm of her hand. She could take it to Israel.

She shivered, sniffed violently, then spat a gob of yellow mucous into the snow. "How," she asked Danny Boy, "does he get into the house if it's all boarded up?"

"I don't know. Guy didn't say."

Snow had drifted up over the front porch and there were no foot-prints, no sign that anybody had been coming or going. Marta went in through the cemetery gates and skirted the side of the building where withered brown vines clung to wind-battered siding. Danny Boy trailed after her, stealing anxious glances over his shoulder, back toward the road.

There were no footprints by the back door, either, and the snow had piled up high there too, drifting over the derelict back deck. A stone statue of an angel sat by the door, only its haloed head and the tips of its wings protruding. After a brief hesitation, Marta stepped off the path, wading through the snow up to the back deck. Cold soaked her jeans, overflowing the tops of her boots, and she shivered. When she clambered onto the deck, the boards creaked under her weight. Here, she paused again, her eye caught by a shiny yellow sticker pasted in the window. It was emblazoned with the crest of the city of Halifax, and the tightly printed text below warned that the premises were monitored with burglary alarms and that all the possessions in the house had been marked to deter theft.

The wood creaked again, as Danny Boy tottered beside her—he was out of breath and she put out her hand quickly, catching his shoulder to steady him. "Is that legit?" she asked, tipping her head toward the sticker. "There's gonna be alarms?"

"Naw, they put those things everywhere. It's just civil bylaw bullshit."

"Maybe you can do something about that when you get elected," said Marta.

"One thing at a time."

Breath catching, she reached out and tried the door handle—it turned easily, but, when she pulled, the door would only open a few inches before it got stuck. She yanked hard, rattling the hinges, but it wouldn't budge. Looking down, she saw that a crust of ice and packed-down snow had formed, wedging the door shut—she worked at it with the toe of her boot, then crouched down and began to scrape the ice away with her bare fingers. Danny Boy stood over her, watching silently. The sound was loud in the quiet that hung over the cemetery and she was suddenly aware that anybody coming up the path to the graveyard would see them. Thomas Zimmerman might not be in there at all, and she didn't know how she could possibly explain to anybody, let alone the police, why they were trespassing. In her head, she began to string together what she would tell the police, constructing a story. They had just been passing and had heard somebody calling from inside the house, somebody who might have been in trouble, so they had tried to get inside to help.

Even in her head, it sounded very thin.

Her fingers were cold, trembling, but she worked her nails in and dug hard until the last chunk of ice broke away. She tried the door again and this time it swung open with a screech of rusting hinges. Beyond, a darkened kitchen, empty. In the split second that she registered this, and quite suddenly, an ear-splitting whir cut the air.

Marta flinched, stumbling backward into Danny Boy, and the door swung shut again with a crack. "Jesus shit! You said there wasn't an alarm."

His gnarled hands caught her, gripping her arms. His breathing was even more ragged than before, but he held her still. "There's not," he said. "Listen."

Marta did, and heard, beneath the high-pitched whirring, a deeper rumble of an engine, and then the unmistakeable beep-beep of a machine backing up—it was only a plow, she realized, churning its slow path down South Park Street. She saw its lights pass by, reflecting bright off the snow in the cemetery, and then the noise was receding again. She was annoyed with herself for getting spooked and even more irritated by the fact that, for a second when she'd thought it was an alarm, she'd been relieved. It would have given her a reason to run, to not go in—a reason to look but not to find.

"Well, all right," she said and wrenched the door open again. She took a deep breath, then stepped into the house, Danny Boy behind her. It was very cold, colder than it had been out on the sunlit porch, and the air had a strange edge to it, sour and mildewed. The house had been stripped down to its bones—there was no furniture in the little kitchen and all the cabinet doors hung open, empty, a thick layer of dust and accumulated grime coating every surface.

"Hello?" said Marta, loudly, and the quiet of the house sucked at the edges of her voice, flattening it out. She looked over her shoulder at Danny Boy, who only shrugged. Clearing her throat, she tried again, raising her voice a little. "Hello? Thomas?"

Nothing. Only the creak of footsteps as, slowly, Danny Boy eased himself back toward the door. "I guess I'd better . . ." he began, only to trail off into silence when Marta turned to look at him.

"Where are you going?"

"Thought I could wait outside. It's bad breathing in here."

"Wait," said Marta, too quickly. She wasn't sure that she wanted to be alone in the empty tomb of a house. Increasingly, she thought that she was seeing things: specks that moved in the corners of her vision, shapes that darted by the windows. She remembered suddenly being very young, with Dina, and how they'd both entertained the fear that something was running around the outside of their apartment, looking in all the windows, that whenever they turned their heads it was always just too quick, around and around, always staying ahead. She'd never asked Dina how exactly she imagined the creature, but in her mind's eye it had always been very dark, like a Taiwanese shadow puppet cut intricately out of paper with firelight shining through its yellow eyes, its yellow jaws. It was here now, she thought, that phantom of her long-gone childhood—or something was.

She took a deep breath, drawing the dust of the place into her aching lungs, then took one step and then another across the stained tiles, picking her way between the discarded cans and odd bits of rubbish, the desiccated remains of flies and hornets crackling under her boots. Through the kitchen and into what she supposed had been a living room—there were traces of wallpaper still clinging to the walls, a faded blue with a darker stripe running through it, and a sagging couch was still pushed up against the far wall. There was another piece of furniture there too, but one that Marta guessed had not been there before the house was abandoned—it was a mattress, stained and bare, shoved up under the window and, spread over it, an incongruously new Hudson Bay blanket.

Marta crossed the room to crouch beside the mattress. Squinting in the dim light, she could see that the floor here was marginally cleaner than the rest of the room and the floorboards were streaked by a ribbed pattern of dust, as if somebody had recently tried to sweep. There was an empty Coke can on the windowsill and the stub of a candle had been wedged into it; it had been lit and re-lit, and wax had made trails down the side of the can, pooling on the swollen wood of the sill.

Danny Boy was hanging back in the doorway, looking as if he wasn't sure whether he was staying or going, his leathered face twisting into an anxious frown. "That his stuff?"

"Yeah," said Marta. "I think so."

She pressed her hand against the mattress, flat, pushing down. It was damp, and a musty smell rose to meet her. He had been here, he *had*, and the knowledge made her almost sick with the suspense of it all. She felt the springs creak and, beneath that, the rustle of something, a soft crackling. On a sudden impulse, she slid her hand underneath the mattress, feeling around until her fingers brushed paper. Drawing it out, she saw that it was a folded page of newspaper—even without opening it, even without reading the penned words that were leaking through the thin paper in blotches, she recognized it; it was the note that she had tucked into the box, before her father had carried it into the hospital.

Still, she unfolded it and read it again. *HELP. . . BOTH crazytown people . . . ONLY thing that happiness is. stay free . . .*

"So," Danny Boy was saying now, "all good, then? Guess he'll probably be back pretty soon, if you just wait for him . . ."

Marta stood up, feeling the crack of sore vertebrae in her spine as she stretched. "No," she said, and the disappointment of it was so sharp it was a knife between her ribs, but she knew, she knew. "I don't think he's been here for a couple nights, not since the last freeze, anyway. That ice was built up in front of the door and the snow looked pretty clean, didn't it? So he hasn't been back."

"Sorry," he said and sucked his lips into his mouth, antsy. "Sorry. I'm sure—I'm sure he'll be back sooner or later . . ."

"Definitely," said Marta, with a confidence she didn't quite feel. There was something abandoned about the little squat, no breath of life. It was sacred with his presence, permeated by it, but there was nothing alive here. Fighting back the twinge of nausea that churned in her gut, she tried to grin at him. "Guess I'll just have to check back sometime, huh?"

Together, they let themselves out onto the porch and picked their way down onto the cemetery path again. Marta, seeing how shaky Danny Boy was looking, gave him her hand to help him down—she was conscious, suddenly, of his age. He was as old as her father at least, and he wore those years much more heavily on his shrunken frame. "Thanks," she told him, brushing the snow off her knees as they stood, together, safely back on the sidewalk again. "I really appreciate you showing me around, coming with me and all. I owe you one."

"It's all right," he said and cuffed her, a little awkward, on the elbow. "I'll be seeing you, I guess."

"Stay safe out there, man. Stay free."

Marta watched him make his way up the street toward Spring Garden again, a bent figure moving quickly along and looking—every so often—over his shoulder at her. Then she turned and started down the street. She trailed her fingers on the wrought-iron fence of the cemetery and felt the metal wet and icy against her skin.

CHAPTER SIXTEEN

In the day, the House of Blues lost all its magic. All the neon signs were switched off and the late afternoon sunlight wormed its way into everything, made it washed-out and ugly—the paint on the old façade was streaky, peeling away, and the desiccated remains of dead flies cluttered the windowsills. Standing outside, Marta counted them in her head and got to seven—seven whole insects, fragments of others—before she had the nerve to go inside. There was a song she remembered hearing, those first few nights on the job, but she couldn't remember who had played it. Only that it had been about dead flies and how she'd stood at the sink out back, up to her elbows in suds and dirty dishes, and listened to the snatches of music that escaped through the swinging doors. *One, two, two dead flies, two dead flies don't tell no lies—* And that night she'd dropped a pint glass and it had smashed into a dozen shards on the floor, while she cried from the sheer embarrassment of it, cried because her mother was gone, and Janice had given her a hug and told her it was okay, dear, it happened to everybody and this, too, would pass.

When Marta went in, the sunlight came with her. Bad inside, too. The tables were all empty, no customers hanging around this early, but Janice was behind the bar and a cluster of men had gathered around the stage in the corner, untangling a pair of amplifiers from a nest of criss-crossed wires. Marta's stomach twisted when she saw that one of them was John Zimmerman. For a second, she hesitated in the doorway—she wanted to turn around and go—but she dug her nails hard into her palms and waited for the feeling to pass. Her body remembered things, even after they'd gone out through the hole in the back of her head. Her body told her things, sometimes, but— *don't tell no lies*—she wouldn't listen. She forced herself to turn away from him, leaning up against the bar.

"Hi, Janice," she said. "Do you remember me?"

The woman had the cash register open and was counting bills, but she looked up quickly. "Sure, of course," she said, but Marta saw the glazed edge to her smile and knew that she didn't, really.

"I washed dishes here a couple years back, before the pandemic. You might not remember—my hair was different, back then. I bleached it more."

"Of course I remember you, honey—always nice to see one of our girls back. How've you been doing?"

Marta grinned. "Great. Really, really great."

"Where are you working now?"

"Nowhere, right now," said Marta. "That's actually why I came by. I was hoping you guys could be a reference for me, this new thing I was thinking of doing. Charity thing. They need a couple numbers to call, so I was thinking you could tell them I was a responsible worker, team player, helped out doing the odd jobs and stuff, and . . ."

She trailed off, gripping the edge of the bar tightly, a knot in the pit of her stomach as she saw the other woman's expression shift. Janice was still smiling, but it was an apologetic smile now. "That's really great, honey," she said. "It's just that it's been a couple years, hasn't it? We've gone through a lot of girls. Don't you think it would be better getting more recent references?"

"Right," said Marta, and bit the inside of her cheek. She was thinking about the flies on the windowsill again, and their shrivelled wings turning brittle under the sun. *Three, three, three dead flies, three dead flies now don't go crying*— "You're right, yeah. It's just that it meant a lot to me, you know? Those were some good nights and we all had a good time. I always felt lucky to be here, those nights."

There was a jingle as Janice shut the drawer of the cash register. "All right," she said. "Why don't I give you my number, then? They call me, I'll tell them you're a solid worker."

Marta pried her fingers from the stained wood of the bar. "Thanks, Janice—seriously. I really appreciate it."

She waited while the woman jotted down a phone number on a crumpled scrap of a receipt, then slipped it to her across the bar. "Can I get you a drink while you're here, honey? On the house, if you want it."

"Naw, I'm okay. I gotta get to the bank before they close, anyway."

She stepped back from the bar, but she couldn't go yet—John Zimmerman had seen her. He was staring at her from across the tangle of wires, and leaving would mean running away. Instead, she forced herself to stand there for a moment in the sun-drenched expanse of floor, staring back at him, cold and level. He had taken his jacket off while he worked and his hat was pushed as far back as it could go on his head, exposing an expanse of mummified scalp, thin and stretched over his skull. When she did turn to leave, he came after her, on her heels as the doors swung shut behind them.

"What were you talking to her about?"

"I don't think it matters to you," said Marta. She didn't want to talk to him, but didn't want him following her up the street, either. She stopped on the sidewalk and waited for him there. Her body was talking again, but only in the slightest twitches around her wrists, the palms of her hands, and the taste of steel between her teeth. Easier to ignore, now.

"I never did anything," he said. The light was doing him bad, too—she could see the speckled skin on the back of his hands, tobacco stains on his teeth. "I'll tell them that if you start making shit up. I never did anything and you know it."

"I know," she said. "Not even for your own cousin, eh? Not even to help him."

For a moment, he stared at her, and she thought she could see him grappling with it, trying to fit it into the space in his head, then throwing it away—the creases in his face smoothed out, with the forgetting of it. "Whatever your problem is, I never had anything to do with it. I was just trying to help you out, just be friendly, and you lost it. I don't want any of that. Coming around my work like this, around my people, talking—it's fucked up."

Suddenly, she was bored with him, of him—she saw him in the daylight and there was nothing of Thomas Zimmerman in his face, no connection between them except the accident of their genetics, the footnote he'd been in the night she'd wanted to die. "Fine. I probably won't be seeing you again. Feel free to forget all about it, if you want. Or don't, you know."

She turned away, out onto the sidewalk, but she'd only gone a few steps before he called after her. "I'm trying to be fucking reasonable!"

"I get it. It didn't have shit to do with you—you just happened to be there, and I wanted to die. It wasn't personal. It was all in my head and you weren't there. I get it."

"You're crazy," he said. "You're fucking crazy."

"It's been looking that way for a while," said Marta. "Good luck with the gig, John."

She got to the bank fifteen minutes before it closed and stood just inside the doors, digging through her pockets—she found her card, slightly bent and scratched-up in the back pocket of her jeans, then began going through her coat for the money Dina had given her. Chest pocket, front, sides—she checked them all once, twice, while the bank teller eyed her from his perch behind the counter. She remembered rolling the bills up tightly, tucking them deep into the pocket—she probed every corner, feeling for holes, but there was nothing. Just lint fluff and her cigarette lighter, a few crumpled rolling papers.

"I'm sorry," said the teller, "but we're starting our closing procedures in five minutes. If you have a transaction you'd like to make, you need to make it now."

"Right, sorry. Just a second. I wanted to make a deposit, send some money, but I don't. . . "

Blushing, she tried all the same pockets again, then her jeans, too, but there was nothing, no money. She'd had it leaving the Zimmerman house that morning, because she could remember stepping out onto the stoop and putting her hands in her pockets, and how her bare fingers, poking out from the ends of her half-gloves, had touched the cold silk of the three twenties, the single five.

"Ma'am—"

"Sorry, I just need a minute to look. I thought I had the money with me, in cash, but—"

But she'd had it leaving the Zimmermans', *had* to have had it at the McDonald's where she'd bought Danny Boy his food. She could remember that as well. And now it was gone.

"Ma'am, I'm really sorry, but you're going to have to come back tomorrow. We open at nine and there will be someone else here to help you with your transaction."

"All right," said Marta. "Right. Thanks. I'll do that."

A weight was settling at the very back of her head, drawing her down through the soles of her boots as she went around behind the IWK hospital. Smoke was billowing from the tall candy-stripe smokestack on the hospital rooftop and she lowered her head to keep it from tangling in her hair, crossing the road to the far sidewalk.

Through the chain-linked fence, she could see the hospital parking lot, ringed with scrubby patches of pine trees and overgrown, desiccated bushes. The snow was melting away, revealing soggy patches of dirt and yellowing grass, but there was still enough of a covering left that she could see a marked trail through it, running from the edge of the gravel and into the bushes. Churned mud coming through the snow like the same set of shoes had trekked back and forth many times. Marta stood for a moment longer, gripping the fence and staring through, then made her way in through the gates. It was quiet in there, a scattering of parked cars but no movement, no sound but the drip of melting ice running off the pine branches. Following the muddied track to the bushes, she saw that there was a gap there, a natural hollow made by the snow-bent boughs.

Crouching to crawl, crabwise, into the opening, the brittle ends of branches tickled her face and snagged in her hair. When she emerged, it was into a small cavity between the bushes and the bramble-tangled fence. There were a few empty wrappers poking out of the snow, flattened tin cans, and—scattered around in the mud—some assorted garbage; an old computer keyboard with some of the keys peeled away, a boxy television trailing its intestines, the shattered fragments of a lightbulb. There were footprints too, some old and fading, some fresh. And, sitting tucked in among the overarching screen of branches was Danny Boy, cross-legged on a stretch of cardboard just like he'd been when she'd first seen him outside Rachel Zimmerman's house.

"Hey," said Marta, and he didn't say anything, only looked at her mutely with his wide and jaundiced eyes. "Why did you take it? Why didn't you ask me?"

"It's very hard," he said.

"Why didn't you ask me for the money?"

"You can't live right, if you don't have somewhere to live. The winter won't stop. If I could get somewhere to live, four walls and a roof, if I could get a tent . . ."

All at once, Marta was rigid with fury. That he'd stolen from her was a betrayal of who he was and, much worse, it was a betrayal of who she was. And—she could hardly bring herself to think it, her mind turned from it—if Thomas Zimmerman was dead on a slab in the morgue, then that would be a betrayal as well. There were things that could not be endured. There were things that the heart could not understand. "I would have given it to you, you stupid fuck," she said and she was too angry to stay there, crouched in the snow with him. She stood up all at once, the branches tearing at her, brambles running tracks into her bare cheeks, her clothes. "If you'd ever asked me, I would have given you the money."

It was maddening to her that he hadn't seen that. Why couldn't he have just looked at her?

He talked on, as if he hadn't heard her at all. ". . .and if I had money, if I could just get some money, and it's very hard, it's hard to—"

He broke off when Marta kicked out at him wildly, the tip of her boot connecting with his ribs. He fell awkwardly, scrambling back through the thicket that snapped and cracked around him, and her second kick missed him. "You don't get it," she said. "It's not me, man, it's not! This doesn't happen to me."

Danny Boy was doing it again—he was rocking himself back and forth, gripped by some internal and awful rhythm. His yellowed eyes were very wet and the gaping hole of his mouth spasmed, lips sucking in and out with each ragged breath.

Looking down at him, Marta felt sick, and sorry, and very cold. Doesn't happen, she thought. *Christ, Thomas, where did you go, man? Where did you go?* If she wasn't the one who got stolen from, who else could she be? She stood back, raking her fingers through her hair and feeling some of the weight dislodge from her cranium, unmooring her from the earth. "Keep the money," she told him. "Buy a tent."

He didn't look at her and, after a moment, she turned and left him there, rocking himself in the muddied snow of the parking lot. She went slowly up through the city, heading back toward Inglis Lodge again. Everything looked pale and washed out in the afternoon light, and the streets were more or less deserted. Dark figures darted in the periphery of her eyes, a car or two rolling by in the road, but nobody seemed to look at her. Dizziness gripped her cresting the hill, and she drifted sideways across the sidewalk, reeling. She crouched down, pretending to be retying her bootlace, and stayed hunkered down until her head stopped spinning—it was a trick she'd learned years ago, for when she got cross-faded smoking and thought she might faint but didn't want anyone to see. She kept going this way, stopping and starting, stumbling, crouching, and made slow progress back through the city streets.

Shaw had picked the blisters off his wrist. The skin underneath was the pearly pink of coral, raw and clean; he couldn't seem to leave it alone, kneading the flesh between his fingertips, with the same distracted air with which he'd once rubbed his moustache. He kneaded and kneaded, and his eyes darted left-right-left-right, following Marta as she paced from one end of the apartment to the other. Kitchenette to daybed, daybed to kitchenette—the fury was in her, still, and it sent her ricocheting across the floor.

"Fucker," she said. "The fucker."

The words felt raw in the back of her throat—she'd cussed herself sick already, telling him what had happened.

On the daybed, Shaw pinched his wrist. He was still wearing his work clothes, his uniform shirt emblazoned on the chest with the logo of the supermarket, the sleeves rolled up to his elbows. "It sounds to me," he began, hesitant, "like maybe he needs the money pretty bad."

Marta reached the far wall again and turned back. It was a bad room to pace in; she kept having to pick her way around the heaps of clutter in her path, all the detritus they'd let build up over the past week. She took a step and felt, through a layer of dirty laundry, something crunched under her foot—an empty cider can, crumpling up. "I know he does," she said and dug the can out with her toe, kicking it across the carpet.

"I mean, if it's upsetting you so much, you could always call the police."

She kicked the can again, sending it rolling past Shaw's feet and away under the daybed. "Don't be stupid. What kind of a person would I have to be to do something like that? What kind of a piece of shit do you think I am?"

"I don't think you're any kind of—"

"Forget it, all right? Forget him. It doesn't matter."

"I just meant—"

"I said, it doesn't matter."

He shuffled over, making room on the cushions and looking up at her appealingly; reluctant, Marta sat down beside him. There was another can of cider on the coffee table. It had been there long enough to leave a ring of residue on the wood when she picked it up, wanting something to fidget with, but there were still a few ounces of liquid sloshing around inside. Gingerly, she took a sip, wetting her throat—it was flat and clear and tasted, now, of something more like apple-flavored lip balm than cider. She noticed that Shaw was watching her; she toasted him with the can.

"Leftovers," she said, giving him a dry little grin. "Fucking score, right?"

A little crease had appeared in his forehead, the lines of his face drawing together in a look of pained concern. "When was the last time you ate?"

"I don't know—why?"

"We could have supper. You might feel a bit better if you had something."

"I am having something," she said and drained the last gulp of cider from the can. She didn't like the way he was talking to her, soft

207

and slow and measured, like she was a skittish animal who needed to be soothed for its own sake. It was the voice on the other end of the crisis hotline, the all-too-familiar voice of a perfect stranger.

With a crackle of aluminum, she squashed the empty can between her palms and then lobbed it, underarm, at the recycling bin. It bounced off the rim and fell, one last trickle of cider soaking into the carpet. They both watched it in silence, but neither of them moved to pick it up. Marta rested her chin in her hands. "Dee will never believe the money got stolen," she remarked. "She'll think I spent it on weed, you know. I was trying to show her I was growing up, I was being responsible, and then . . ."

"Oh."

"And I can't tell her. I can't ask her for more."

"Oh," said Shaw, and picked at his wrist again. This time, he dug his nails in hard enough that he peeled the skin away in a single translucent flake. Holding this between finger and thumb, fidgeting with it, he went on, the words spilling out in a sudden rush, "I could give you the money."

Marta didn't raise her head. "What?"

"I mean, I could write you a cheque for it. So you'd be able to apply for the program. I get paid this Thursday, so I'd be good for it, and that way you could apply, and, eh, you could. . ."

He trailed off by degrees, seeming to run out of steam. Marta hadn't raised her head. Out of the corner of her eye, she watched him fidget, but she couldn't bring herself to look at him straight on. "It's all right," she said, after a moment. "You don't have to do that."

"I wouldn't mind at all. Honestly, I wouldn't."

"No," said Marta. "You'd only be wasting your money. It's not worth it and I don't know if I want to apply at all, anyway."

"What? Why not?"

She shrugged. How could she explain the fury that had set in, ever since Danny Boy had taken the money from her? How could she explain what it had attacked in her? That purest shred of her own identity, the certainty of where she stood.

"Listen," said Shaw. "I know you're shook up, but you shouldn't forget why you wanted to do it in the first place. You need to do something, you need to have some kind of work, not just run around playing detective games. You need to have something in the real world, something to hold onto, or you're going to keep sending smoke signals. You'll keep on going down."

"Like you, you mean."

But he ignored the jab and only knocked his knee against hers, shifting closer on the daybed. She could hear the breath quickening in his chest as he reached a point of crescendo in whatever piece it was that he was composing for her benefit. "Listen," he said again. "That was the happiest I've ever seen you, when you decided to apply for this job. You were sure this morning—why can't you just be sure now?"

"What the fuck do you know about what makes me happy? What gives you the right to tell me what to do?"

"I don't, but—"

"But what? What?"

"I love you," said Shaw.

Marta stared at him. They were, she thought, speaking two entirely different languages—she could barely follow the drift of his words. *I love you.* What difference did it make? What did he think it meant to her? "What," she said, "do you want me to say?"

"I don't– Jesus Christ, I love you, Marta."

She was blind with anger at him for what he was doing, for thinking that he could change her mind. Did he really think that he was the first—the only—person who'd ever loved her? Her mother, her father, Dina, Nicky—their love hadn't been enough to tie her to the earth, hadn't been enough to keep her in the window of tolerance, of sanity, so why would his be any different?

"Marta—"

Dimly, she felt something buzz in her jacket—her phone ringing. He was waiting for her to say something, but she wouldn't. The buzzing went on, insistent, and she dug the phone out of her jacket; anything was better than looking at his face, so painfully expectant. The number that flashed across the screen was an unfamiliar one—a local area code for Halifax, but no name attached to it.

Shaw cleared his throat wetly. "I didn't say it to upset you or anything."

"Someone's calling," she told him.

He opened his mouth but she didn't give him time to say anything, twisting away from him and, with a flick of her thumb across the "answer" icon, putting the phone to her ear. "Hello?"

For a moment, there was only a distortion of noise on the other end, a faint buzzing of distant activity. Then, "Are you still looking for Thomas?"

The voice was so low and hoarse that it barely differentiated itself from the static.

"What?"

"Thomas. Thomas Zimmerman."

Marta stood up quickly. "Sorry, who is this?"

"I got the number off a paper bag," said the voice, and she heard a crackle of noise that might have been a laugh. Out of the corner of her eye, she saw Shaw raise his head, looking up at her questioningly—she ignored him, wedging a finger into her other ear to block out the hum of the radiator. She was listening hard. The voice went on, "You wanted a tip? You're still looking for him?"

"Have you seen him?"

"He's staying at the shelter on Gottingen Street. Not the Sally Ann, the one at the corner of Cunard. He's there now."

"Who—" she began, but there was only a rustle and click, then the drone of a dial tone starting.

"Who was that?" asked Shaw.

Marta looked down at her phone. Her thumb moved slowly, as if drawn by a magnetic force, entirely separate from her—first to hang up the call, cutting the dial tone off sharply, then pulling up a map. She punched in "Gottingen Street" and "shelter," and watched as a little red marker popped up, far to the north end of the city.

"Marta? Who was it?"

"I don't know," she said. Twenty-six minutes away, said the words that popped up beneath the shelter's icon. *He's there.* She could be there in half an hour—she could be seeing him in half an hour. She began to button up her jacket.

He sounded panicked now. "Where are you going?"

"Gottingen Street," said Marta, and gave him a flat little grin, shoving her phone back into her pocket. The boots were by the door and she wedged her feet into them, yanking them up. "More detective games."

"Are you serious? It's almost midnight—you can't go up there now!"

She ignored him, stooping to knot the laces.

"Please don't," Shaw went on, voice rising in consternation. He was standing now as well. "Please just stay and talk a while."

"Stay easy," she said and put her hand on the doorknob. "I'll be back in a while."

She felt a little guilty, but that faded quickly as she went out into the road. Behind her, Inglis Lodge had ceased to exist, and so had Shaw. Cutting up toward Spring Garden Road, she passed the corner where the woman with mould in her ceiling sat. The woman raised her cup and Marta walked past her quickly, not pausing. She felt guilty about that, too, and the feeling was just as guilty. Piece by piece, the world bled away behind her, and the fog closed in ahead.

CHAPTER SEVENTEEN

"It's late," said the man who sat at the desk in the entrance of the homeless shelter on Gottingen Street and Cunard. Marta looked at him and he looked right through her, like he was counting the stains on the wall behind her left clavicle. "There's no beds left in the women's dorm."

"That's all right," said Marta. "I don't mind going in with men. Uh, the unisex. Whatever."

He shrugged, shoving the clipboard across the table toward her. "Just sign yourself in, then."

The pen was attached to the desk by a loop of chain and she fidgeted with it for a moment, scanning the list of names that ran down the page above. The signatures ranged from illegible scrawl to neatly looping letters, but none of them were familiar—none of them were Thomas Zimmerman's. Marta lifted the corner of the page, trying to see the previous set of entries, but the man at the desk had resumed his x-ray staring. Quickly, she scribbled "Marta Klausner" on the first empty line and dropped the pen as if it had scalded her. "Where do I go?"

He tipped his head toward the door on the left. "Down the hall. One blanket, one mattress. No smoking, no drinking, no illicit substances or sexual activity permitted in the dorms."

"Great," said Marta, her grin fading in the face of his bleary-eyed indifference. "Guess I'll bear that in mind." And then, when he only bowed his head over the clipboard again, "You have yourself a real good night, man."

There were twenty-four beds in the men's dormitory, arranged in twelve sets of bunks, and only one of these was unoccupied— the lower bunk in the farthest corner. Marta went down the aisle slowly, looking left and right as she passed each bed; the floor was made of the same springy stuff as the inside of a school gymnasium and the soles of her boots squeaked softly with each step. None of the beds' occupants seemed to hear. Most of them were lying very still, cocooned in mismatched blankets. Only little pieces of each one protruded: the sliver of a cheek, a clenched jaw, a tightly curled fist. Some had draped their coats over their headboards, some had left their bags and backpacks in a jumble beside their beds. The overhead lights were switched off, the dorm illuminated by faintly glowing emergency strips along the floor, and Marta had to squint hard at each chrysalis, looking in vain for Thomas Zimmerman's dark hair and fine features.

When she got to the empty bed, she stood looking at it with a similar kind of scrutiny. This, too, reminded her of the gymnasium at their high school. The mattress was made from the same stiff, shiny canvas as the old tumbling mats they'd done acrobatics on. It felt oddly sticky when she touched it and, when she pressed down, it let out a faint wheeze of air.

There was a sudden creaking from the upper bunk and a head appeared above her—a man, his hair tousled, his chin resting on the metal safety rail. "Are you worried about the stain?" he asked, voice pitched to a low murmur. "Do you want to switch with me?"

Marta blinked. "The . . ?"

"Piss stain," said the man, and poked his hand through the railing bars, pointing downward. "On the mattress."

Looking down, Marta saw that he was right. She hadn't noticed it before in the darkened room, but there was a dark patch at the very centre of the mattress, discoloured like a bruise, and a smell of ammonia rising from the mattress seams. She shuddered in spite of herself, then shook her head. "Naw, it's okay. I'll, uh—it's okay. It's all good."

"You sure?"

"Yeah."

"I don't mind switching."

"No, thanks," said Marta, who wanted to switch very badly but couldn't think of a single reason why he should sleep in a puddle of urine and she shouldn't. The single permitted blanket was folded neatly at the end of the bed and she shook it out, spreading it over the stain. When she sat, the mattress let out another asthmatic groan and the smell enveloped her—she swung her legs up and lay there for a moment, awkward and stiff in her clothes. She didn't want to take her boots off, but held them slightly raised off the bed, conscious of the mud crusted on the soles. When she turned her head on the pillow, the pillowcase felt scratchy on her cheek—the texture reminded her of the bandages on Shaw's arms and she shuddered again.

The heat in the dormitory was cranked up high and the air felt suffocatingly thick. The man had drawn his head back. She looked up at the metal slats of the bunk above and saw his weight making a bulge in his—unstained—mattress. After a moment, she reached up and tapped on the slats. "Hey," she said softly. "D'you know if there's any other rooms here? Besides the women's dorm. Is there anywhere else people go to sleep?"

For a moment, she thought he hadn't heard, and then, "Why?"

"Just wondering."

"We can switch, if you want to. The smell's not so bad up here."

"Naw, I'm all right. I'm just, uh—I thought a friend of mine might be here tonight. I don't see him."

Above her, the mattress shifted, the railings rattled in their sockets—him rolling his bulk to the edge again, peering down at her. "Yeah? Who's your friend?"

"Thomas. His name's Thomas. I heard he'd been staying here a couple nights."

"I think—" the man began, then stopped as someone in the next bunk along sat up suddenly; a hoarse voice, thick, dredged from the deepest part of the lungs, whispered—"Shut the fuck up. I'm trying to sleep."

Quiet for a while after that. Marta stared blindly up at the shadowy mass bearing down on the mattress, stared at it long enough she lost sense of it and it all swam into static distortion. I think, he'd said, he'd started to say, and something in his voice had made her heart stutter. Hopeful. She sat up again very gingerly, leaning out of the bed, peering up at his bunk. Neck craned, she whispered. "What were you going to say?"

A pause. Then, "Nothing."

"Do you know a guy named Thomas?"

His hand appeared, gripping the railings. Then his face again, chin resting on the rail as he looked down at her. Shadows were dark in the pits of his eyes, the hollows of his cheeks, a chiaroscuro effect that threw his features into sharp relief. "Might," he said, matching her whisper. "There was a guy—a Thomas—here a couple days this last week. Talked some."

She could hardly believe it. She swung her boots down onto the floor, standing. "Yeah? What did he look like?"

"Dark hair. Tall. Maybe in his thirties, mid-thirties, said his name was something kind of Jewish, you know . . ."

"Zimmerman?"

"Yeah. Eh, maybe—yeah."

She grinned. She bit the inside of her cheek to stop herself from laughing from pure exhilaration. There was a feeling in her flesh, a buzzing just under the skin. A breath, then, struggling to get her jumbled thoughts in order again. "When was the last time you saw him? Did he say where he was going?"

In her excitement, she'd forgotten to be quiet. Again, in the dark, an aggrieved voice rising, "I said, shut the fuck up!"

"It's four in the goddamn morning," said somebody else, piping up from a bed further down the row.

The man's face dipped, pulled away, and then he was sitting up and swinging his legs over the edge of the bed. She had a brief look at his feet, encased in grubby running shoes, grappling blindly for the top rung of the ladder, and the denim of his jeans, worn threadbare at the knees and cuffs, and then he was lowering himself down. He hadn't undressed before bed, either, then it struck her as odd and she wondered briefly if he'd felt as uncomfortable lying down as she had or if there was some other reason.

"Come on," he said softly, reaching up to rake distractedly at his hair, which was nearly as long as hers, falling to his shoulders. "We can talk in the hall."

Marta nodded. She followed him back down the row of bunkbeds and through the door, back out into the dingy corridor beyond. It was cooler here, the breathing better, and the cold fluorescent strips above bathed them both in a cold light. Looking at him now, she saw that he was dressed in an odd mismatch of clothing, a battered rain slicker that stuck out in bunches from under an equally battered vest. He looked more familiar than ever to her now—the resemblance that had, before, been tugging at the back of her mind became more insistent. "We don't," she began uncertainly, "know each other, do we? I mean, I haven't met you before, yeah?"

He made an impatient gesture, twitching his head like a mosquito was at his ear, but didn't answer. Instead, he said, "Your friend, Thomas, he was here tonight. I saw him in the cafeteria, getting supper."

"His name wasn't in the registry. . ."

"No, he didn't want a bed. He said he wasn't sleeping here tonight."

She frowned. "Yeah?"

"He said he'd found someplace better. He's staying in a house uptown from here, him and some other guys."

"Did he say where?"

"I know the house," said the man.

She was starting to get impatient. "Yeah? Where is it?"

His eyes cut away from her, seeming—for the first time—vaguely uncomfortable. "We're not supposed to, you know, talk about this stuff. People get real paranoid. We're not supposed to say."

"He's my friend," said Marta. "I just want to see him."

"I could take you there, I guess."

"Is it far?"

"Not really."

She followed him out of the shelter, back past the desk and the man who watched them go with the same quiet indifference with which he'd taken Marta's name. Out into Gottingen Street, where the streetlights hung above them in the hazy night, the pre-dawn dark. No stars. "You could tell me where it is," she said. "The house. I don't want to, uh, trouble you."

He shook his head. "They won't let you in if you go on your own. I'll have to show you."

Snow was melting along the sidewalk, making the pavement slick, reflecting the lights back. They had just passed the darkened storefront of a Salvation Army when he stopped suddenly, so quickly that she almost tripped over him. He was standing at the very edge of the sidewalk, where the muddied snow dropped away sharply in an embankment, sloping down into a paved parking lot that stretched all the way to the next street over. It was dark, no lights down there. She could see that and see, too, that once they got down the hill, they would be out of sight of anyone on the road above.

"It's this way," said the man.

"The house?"

He nodded. "It's just down here. A little farther."

Marta looked at him uncertainly. He started down the slope, footsteps crunching in the muddy snow, holding his arms out on either side for balance and half-raising them, fingertips held rigid and trembling slightly with each step, like the wings of a bird.

"Did you call me?" she asked him.

He looked at her, head tipped to one side, that same twitchy discomfort. "What?"

"Were you the one who called my number? The one they've been passing around?"

"No," he said.

But he had been. She was sure, suddenly. If he hadn't, he would have asked her what she was talking about. He knew, he did, and that meant that he'd been the one to call. Marta stuck her hands deeper into her pockets. She looked up the street, then down.

"It's just down here," he said again.

She followed him. They went down the slope and she slipped, slid, the soles of Thomas Zimmerman's boots grasping for purchase in the slick iced-over grass, the mud, and he looked back at her often. In the parking lot, he stopped again, and Marta stopped too. He had turned to face her. They stood looking at each other, and she saw the lights of his eyes in the dark. "You said you'd take me to where he was," she said.

He nodded. He stepped toward her and she didn't move, only held herself very still and rigid. "You look scared," he said.

"I'm not," said Marta. "I'm not scared of anything. Were you lying about there being a house?"

The man looked at her.

She said, "You never met Thomas at all."

"I thought you knew," he said. "You wouldn't've come with me, if you didn't know."

Again, he took a step toward her. Marta watched him. She didn't feel frightened, really, just sick in the pit of her stomach—a falling feeling, a knowing feeling. An inevitability to it. He was so close to her now that she could feel his breath on her. She could see he meant to hurt her. She wondered if he could. "You can do whatever you want to do," she said. "It doesn't matter to me. Just get it over with."

Get it over with. She pressed her legs together tightly and he worked his hand between them. She wondered if he would be able to tell, when he did it, that John Zimmerman had been there already. Would her body be like new again? Would it offer all the same resistances, all the same hardness, or would it spring open like a key had turned in a lock?

"It's okay," he said. "It won't feel bad."

"Feels cold," she said.

It didn't matter, she told herself. It wouldn't matter. It might even be a good thing. He'd make a hole in her, a wound in her body to match the one in her head, and she'd have something to show them, then. Something to point to and say why. It would be a blessing, it would be a relief, and it would be the final piece, the final push, the thing that would keep her in the hypozone for good, forever and ever and—

"It's okay," he told her, and his other hand gripped her chin, squeezing, coaxing her mouth open. "You don't have to do anything."

Marta bit him.

She bit him hard. It had been years since she'd bitten anyone— not since she and Dina had been little and fighting—and she'd forgotten how hard it was; she bit him and tasted no blood, only the spongy sensation of his fungal-soft flesh pushing back at her.

Still, he jerked his hand back quickly. "Jesus!"

"Go fuck yourself," said Marta, and he slapped her, shoved her down, and there was the blood she'd been looking for. It flooded her mouth, scalding-hot, and she parted her lips and dribbled a laugh down her chin. Don't have to do anything, he'd said. She told him, "Go on. Fuck off."

For a moment, he only stared down at her, and the skin around his hollowed cheeks looked slack and loose—like she'd knocked the muscle right out of him. He looked hurt, she thought.

"Bitch," he said, his voice gone flat again. "You fucking bitch."

She began to stand and he shoved her down, driving the toe of his boot hard into the back of her calf, forcing her back to her knees. When she tried to push herself up, he half-raised his fist. "Stop it," he told her again, and a sharp blow took her across the side of the head, so that pain went crack in her left ear and she only heard the tail-end of the next words. "—it. Stop it, stop it, stop—"

But Marta ignored him. She thought about Thomas Zimmerman's bare feet caked in mud, and about the bandages on Shaw's arms, and about Dina in her funeral dress, and she tried again to stand. He shoved her harder, knocking her down onto her side so that her hip struck the asphalt with a jolt, and then she felt the whole weight of him bearing down on her. Her ribs creaked. Again, she heard him begging her to stop, stop, but she knew that she couldn't. She never could. That was just the way it was when you walked along those lines, looking for the Window of Tolerance; you couldn't stop, you couldn't do nothing, because you were always waiting for the very last second, the moment when somebody would open the window or shut it forever, and the only thing you knew was that you couldn't just—

"Stop!"

Her arms were pinned against her chest, forced down by his weight. She looked up at his face and saw that his eyes were very wide—hare eyes, mad eyes. Scared. She was lying on the asphalt and he was over her, and his hands were fumbling at her sternum again and for a moment she thought that he was still trying to take off her jacket. Then his fingers touched her throat.

"Stop it," he told her, the words sounding nearly mechanical now, a monotone chant. He was pressing down hard on her neck, one thumb over the notch of her Adam's apple. There was a bead of saliva hanging from his lower lip, translucent and trembling slightly with each ragged breath he drew. "Please, stop, please just . . ."

She tried to breathe and couldn't. Her ribs bowed inward, her lungs compressed, and he crowded in, filling up every inch of space she left behind. He seemed to fill up everything now—his face was the entire world, nothing left at the edges, and she watched as the droplet of spit stretched thinner and thinner, longer and longer. She couldn't breathe.

"Stop," he pleaded, and it didn't even sound like a word anymore. *Stopstopstopstop.* The sibilant hiss of each S ran together with the next, becoming the hum of the radiator in the spare room of her family's apartment, the sound that Shaw had made when the knife touched his skin, the sound of the air whistling between Thomas Zimmerman's front teeth. Stop. But she couldn't think about that anymore.

She couldn't think about anything.

One moment, his face was all she could see and the next, it was nothing; it fractured, the proportions growing stranger and more alien, and then a breath of wind blew it apart completely. Behind it, she saw the dark. It spasmed, contracted, capillaries breaking behind her eyelids, and she dimly realized then that she'd been wrong. She wasn't lying on the wet asphalt, but on the bed in John Zimmerman's apartment, and the weight on her chest was only the figure that crawled to her across the blankets. The pressure on her neck was the bedsheets tangling around her. Vaguely, she felt relieved—all she'd have to do was open her eyes, then, and she'd be able to breathe again. Already, she could hear the voice of shattered porcelain babbling in her ears, rising higher in pitch and urgency. And one voice sharper than the others, clearer, cutting clean through the haze, "—cops!"

Suddenly, the weight lifted from her ribs. There was a crunch of rapid footsteps very near her ear, making her flinch and turn her face away, and then the voice began to speak again. "—mean it," it said, sounding high and tight and a little frightened. "You leave her alone!"

Marta took a breath and the dark receded, the filaments of the world knitting themselves back together again. At first, she could only see a field of white, shot through with veins, and she had the irrational thought that she was looking at the inside of her own eyes. Then she realized that she was looking up at the grey sky and the veins were the bare limbs of the elm trees that grew around the edge of the parking lot—an arterial network of branches, clotted here and there with the smudged shapes of squirrel dreys. Marta took another breath and then, pressing her hands flat to the asphalt, pushed herself up—first onto her elbows, then rolling herself painfully onto her side. She looked around. The man was gone. She could still feel the push of his hands against her neck, but his actual self—the breathing, crawling weight of him—had vanished.

But the parking lot wasn't empty. The woman in the red anorak was standing there, staring at her. The woman who'd had black mould in her walls. She'd dropped her bags, and they lay in a jumble around her feet, spilling bundles of cloth and packets of food onto the pavement. "Honey," she said, "are you okay?"

Marta looked at her, then down at her own feet, at the toes of her borrowed boots. She saw that one bootlace was untied. Then she started to laugh.

CHAPTER EIGHTEEN

The woman was still staring at her. "Honey—"

"I'm okay," said Marta.

Slowly, she got to her feet. Her head didn't really hurt, only felt light and buzzing and somehow bulkier than it should have been. Like there was a cold lump of something now lodged at the very back of her cranium. She reached up to prise that alien matter out but found nothing except for her hair, tangled with damp. Gingerly, she probed at it, at the tender scalp underneath, following the soreness down to the base of her skull. Brain stem, she thought. Vaguely, she remembered that from one of Quyen's diagrams, sketched out in cartoonish shapes on the whiteboard. A big knot, coiled like licorice. Base brain, lower brain, animal brain: the most basic functions that kept a body up and breathing, even when all the other lights had gone out. Marta touched her animal brain, felt it whole and intact under her fingertips, and thought, *That's okay, then. That's okay.*

"Don't you want to go to the hospital?"

She shook her head and the world went skewed for a moment, everything—the woman's face, the asphalt, the graffiti and the crumbling brickwork beneath it—twinned with its own reflection. It struck her suddenly that this was the closest thing to high she'd felt in days and she bit down hard on the inside of her cheek to stop herself from laughing. "No hospital, thanks. I'll be all right."

"Are you sure? Somebody could drive you. Your neck—"

"Naw," said Marta. "I just want to breathe for a second and get my head okay. That's all."

That was all, sure, but it wasn't easy. Every breath seemed to come from very far away, dredged up deep from the pits of her lungs, and the air crawled its way past the obstruction of pain in her throat. She gagged, spat a clot of red-edged mucous onto the asphalt between her boots, but the obstruction still remained. After a moment, the woman dug around in one of her bags and pulled out a crumpled Kleenex. She unfolded it, smoothed out the creases, then offered it to Marta. "Yes," she said, uncertain at first and then again, more decisively, "Yes, you'll be all right, honey. You just keep your head up. Keep going."

"Thank you," said Marta and stared at the Kleenex. She blinked and felt her animal brain flicker—off-on, off-on—like a set of faulty Christmas lights.

"For your eyes," said the woman.

"Oh. Thanks."

She hadn't realized that she was crying.

"You're a strong one, aren't you?" the woman went on, watching as Marta daubed gingerly at the tears. She seemed to be speaking half to herself, not expecting an answer. "Resilient. I knew you were resilient when I saw you. You just keep your head up, just like that, and you'll be all right. Did you know him?"

Marta shook her head.

The woman nodded, then asked, with an odd kind of briskness, "He didn't get inside you, did he?"

"No," said Marta.

"Then don't bother calling the cops. They'll swab you, that's all, and they won't find anything if he didn't come inside, and they might not let you go again if you don't give them a fixed address. You just keep your head up, honey. Keep on going, cry later."

She balled the Kleenex up tightly, gripping it in her first. "Yes," she said. "Later."

Later, much later, there was gravel in her knee. She took it out with tweezers. Standing by the sink, one foot propped up against the toilet and her pajamas rolled up, she gripped the tweezers in her right hand, then gripped her wrist with her left hand, to stop the shaking from getting too bad. She pinched at the skin, teasing the fragments of gravel and grit up to the surface, and blood came up too. Dark and a sheen of pus on it, too—not the waxy something that had drained from Shaw's blisters, but yellowish and thick. she coated the raw skin with a dollop of Polysporin.

Through the door, she could hear Shaw speaking on the phone in a low voice, the sound growing and then fading as he moved restlessly around the apartment. She heard him clattering around in the kitchenette, and—after a few moments—the shrill whistle of steam escaping the kettle.

Of the meagre first aid supplies they'd had, every single one of the Band-Aids and most of the gauze had gone to treating his burns. All that was left was a couple inches of bandage from the very end of the roll—she folded it in two, then pressed it to the gash on her knee, which was still oozing a thick trickle of blood. She pinned it in place with a few pieces of electrical tape, then— very gingerly—stretched out her leg to see if it would stick. It did. The bleeding didn't bother her as much as the pain did. The skin was a mottled and swollen purple and, even now, nearly six hours later, it felt like her kneecap was being pried off with a claw hammer. She could feel where the pain had lodged itself inside the bone, another lump of alien matter, and she stood on one leg to stop herself from thinking about it.

From the other side of the door, she could hear his footsteps, very quiet and deliberate across the carpet, then an even quieter knock.

"I'm leaving the tea just outside," he said. "Just on the floor, here, all right? On the left, when you're coming out."

She bit off another strip of tape, then wrapped it over her knee, an extra layer of protection—it would stick until she showered again, at least, and maybe longer. "Thanks."

"Sorry?"

She tried again, raising her voice a little louder, pushing the words past the soreness in her throat. "I was just saying thank you."

"Oh. You're sure you don't want me to help?"

"Yeah," she said. "I'm sure. Be out in a minute, anyway."

There was a breath's pause, then, "All right. Don't forget the tea's here. It's real hot."

"I won't forget," said Marta, and listened as his footsteps receded again, then wet another wadge of toilet paper and used it to wipe the crusted blood from around her nose and down to her chin. Her lower lip was raw and swelling. She made herself smile at her reflection in the mirror, grinned, and saw blood on her teeth as her mouth began to tremble. That would stick for a while too, she thought, and there was nothing much she could do about it.

Nothing she could do about her neck, either. She'd been scared, at first, that the bruises would look like phantom fingerprints on the skin—that she would look at them and see hands around her neck—and was faintly relieved to see now that they didn't. The marks were livid and red, but they were shapeless, too. One at the front and one on each side, darker, just under the jaw. She touched them tenderly with her fingertips and smiled again, kept smiling as her cheeks twitched and convulsed. The wool scarf she'd dug out of the bottom of Shaw's closet was hanging where she'd left it, looped over the shower rod, and she took it down now and wrapped it gingerly around her neck. Twice around, she knotted it, then carefully smoothed out the edges until the bruises were out of sight. She turned left, right—in the mirror, she checked her reflection.

"Done," she said aloud, and let the smile go.

When she stepped out of the bathroom, Shaw was sitting on the very edge of the daybed, bent over his phone, but he looked up very quickly when the door creaked shut again behind her. "How am I looking?" she asked, stooping to pick the mug of tea up very carefully, contorting herself from the waist to keep from bending her knee. It didn't work—the pain sparked up again and she hissed out a breath, then turned it into a reedy little laugh. "I've heard scarves are real fashionable this year, you know. They're gonna be the big thing of 2023."

"Marta . . ."

There were red rings around his eyes and she could see his jaw working, twitching. He was going to cry.

"Don't," she told him. "Don't do that, when I'm trying to be all brave and devil-may-care and shit."

"Listen—"

"I'm serious. If *you* start crying now, *I* won't ever be able to, and I'll just have to keep laughing and keep saying stupid stuff, and I don't think I can do that. So. Don't."

He opened his mouth, then shut it again. "Sorry."

"Good," she said and made her way stiffly across the room to him, holding the mug ahead of her as scalding tea sloshed on the carpet. "Come on, move over. Knee's really messed up."

Shaw did, and they sat on the far opposite ends of the mattress with the silence between him until he asked, "Did the aspirin help at all? Is your neck feeling any better, now?"

"Kind of," she said. "Bad when I breathe. I guess I won't be smoking much for a while."

"Oh."

She didn't particularly want to drink the tea, but she held the mug to her breastbone and felt the heat seep through the fabric of her T-shirt, a warmth that spread outward from her sternum, and that was good enough. "Wouldn't hurt to cut back, anyway. Couple days. It wouldn't hurt."

"I called the shelter," he said. "Woman I talked to said they'll keep an eye out for him, if he comes back tonight, tomorrow night, but all they've really got is the name he signed in under and nobody remembers seeing him before. They said there's not much they can do, unless you want to file a police report. And you—"

"Won't do that."

"Sure. Yes. I mean, you don't have to decide now, if you wanted to think about it for a while."

"I already thought about it," said Marta, who was looking at the rising bubbles in the wallpaper, the patches of damp that stretched up toward the ceiling, and seeing none of it. She'd thought about it the whole staggering, limping way home, and in the time it had taken her to patch herself up, and she'd thought—more than anything else—about Danny Boy. When she breathed, air whistled in her lungs, crawled down her throat, but the breath that came out was rancid and what came in was clear. Danny Boy on the ground, and her putting her boot to him. Breathe, and clear, and breathe, and clear. "So I won't. Not the way shit is now, not the way it's getting around here. Not the police."

Out of the corner of her eye, she saw his shoulders sink a fraction, but he only said, "Okay, whatever you want."

"They wouldn't find him anyway," she said. "It's really hard to find anybody in this city."

And she laughed, then, because she couldn't stop herself. It tore her throat up, and scalding tea slopped down her chest, and she hissed and wheeze and swore, and laughed again. For a moment, he only stared at her in bemused horror and then, to her relief, he laughed, too—just once, just a single, nasal little giggle, but it was enough, and she felt dizzyingly grateful. Then he got up and went to get her a paper towel, and she was even more grateful for that.

Mopping herself up gingerly, daubing at her lap, she said, "I was thinking about the money, too."

He was back at the sink, yanking another fistful of towel off the roll, but he turned to look at her quickly, his face twisting into a frown. "What?"

Again, she forced herself to enunciate, raising her voice beyond the breathy creak she'd fallen into. "I – was – thinking – about – the . . ."

"No," he said. "I heard you, I just meant: what money?"

"For the job application," she said. "The background check thing. If you could just transfer me sixty-five dollars, I could pay the fee with that. And then you could have it back out of my first three pay cheques, if I get the job, and if I don't get it—"

"Marta—"

"—then I'm gonna drop my resume off at the superstore, drugstore, wherever. I'll find something else."

"Marta—"

"I'd pay it back sooner, but it's gonna take me a while to get even on the rent, too."

"You're kidding," he said and Marta broke off, reaching up to tug the scarf a little looser around her burning throat as she looked at him. He had turned all the way around to face her and the paper towel was crumpled in his hands. There was a particular note to his voice she couldn't remember having heard before, not just anger but a kind of amazement as well. Knotting his fists into the paper, he went on. "You're fucking kidding. You're not really going to apply, are you?"

"Why not? You were wanting me to, last night."

"Last night was different."

She screwed the tea-sopping paper up, tossed it in the vague direction of the garbage. It slid off the rim, hit the carpet with a faint *th-wump* that they both ignored. "I know," she said. "I was chickening out and that was stupid. And you were right, too. I don't have any good reason not to go for it now."

"You're kidding," he said, and now his voice was so sharp, so unsteady that she wondered if his mental needle was getting stuck. If that was all he was ever going to say. His jaw was working again and he waved the paper towel at her wildly, a single erratic arc that went from the scarf around her neck to the gauze taped to her knee. "You're kidding," he said. "You don't have to keep doing this stuff. Going to these places. Not when it's fucking you up, when it's—when it's going to be like this. You tried for Thomas, I get it, and you did your best, but there's nothing else you can do."

"I know."

There was nothing else she could do for Thomas Zimmerman. She could see that clearly enough; there were no more leads to follow, no more places to look. He was gone now, she knew, but the notion didn't paralyze her the way she'd expected it to. Maybe he'd been gone for a while—or maybe he'd been gone since the beginning. Either way, it made no difference to her; it hadn't mattered when she'd been down on the asphalt on Gottingen Street and it didn't matter now.

"You shouldn't go back," said Shaw. "Christ, Marta, you could have died. You don't have to go back."

"I know," she said again. "I know I don't have to."

"And if you get hurt . . ."

If, thought Marta. If. She looked at him, at the wallpaper over his shoulder, and she breathed in and out, and out, out, until her chest ached and her head was so clean it was spinning. Then, quite slowly and deliberately, she shrugged. "He told me to stop," she said. "That was what he said, you know—over and over, that's all it was. Stop. He just wanted me to stop."

Shaw was looking at her wide-eyed now, stricken, and in his silence, she went on. "You don't have to give me the money, if you don't want to. I get it. I think we both do."

For a long moment they only looked at each other, and she thought she could see the circle between them, around them, like they were back at Barrington and passing the ball to each other across the kitchen. Then he put the paper towel back down on the counter and wiped his hands clean on his jeans. She watched him as he crouched in the corner, dredged his coat out from a heap of laundry, as he rooted around in the pocket and drew out his cheque-book. She listened to the scratch of the pen nib as he wrote, then the paper tearing. Then, "Do you want me to write it out to you, or to the charity directly?"

"The charity, thanks," she said.

Again, the pen went scritch-scratch, and then he was running the cheque between finger and thumb, smoothing out the crumpled paper. He held it out to her, but she didn't take it.

"Go on," he said and tried to smile at her. "Sixty-five whole Canadian dollars, payable to the Open Hands Charity Foundation." And then, "Go *on*."

Looking at the cheque, Marta took a deep and careful breath, feeling the air scrape the bruised innards of her throat. "Listen," she said. "I remember what you said, yeah? About how you felt. I'm not going to forget it. And—" She saw his face seize with a look of petrified horror, saw him opening his mouth to interrupt, and plunged quickly along. "And whenever I was with you, I always wanted to be there. I never felt like that with anybody else. So I won't forget that, either."

For a moment, she saw the look of horror fade away into something else—a flicker that passed across his face too quickly to take stock of—and then he only looked tired and a little gratified. "So you still want the cheque, eh?"

"Oh—yes," said Marta, and felt the blush she'd neatly been repressing for the last half-minute start to come up on her, inescapable. "Yeah, I do. I just wanted you to know . . ."

"Good," he said. "So is there any reason why you can't take it?"

SUSANNA CUPIDO

Marta thought there probably wasn't. And only after she'd taken the cheque and tucked it safely into the inner pocket of her coat, did he say, "And is there any reason, now, why you can't go and get some sleep?"

There wasn't.

By the time she was called into the downtown offices of the Open Hands Charity Foundation, most of the snow in the city had melted into a brown April slush and Marta's throat had healed sufficiently for her to take the interview. Mostly, it only ached a little when she swallowed too hard or turned her head too quickly, and there was still the slightest of rasps when she talked. She didn't mind that much. It sounded, to her ears, pretty decently cool. She told the woman who interviewed her that she was just recovering from a protracted bout of Long COVID and, when they gave her the paperwork to sign, she held the pen crookedly between her third finger and her thumb. A fractured metacarpal, the doctor had said. If the woman—whose laminated plastic nametag identified her as Debbie Halloran—noticed this, she didn't mention it.

"We've been notified that your background check's cleared," she told Marta, and offered her a brightly wrapped candy from the bowl beside her computer. "And all your references were excellent, all very enthusiastic. A+ material, all around."

Marta stuck the sweet in her pocket. "So I'm good to go, yeah?"

"Well—yes. I should say that we *usually* prioritize candidates with a bit more 'field experience,' as it were, but we've been a bit short-staffed these last few months. And, if you're willing to undergo a few weeks of training, shadowing some of our other outreach specialists—"

"Yep, no problem."

"—then we'd be very happy to have you on the team."

"Couldn't be happier to be here," said Marta, giving her best

232

approximation of Quyen's most-kindergarten-ish smile, and was rewarded with another rattle of the candy bowl.

"I should maybe warn you, too," Debbie Halloran went on, "that it's not *pleasant* work. I mean, I don't know how much research you've done on our website, but as an outreach specialist, you'll be spending time with people at the very lowest points of their lives. I know it can be hard to imagine, but even in a beautiful city like Halifax, there's a lot of suffering going on right under our noses."

Marta thought about this for a moment. "I think you're probably right," she said and reached across the desk to take another sweet. "I think I can imagine it pretty well."

She gave the candies to Nicholas later on, flicking them across the dinner table to him, and he put up his knife and fork to make a set of improvised goalposts. Two scored, one ricocheted off the butter dish with a resounding *ping* of glass. They both looked around guiltily, but Dina was pretending not to notice. She'd been telling Shaw about Nicholas's exploits on the hockey team. "—long as it keeps him *active*, you know? I think that's really the most important thing, for kids that age. They have to keep *active* and *doing* things, don't they?"

"Absolutely," said Shaw, and reached up to rub the place where his moustache had once been.

The table was too small to sit all five of them comfortably and they were jammed in elbow-to-elbow, knocking over glasses and poking each other with forks. Under these circumstances, Marta couldn't catch his eye and grin at him, not without contorting her already-aching neck around impossibly, so she settled for kicking him under the table.

"We're getting a bigger TV," Nicholas told her, dismantling the makeshift goalposts in order to finish eating his casserole. "And putting it where your room was. It's got a flatscreen."

He'd been saying this kind of thing increasingly often, Marta noticed, as his seventh birthday approached—always a little bit defiant, a little petulant, jutting out his chin as he watched carefully for her reaction. Punishing her for leaving, she thought, but there were worse ways to be punished.

She only grinned. "Great. Maybe I'll come over sometime after work and we can watch some movies. Some real horror shit."

"Mind your language," said Jacob.

It was only after dinner that the feeling started setting in again, after she and Nicholas had cleared most of the dishes away and Shaw had helped wash them, after dessert had been brought out and served. Nothing she could put a name to, exactly, just a restless pricking under her skin and a constriction in her chest like someone was bearing down on her with its full weight. She sat in her place, gripping her wine glass with a sudden rigidity, and imagined—just for a moment—that someone was crawling across the table toward her. The table bowing inwards, buckling, and the crash of glassware on the floor when the tablecloth slipped away.

After a while, Nicholas decided that he didn't like the mille-feuille cake, and Dina sighed and got up to find her coat. "They've opened up the ice cream shop on the wharf again," she said and shot Marta a tired little smile. "Tourist season is almost upon us, I guess."

Shaw offered to go walk down to the harbourfront with them, and Marta wondered privately if that meant he knew what was happening to her, or if it meant he *didn't*.

Then it was just her and her father left at the table, picking over the bones of dessert. Neither of them said anything. Marta dug the cork out of the wine bottle and poured herself another glass, then decided that she didn't want it after all. She pushed back her chair to stand up and saw, just briefly, a look of relief cross his basset hound face.

That, more than anything, decided it.

"Dad," she said, "do you remember what I did at Mom's funeral?"

"Is this one of those neuro-tricks? Alzheimer's test or whatever? Worried the old man's cracking up?"

"It's just a question."

The expression of relief had vanished, now, but his face was otherwise perfectly composed. With the edge of his fork, he scraped away the last scraps of pastry from his plate. "Oh. Well, you were wearing one of her dresses, weren't you? The corduroy one with the pearl buttons down the front and the big sleeves."

"I think they were silver buttons," said Marta. "Shaped like little shells."

While Dina had been fixing dinner, she'd gone through the closet and taken out the family photo albums to check.

"Right, and you looked very pretty. So did Dina. And we all threw a bit of dirt into the grave, after, and your uncle from Mahone Bay played the bagpipes for us. I think he played 'The Mist Covered Mountains,' because that was her favourite."

"Her favourite was 'The Bonnie Lass of Fyvie,'" said Marta. "But Dad, do you remember what *I* did?"

He hesitated, frowning; his fork, crumbs of pastry wedged between the tines, hovered an inch from his lips and then dropped again. "Well, I think we asked you to read some scripture during the service, but you didn't want to. Dina did, instead, or one of your cousins—I'm not sure."

Marta nodded. She looked at the table and saw, tucked away among the wine glasses and bits of silverware, the dandelions that had grown around the parking lot of Fairview Lawn Cemetery.

"I was high on ketamine," she said. "I was so high I couldn't talk, and I could hardly walk, and I kept looking at the coffin and thinking she was breathing. Everybody stared at me. You remember that, yeah?"

"No," he said, and she knew that he did.

235

"I was so high I couldn't stand up to sing, or sit down to pray, and she kept breathing in her coffin, so you told me to go and wait in the parking lot until it was over. I walked around in circles, around and around, and Dina came and got me later. I wasn't there when you threw dirt in the grave. I was your oldest and I should have been better, and I was worse. You don't remember any of that?"

"No," he said. "I don't."

"You must have been so fucking ashamed of me," she said and wiped her nose on her napkin. If she started to cry now, she thought that the tender pulp of her throat would split right open and choke her. And she didn't *want* to cry, anyway. "I'm sorry, anyway. Whether you remember it or not."

She looked at the table and tried to see something else, *anything* else. She told herself that it was the Halifax pier she was looking at, the far end of the wharf where the ice cream shop was, and that she was seeing Dina and Shaw and Nicholas all ambling along the table-cloth. It didn't quite stick. Your brain could fool you pretty well, sometimes, but you couldn't fool it.

After a moment, Jacob Klausner picked up his fork again, snapping her out of the reverie. "I don't know what you're talking about," he said. "But I think I'd remember if I'd ever been ashamed of you."

The second time she turned the bedside lamp on, Shaw didn't open his eyes. He kept them screwed shut, the comforter pulled up to his chin, and only the too-measured rhythm of his breath told her he'd woken up at all. After a while, he said, "There's no one in the bed."

"I know," said Marta.

"No one else, except us."

"Fucking Christ, I know that," she said and switched the lamp off again. "Just go back to sleep, man, I'm sorry."

But she kicked the bedsheet away and pushed all the blankets off her side of the daybed, piling, them at her feet. *Treat the problem and not the symptoms.* She lay back, feeling the weight of nothing on her chest. "I'm not like him," she said.

"You aren't," said Shaw. "Just go easy, that's all."

They never talked about Thomas Zimmerman again, after that.

CHAPTER NINETEEN

It rained on the night that was the first of May and the last of April. The rain lashed through the birch trees that grew in the Halifax Greenway Urban Park and turned its winding pathways to rivers of mud, and Marta, feeling the currents washing over her boots, wished again that she'd taken the bus home instead. Shaw had warned her before he'd left for work that it was going to rain, but she'd still had her head buried under the comforter and hadn't listened. He said a lot of things in the mornings that she didn't listen to: that one or both of them were going to have to move out of Inglis Lodge, that he was sick of living in the city and was going back to Yarmouth, that they needed to buy a second bed. None of these resolutions ever lasted much past noon.

He had called her with a different one that evening, while she'd been stacking tin cans of donated food in the Open Hands pantry. He'd said, "I think I'm going back to therapy. I miss doing the sessions, you know."

"Good," Marta said, holding the phone wedged between ear and shoulder while she juggled tins of tomato soup and creamed corn from hand to hand. And there was a pause, like he was expecting her to say something more, so she said, "That's really good."

He sounded inexplicably taken aback. "Is that it?"

And Marta grinned at the can of soup in her hand, and said, "I love you, man." She heard him laugh.

"Fuck you."

And she laughed, too, and hung up and went back to sorting the tins. That was, it turned out, most of what being an "outreach specialist" entailed. She'd been disappointed at first, finding it much the same as what she'd done as a janitor and dishwasher. The supervisor said it would change when she had a bit more on-the-job experience, that pretty soon she'd be out on the streets making connections, but mostly it was just mopping the floors and answering phones and making inventories of the donations they got. It wasn't too bad. It was all worth it, in fact, for two nights a week she did shifts at the Open Hands shelter—where she sat at a table outside the women's dorm, marking names off her clipboard, and held herself very still, and listened to the sound of their breathing in the night.

That was why Marta had gotten in the habit of walking home through the park, coming off those shifts in the early hours of the morning. She didn't like to give up the quiet until she absolutely had to.

But it wasn't quiet now. Rain drummed on her head, on her shoulders, made the ends of her bobbed hair—Dina had cut it shorter than she'd been expecting—curl into clumps and stick to her cheeks. She picked her way down the muddied trail, following it when it cut sharply right, becoming a bridge that spanned a wide ravine. Away on the other side, the road went on, vanishing into the dark woods. If she followed it, she would get to the waterway of the Northwest Arm, where a string of yachting clubs and private homes lined the shore, but Marta had no intention of going that far. Instead, like she always did, she stopped halfway along the bridge. Like she always did, she leaned over the parapet and saw the train tracks down below, slick and bright as they cut the ravine, bisecting it down the middle like the first incision of an autopsy.

It was six in the morning and dawn was lost behind a veil of rain, and Marta wondered whether it could *really* be May if the sun never came up to see it. She wondered if the city would drift along forever in this wet and hazy nothing, left stranded with the cicada husk of April behind them.

And dimly, wondering this, she became aware of something else, too, through the downpour—just a smudge, catching the corner of her eye, but it was enough to make her lift her head. For a second, squinting into the not-dawn, she thought that it had only been a trick of the storm. Then she saw it: a shape was moving down in the ravine. A person, bent low, picking their way slowly along the tracks. She could only see the hood of their coat and their shoulders, hunched up against the wind and the white and lashing gusts of rain. Still, as they trudged closer to the bridge, she saw why they were going so slowly.

They were dragging something along the ground behind them—a dark bundle. The figure stopped just short of the bridge and, as Marta watched, the head tipped back slightly. Below the hood, she saw the pale sliver of a face and a hand rising, waving in a big and expansive arc. Through the rain, she heard a voice calling up to her, but the wind tore the sound away and all she could make out was the vague edge of the words.

She wiped the rain from her face and then leaned forward until the rails were cutting into her stomach. Cupping her hands to her mouth, she called down to him. "What?"

Below, the figure did the same, dropping the bundle down into the mud in order to use both hands. This time, she caught the words more clearly, and the voice, too—a man's voice, and a booming, bullfrog croak in the night. "Please— come— down!"

"Fuck off!"

"Please—come— down!"

"Fuck— off! Why?"

But there was no answer. The figure had only gone back to gesturing, waving his arms urgently like he was trying to signal her with semaphore. Marta stayed rooted to the spot, leaning against the parapet as she stared down at him, and eventually he seemed to get tired and the waving slowed, each movement stretching into a wide and lazy arc. Slower and slower, until he stopped completely, dropping his arms abruptly to his sides, like an invisible hand had cut his strings. He stood there for a moment, staring up at her, and then bent and picked up whatever it was that he had been dragging. Again, he began the slow trudge along the ravine, but he seemed to be having even more trouble than before, staggering and swaying wildly. He hadn't even gotten under the shadow of the bridge before she saw him stumble and fall, down on his hands and knees in the mud.

Marta waited to see if he would move, but he didn't. She hesitated for a moment longer, gripping the railing tightly. She looked around, back down the bridge and through the screen of pines to the road where, distant, the lights of cars tore and screamed. She looked up at the falling sky. "Christ," she said aloud, and then leaned over the parapet again, holding her hands up, palm outwards. "Just— wait— there! Jesus Christ, man, just wait!"

She went to the end of the bridge again and, with a little difficulty, swung herself up until she had her knee up on the railing. She worked one leg over, then the other, and let herself carefully down into the bracken. Crouching in the muddy-clogged brambles that grew down the ravine, she felt the blood stinging in her fingertips. Below her, under her, the ravine sloped away at a steep angle, some of it exposed rock and some covered in desiccated bushes, and all of it slick with streaming water. She went down slowly at first, gripping fistfuls of bramble and weed that cut into her hands, and then her feet went out from under her, the soles of Thomas Zimmerman's boots sliding off the stone.

A crackling, jolting pain shot through Marta's arms and down to her wrists, and only the brambles kept her from falling entirely. "Shit, fucking shit!"

Gritting her teeth against the wrenching agony in her shoulders, she went the last ten feet in an awkward sideways scramble, bringing down a shower of debris with her as she landed in the muddied gravel that ran along the train tracks. A fresh damp soaked into her jacket, rucked up high over her ribs, and through her T-shirt.

Marta stood slowly and saw that the man who had called to her had picked himself up, too. He was standing a few feet away and watching her from under his hood. She looked back at him and, only now, saw his face properly through its sheen of dirt and grime. She recognized him, not with the surprise she knew that she ought to have felt, but with a certain resignation. "Oh. I didn't know it was you, from all the way up there."

Danny Boy looked back at her anxiously. He was wearing a windbreaker that was several sizes too large for his shrunken frame, that hung off him strangely, bulging in places and hanging loose elsewhere. "I can't get it set up on my own, you know," he said, motioning vaguely to the bundle now lying at his feet, and then, "You're looking very well, dear."

"Yeah. Less well than I was a minute or two ago."

He hesitated for a moment. "I'm sorry about the money. You got to understand that I don't always listen to the angels."

"It's all right," said Marta. "Call it a donation to your campaign for mayor."

She glanced down at the bundle and saw that it was a mass of dark and mud-caked canvas. Over a metre long and wide, it was disc-shaped like a frisbee or the sack of a trampoline: a camping tent, furled up and flattened. Danny Boy was crouching down, fiddling with the straps and ties—he hefted it awkwardly, gripping one edge with both hands together, like he was pulling a sledge.

Marta looked around, at the steep walls of the ravine rising up above them, the tracks stretching away into the night. "You want to set it up here?"

"No," said Danny Boy, and jerked his chin in the other direction, along the tracks and running parallel to the path she had followed before. "Down there."

She hesitated for a moment and then reached down to grip the opposite edge of the tent, helping him to lift it. It was slow going, even with two of them carrying, not because it was particularly heavy but because the canvas was slick with mud and slipped often, and because the ground was all gravel and mud, thick and sucking at the soles of their boots, and the rain was white and blinding. They stumbled and tripped and dropped the tent, and as the ravine got narrower, the rocky walls pressing in close until there was only a few feet of clearance between them and the rails, Marta wondered just what they were going to do if a train came along.

"You come around here pretty often?" asked Danny Boy, easy and oddly conversational, as the tent slipped again, splashing down into a puddle of rainwater that had gathered between the tracks. Mud made warpaint streaks across his withered face and his lips were puckered, breath escaping in reedy little whistles.

Stooping, Marta shook her head. "Only lately. And my mom brought me, sometimes, when I was a kid."

"Oh," said Danny Boy again, then seemed to fall back on familiar territory. "I just called 'cause I can't get it set up on my own, you know. I'm not really a camper and it's all kind of awkward. You need two people to hold the poles up."

"It's all right," said Marta, and gave a one-shouldered and awkward shrug, hoisting the canvas higher when it sagged.

The ravine got narrower and narrower and then, all of a sudden, opened up again. The rain was slackening off by degrees, now only a cold and persistent drizzle and, in the reddish light cast by the railway beacons, Marta could see that the tracks ran past an old signalman's booth and, behind that, an empty lot. A scattering of tents had been pitched here already, she saw, and a few figures darted here and there between them, wrapped up in their coats, some of them holding magazines or a bundle of newspaper pages above their heads as makeshift umbrellas.

"See?" said Danny Boy. "Not far."

"Lead the way, man."

He chose a spot near the edge of the encampment, between a dark green tent and a blue one, and together they spread out the groundsheet and got to work. If carrying the tent had been hard, then pitching it seemed almost impossible to Marta. It became a living creature, squirming out of her hands, and every time she tried to drive the fat metal pegs into the mud they only slid away. She had never fixed a tent before and she suspected that Danny Boy hadn't, either—his lips were bunched up, sucked inwards with concentration, and his yellow eyes were slits in his head.

"Tough one," he said. "Ve–ry tough."

"S'a real bitch, yeah."

Her fingers were getting numb and bloodless, clumsy with cold, and she stuck them in her mouth. Danny Boy shook his head. "Under your arms," he said and then showed her how, tucking his hands down the front of his coat and wedging them into his armpits. "Warmest spot."

"Oh."

The groundsheet kept getting bunched up, too, sucked down by the mud, and one of them would have to stop and straighten it out again. It wasn't raining anymore, and everything looked muck-brown with the early morning haze. After a while, a woman emerged from the green tent and stuck her hand out to test the rain; feeling nothing, she stayed and watched them struggling for a few moments, her head tipped to the side. "You want any help?" she asked.

Marta's clothes had stiffened with grime, hardening into a shell. Her hair was plastered clammy to her cheeks, her neck—she reached up to brush it away with one muddy hand. She looked at Danny Boy, who nodded. "Please."

"I think you need something to wedge the stakes in," said the woman. "There's nothing for them to stick against, in all the mud. That's why they keep sliding."

Hesitating, Marta looked at the deep and gouged-out grooves that the pegs had left in the mud. Then she reached down and began to tug at the knots of her bootlaces. She kicked them off one at a time, until she was standing in the sucking, clutching mud, and wet was pushing up between her toes. Then she took one of the boots and mashed it down as far as it would go, until the entire toe and most of the lacings were entirely submerged. Carefully, she lifted one of the tent pegs and shoved it down into the laces as far as she could, nesting it between the tongue and the leather of the inner boot. For good measure, she stripped off her sock and wedged that in as well, then pulled the bootlaces tight and knotted them around the peg. When she let go again, it shifted slightly in the mud, but it held in place. "There," she said. "That's gonna work for two of them, anyway."

"I don't have any other shoes," said the woman, and then, turning, called out to someone away and out of sight within the warren of tents "Hey! Hey, you got any extra shoes?"

Squatting down, Marta rammed the second boot into the mud. It wouldn't go as deep as the first one, but when she wedged another stake in and tested it, sock bunched up inside, the whole rig seemed to hold. Vaguely, away in her periphery, she was aware that somebody else had joined them—another brown blotch that might have been a person, picking their way around the edge of the tent, and a voice that Marta could barely hear over the beat of her own struggling pulse, saying, "Why shoes, Val?"

The woman whose name was Val let out a sharp huff of laughter through her nose. "These guys've got a dumb tent."

"It's just my tent," said Danny Boy. "Not hers."

Up close, Marta could see that there were a number of dangling laces all down the tent's canvas, meant—she thought—to be lashed together around the poles. When she tried to tie the first knot, her fingers were too numb to guide the end through the loop. She tried twice and couldn't do it. Under the skin, her veins stood out stark and prominent, and the scratches on her hands from the brambles of the ravine were purpling around the edges, showing the ugly colour of bruised flesh.

"So," Val was saying now, "you got any more shoes, Tom? They need something to go like runners under the stakes."

"I don't think so, sorry," said the new arrival. "I lost my other ones, you know."

"Could use some takeout cups," said Danny Boy. "Make a hole in the middle and then bottom part of the stake goes through and sticks, and the whole thing gets held in one spot. How about that?"

"Sure, we could ask—"

But the tide in Marta's ears had receded just far enough that she heard the arrival's voice, really heard it, and now she could hear nothing, because the sea had come back. She looked at her hands, still gripping the stubborn ends of the canvas laces, and saw them—everything—begin to pulse and seethe, distorting with each ragged breath. She closed her eyes very tightly. Then she looked up.

He looked older than she remembered, and his long hair was tied back from his face, but he had kept the heavy duffel coat. And, when his lips parted, she saw the slight part between his teeth, dividing his grin neatly in two.

"Hey," said Thomas Zimmerman, and grinned at her. "I thought it was you."

In her head, Marta had gone down the same road a hundred times. She had imagined over and over what it might be like if she saw

Thomas Zimmerman again. It had been pure anticipation at first, then hope, and then—finally—just the nonsense that her mind's eye had scrawled across the walls of Inglis Lodge, but the shape of it had always been the same. She had imagined that she would feel a little numb, that everything would turn quiet as the world fell away from under her. But it didn't. If anything, the world was more there than it had ever been before. Looking up at him now, she was acutely aware of how her clothes were starting to itch where the mud made a crust. She thought that she could even feel parts of herself that she had never noticed before—she felt the pores of her skin expand and retract, felt a twinge in her lower left side that might have been her appendix.

Val had vanished into her tent and re-emerged a moment later with a pair of dilapidated plastic cups. She thrust one into Danny Boy's hands, then tossed the other to Marta, who caught it mechanically.

"Uh, thanks. Thank you."

Thomas Zimmerman looked taller than she remembered him being, too, but she couldn't be sure if it was just the angle she had, kneeling below him in the dirt, or if he was holding himself differently now. She had carried the image of him around for so long that he'd become a photonegative, imprinted in opposite hues on the inside of her mind. Now, seeing the real thing, she was startled by the vividness of him, the life. Even standing in the early morning haze at the bottom of the ravine, he was sharp and clear in his colour and Marta could see nothing through him.

Beside her, Danny Boy drove the metal tip of the tent peg through the bottom of his cup, then squatted down to wedge both into the ground. He seemed entirely indifferent to Thomas Zimmerman's presence—he barely looked at him—but, when the stake stayed wedged in the mud, he let out a delighted, wheezing laugh, swatting Marta's arm. "Pretty good, huh?"

She flinched and, for the first time, looked away from Thomas Zimmerman. "Yeah," she said. "Yeah, good."

Slowly, mechanically, she followed his lead, and the last peg went deep into the mud. Danny Boy held it steady while she put her knee on it, bearing down with all her weight to drive it in. She tried to tie the canvas lacings next, but her hands were trembling worse than before—after a few moments' struggle, Val nudged her out of the way. "I've done about a million of these," she said and deftly brought the bones of the tent snapping together. It was coming together properly, now, the canvas stretched over the bent poles to make the black carapace of a beetle, and Danny Boy was whistling reedy breaths between his few teeth as he stooped to fix the remaining ties.

Marta sat back on her heels, running her numb fingers through her bobbed hair again, feeling the snag of knots and tangles. She was unneeded, now, and unsure what to do with herself, and she looked at Thomas Zimmerman. He had been standing back too, watching the construction of the tent with a quiet interest, but he held out her hand to her now.

"Here," he said. "Come on."

"Thanks."

She took his hand, letting him draw her up to stand beside him. His bare fingers felt pitted and rough against her skin, but very warm; she held on tightly and Thomas Zimmerman let her, but when she tried to hug him, he pulled away quickly.

Marta faltered, her arms dropping uselessly to her sides. "Sorry."

"It's all right."

"I didn't know what happened to you."

"I've been around," said Thomas Zimmerman, and then, giving her another halved grin, "You changed your hair. And it was all blond before, wasn't it?"

"Oh—yeah. Just stopped bleaching it, I guess."

"It looks like you," he said. He tipped his head back and she followed the line of his throat, the straining protrusion of arteries and sinews, and the speckled flesh where his beard was growing in uneven patches, all parts of him fitting together with an evenness that made her breath catch. Above them, the sky was changing, indigo turning paler by degrees as the sunrise reached it. It was May after all, then.

"Are you staying," he asked her, "or going?"

Looking over her shoulder, Marta saw that Val had vanished away into the encampment again, but the flap of Danny Boy's tent was hanging open; looking through, she could just make out the shape of him sitting cross-legged on the canvas groundsheet, his coat shrugged off and his rucksack propped up against his knees. As she watched, he reached inside and began to pull one thing out after another—crumpled papers, bundled scarves and hats, a package of granola bars, a can opener. One by one, he arranged them in lines on the groundsheet in front of him. When Marta caught his eye, he glanced up at her, gave her a distracted little nod and smile, but she could see that he was already forgetting her. He'd found the four walls of his canvas world and she was on the outside of it now. She watched him from the wrong side of the glass, looking in on him from the outside of his unvarnished carapace, and felt very cold.

She would have stayed if he had said anything, but he didn't, only smiled and lowered his head and went on arranging the workings of the world.

"Guess I'll go," said Marta.

Thomas Zimmerman nodded. "Come on, I'll walk you back. We can go down the rails a bit farther and get out through the trainyard."

The ground was still churned up and sucking, but he moved very easily along the slatted boards of the train tracks, and she followed him, past the edge of the encampment of tents, where some people looked at them and some didn't—but mostly, Marta noticed, they looked at him. A few of them nodded to him and he nodded back, and she drifted after him, some stray bit of debris in his orbit. He was wearing a pair of tennis shoes, she noticed, so dark with ingrained dirt that it was impossible to tell what colour they'd been new.

"Did you know I was looking for you?" she asked the back of his duffel coat.

The collar twitched. He shrugged. "I got your note."

"But you knew I was looking, and you never called me," said Marta. "I was going crazy for a while. I was looking for you everywhere, all over the city."

He glanced at her sideways and she saw in the dawn light that his dark eyes were bright and very wry. "I never got that far out," he said. "I saw you at that party at Allan's place, that Saturday night back in February. You looked like you had your own stuff going on."

"Oh. Yeah. I took your boots, you know."

"I wondered."

"I can't exactly give them back, 'cause they're holding up Danny Boy's tent, but . . ."

Again, he shrugged. "It's all right. They didn't fit me so well, anyway."

Marta didn't say anything to that, only looked down at her bare feet in the dirt, at the blue veins in them, and shivered. Her soles had been tender at first, but now they were numb from the cold and that was better. It felt like everything underfoot was covered in a thin carpeting of some wet and fibrous webbing. Ahead, the ravine narrowed into a tunnel, the road running over top—a car passed by, rocketing through the blue of the dawn, and then another one. Already, Marta thought, people were on their way to work. It seemed like a perfectly absurd thing. Down in the dark of the tunnel, Thomas slackened his pace and she grew acutely conscious of him beside her, his fingers snagging the sleeve of her coat to pull her along with him.

"Mind your feet," he said. "People throw all kinds of trash down here. Bottles, broken glass."

She managed a few steps on her tiptoes, numb and tottering along like she was on stilts, then stumbled. He tightened his grip on her sleeve, bearing her up, and she let him lead her along after that. Plucking and picking at her clothes with fastidious little touches, steering her around things she couldn't quite get the shape of in the dark.

"I think your mom really misses you," she said. "I mean, I'm not saying you have to go see her or anything, if you don't want to, but—but I think she'd really like it if you did. Just so she'd know you were all right and all."

He made a noise in the back of his throat, too indistinct an acknowledgement for Marta to tell if he was pleased by the news or not. It could have meant anything. His hand was still brushing against her side. She wanted to reach out and take it, hold it, cling on tightly, but she was almost sure he'd pull away again if she tried.

Instead, she went on. "It seems to me like she felt pretty guilty, not telling you about your dad. And she feels responsible, because of the genetic component, the inheriting, the passing on of—of . . ."

"Schizophrenia," said Thomas Zimmerman.

Marta felt herself flush. "Yes."

"My mom never wanted to say the word either, you know. She used to just call it my 'condition.'"

"I don't—"

"She never told me it was genetic, but I always figured it was. Or maybe I—" In the shadows of the tunnel, she thought she could see him raise up his hands, fingers fluttering as they pulled shapes from the air. He seemed to be searching for the right words, or else trying to craft them. "I didn't know, maybe, until the doctor told me it was. I didn't know he had it, too, but I always thought they were both the reason why I ever had it at all."

"Is that why you stopped going to therapy? The doctor telling you that?"

"Maybe. Or—" Again, his hands moved in the dark. "—I think so. Yes. I couldn't see the point, if it was in me like that. Before I was ever born, you know."

"I guess it must be pretty hard."

He seemed to think about that for a moment. "I don't know if it is or not," he said. "But it scared me when the doctor told me. I got scared for a while, after that."

At the other end of the tunnel, the single set of train tracks split, became two and then three—more and more, a whole network of veins, intricate neural pathways of steel, snaking away across the railway yard ahead. It was deserted. They walked in the shadow of more rusted freight boxes, of the dark and waiting trains. Marta could see the spindly cranes of the dockyard away to the right, silhouettes against the gold-tinged morning sky. On the left, the old granary tower, the sky-high apartment blocks of the South End—she caught herself searching for the brick red of her family's building, then looked away quickly.

"Is it easier now?" she asked Thomas Zimmerman.

She heard his breath catch, but he barely hesitated a second. "Sometimes, sure. I come and go."

"Oh."

"Sometimes I just see something moving in a glass, a vase, a window, a reflection of the thing, behind the curtain and coming, and I see it coming, and—" His voice rose, fell. She heard him draw a deep breath, "—things get to me, sometimes, when I see them like that."

"I'm sorry."

"I understand it better now, anyway. I know it wasn't her fault. I mean, it wasn't his fault, either. I understand the way it is for him, and me, and nobody was ever trying to poison me or putting things in my food or anything like that. You can tell her that, if you see her. I won't. I know that it wasn't her fault, I know that in my head, right now, right this second, but that doesn't mean I'll know it tomorrow or any other day—you see what I mean?"

"I think so."

"That's why I never went home. That's why I went to stay with John, instead of her."

"Yes. I met him, too."

He grinned. "I heard something about that. He might have told me, maybe. But he's not so bad, you know. He's not bad all the way down. He let me stay 'til his girlfriend wanted me out, and he still brings me bags of groceries sometimes, and cans of beer, and he says he'll get me one of those little camper stoves, so I can sit out in the evenings and eat supper."

"Sounds nice," she said. She could feel herself teetering on the edge of crying and bit down hard on the meat of her cheek, jamming her lips together against the trembling of it.

"I can't know if it is, yet," said Thomas Zimmerman, with that same air of thoughtful exactness and then, briskly, "Come on, then."

He led her sharply left, to the edge of the tracks and up a sloping embankment, to where an old chain-link fence cut a line between the railway yard and a long parking lot. Marta knew where they were, now—barely three minutes from her home, just behind the row of superstores and fast-food restaurants that she had walked past nearly every day of her life. Here, there was a gap in the fence, the chains eaten clean through by rust, and he leaned down and drew it back for her, making an opening just big enough to crawl through. "You can go through the parking lot, there, and come around onto Barrington Street."

She didn't move.

"Go on," he told her. "I should get back soon, anyway. There's people I need to see."

She wiped her eyes, her nose, and crouched to drag herself through the gap. Rusted metal snagged her hair and she had to jerk her head to get loose—she hooked her fingers into the fence and slowly, painfully, drew herself up to stand. From the other side, Thomas Zimmerman was watching her seriously, not smiling but very alive in his face, nothing vacant. He hesitated for a moment, then said, "I liked knowing you were looking for me. I never minded that."

"I wish I'd found you sooner," said Marta.

He put his hand out. Not quite touching hers, the hair's breadth between his thumb and her finger, but she felt the fence rattle as he wound his fingers through the links. He let out a breath and she felt the vibrations of it through the cold metal. "I tried to think my way out of it, and I couldn't," he said. "That's why I had to leave, you know? You can't get out of it inside your own head, or you just get lost."

Marta only nodded. She couldn't think of anything to say.

"Mind how you go," said Thomas Zimmerman, and he stood by the fence and watched her as she went down into the parking lot. He was there the first time she turned and looked back, and the second, too. The third time, he raised his hand to the level of his shoulder, fingers curled in tightly, and Marta did the same.

The fourth time she looked back, he wasn't there.

The wind picked up as she crossed the parking lot, carrying with it the cries of the gulls and the sound of distant motors, the screech of shifting metal. That was the construction sites, Marta knew, all up and down the harbour and away over on the far Dartmouth shore. The sound came very sharp over the water. At the far side of the lot, she stopped and stood at the edge of the road. If she followed it left, she knew that she would get to her family's home and, if she went a little farther, she would get to Inglis Lodge again. She felt a drop of rain on her cheek, then one glassed her eye. That was May in Halifax, she thought—it would be like this from now on, until the heat of the summer came and went again, and then it would rain, and it would go on in this way for as long as she could stand it.

She stood in the window.

The mud ran in rivers around her bare feet.

ACKNOWLEDGEMENTS

First and foremost, I'd like to thank all my family for supporting and encouraging me—not just in the writing of this book, but in everything. From reading my drafts to giving me much-needed advice to bringing me cups of hot tea, I could never have done it without all your help. I owe an immense amount to my mum and dad, who raised me to be a reader and a writer and a thinker; to my sister, Marina, who I did my earliest storytelling with; to Deborah Wills, my honorary aunt, who read books to me when I was small and taught me so much about the written word. With all my heart, thank you.

I'm deeply indebted to Kilmeny Jane Denny and Lynn Duncan at Tidewater Press for giving me the opportunity to bring this book to life and for all their tireless work in editing, revising, and publishing it. The experience has been truly life-changing for me and it wouldn't have been possible without you; I'm more grateful for your help than I can ever say. I'd also like to thank Tracy Hetherington for providing the beautiful illustration that appears on the cover. Thank you.

I'm also immensely grateful for the people who, in any way, influenced or helped to shape my work. I'd like to thank my dear friend Melissa Glass for reading my rough early drafts and providing me with so much helpful feedback. I'm equally indebted to Margaret Torrance, my first and always-best friend, who once told me an anecdote that became an episode in this book. And I'm grateful to Frank, without whom the story would have been very different. Thank you.

Last but not least, I'd like to thank Kim Alley, Adrienne Buckland, Krista Royama, Susan LaVoie, and Katherine Goldberg, the wonderful therapists who have helped, supported, and encouraged me over the years. Much of this book has been inspired by what you taught me about mental health and perseverance, and I owe you immensely. Thank you.

ABOUT THE AUTHOR

Susanna Cupido is a Canadian writer from Sackville, New Brunswick. She earned her undergraduate degree in English and Psychology at the University of King's College in Halifax, Nova Scotia. She's currently completing an MFA in Creative Writing at Cornell University in Ithaca, New York.

Window of Tolerance is her first novel.